Hot Bayou Nights

by

Elizabeth Shore

Hot Bayou Nights

Contact Information: info@thewildrosepress.com

Cover Art by *Diana Carlile*

The Wild Rose Press, Inc.
PO Box 708
Adams Basin, NY 14410-0708

Visit us at www.thewilderroses.com

Publishing History
First Scarlet Rose Edition, March 2014
Print ISBN 978-1-62830-320-9
Digital ISBN 978-1-62830-321-6

"You made me lose sleep, you know?" He caressed her arm and along the side of her neck. He slipped his hand into her hair. "I couldn't get you out of my mind."

With the tips of his fingers he lightly stroked along her collarbone and the base of her throat. His eyes glittered as he looked down at her. She heard a change in his breathing as it grew heavier, more pronounced. "You're a very bad girl, Carla."

Her voice was little more than a whisper. "Am I?"

"Oh, yes." He leaned in and brushed soft lips against her neck. "You distract me."

"And that's bad?"

"Of course it is. I have work to do."

She glanced down and saw the rise in his jeans. Emboldened by her effect on him, she put her hand on his chest and felt his thundering heart. A rush of excitement heated her blood. Jackson wanted her. Badly. Still, her mind clouded with confusion.

"I don't get it. Last night you made it pretty clear—"

"That we weren't doing this. I know; we shouldn't." He kissed her neck once more. She nearly purred. "I have work to do, you have an internship to complete." He murmured the words against her skin. "But I can't stop thinking about getting you naked."

"Oh really?" She pulled back to look at him, attempting to be stern even while her pussy throbbed with need. "You had your chance last night and didn't take it. What makes you so certain I'm going to let you do that now?"

He stood stock still, intensity blazing like fire. "I can be very persuasive when I want something bad enough."

Her pulse shot to the sky. "And you want this bad enough?"

His jaw set. "I want *you* bad enough."

Dedication

For Dad

Chapter One

Carla Saunders gripped the steering wheel tight as she shot a glance out the window to check her surroundings. Trees, bayou, and empty road. No signs, no buildings, not even another vehicle. The screen on her rental car's GPS still read *No Matches Found*. Her heartbeat shifted up a few gears as her nerves began humming like a live wire. She let out a shaky sigh and finally accepted the truth. She was lost. *Damn it.* Not a good way to begin her assignment.

A bead of sweat trickled down the side her face; hair stuck to her forehead like wet confetti. Inside the car was hotter than dog's breath. She'd purposely kept the A/C off and the windows down, wanting a full sensory experience of her first trip to the Louisiana bayou—sights, sounds, smells, everything. But with the temperature north of a hundred degrees and thick, humid air streaming into her car, she felt like she was sitting in a pot of warm stew. She needed cool air, and she needed it now. She brushed sweat from her eyes and flicked on the A/C switch.

Nothing.

She frowned; flicked it off and on again. Still dead. What the hell? A rare trace of unease slithered down her spine as she mentally ticked off the latest events. No signal on her GPS. Air conditioner busted. Not another car in sight. No clue of her location. She was made of sturdy stuff, but this was starting to creep her out. Could it all be some weird part of the assignment? She grabbed a handful of chips from the open bag on the passenger's seat, stuffing them in her mouth. *Think, Carla. Think.*

She whipped her head around, looking for a sign or marker, anything to indicate her whereabouts, but came up empty. Green bayou and giant cypress trees as far as the eye could see. She *had* to have missed the turn. Yeah, definitely. All she had to do was get this car going the other way and then—

Shit, monster!

She drove her foot to the floor and slammed on the brakes. Her car fishtailed, back-end flailing as the tires screeched across the road. Sprays of gravel pelted the doors. She grabbed the steering wheel hard, fighting for control. The car careened toward an enormous cypress and she screamed, certain of a head-on collision with the tree. But suddenly her front tires hit the soft dirt by the roadside and her seatbelt snapped tight. The car lurched to a stop.

She rested her head against the steering wheel, gulping air. Her whole body trembled. She sent a prayer of thanks upstairs before turning to look out the back window at what had so scared her. In an instant, every hair on her arm rocketed straight up and she shrieked. Perched by the side of the road, like a horror movie prop, a giant alligator stared her down.

Revulsion and fear stopped her heart. She looked away, steeling herself, before looking back again. The alligator hadn't moved. At least it wasn't walking forward to sniff out her car, wondering if lunch had arrived.

Carla, what in the hell are you doing here? You're a city girl. Honking horns and rude people she could deal with. Alligators and swampy bayous? Not so much. But as she thought back to her boss's final instructions before she'd left for this assignment, she knew she'd have to deal with alligators and more. Or else.

You know what's on the line here, Carla. We expect nothing less than total success. You do this right and get this client signed on with us, Paris and the V.P. title await. If not...well...

He hadn't needed to finish the sentence, and they both knew it. Her ass was on the line if she didn't pull this off. No promotion, no Paris assignment. No job. Period.

She sighed and checked on the alligator. Still in the same spot. Refocusing her attention back on the road, she decided there was no way she'd passed the exit. She'd been paying attention and it had to be up ahead. She grabbed her soda from the cup holder, took a long, cooling swig, and stepped on the gas.

At last, after twenty more minutes, a small hand-written sign stuck in the ground indicated the exit for Rivard Research. Her shoulders sagged with relief. Finally.

The turn-off was more a stretch of dirt than an actual road. Every bump and ditch bounced her around in her seat, and she started to regret stuffing herself full of chips. They were settling in her stomach like a bucket of pig slop.

Her surroundings became darker and more wooded as an enormous canopy of live oaks, dripping with silvery Spanish moss, transformed into a roof above her head. Pea green bayou bordered the left-hand side of the road, and the dense, earthy smell of vegetation hung thick in the air.

She slowed her speed to little more than twenty miles an hour and noticed several small outbuildings as she drove past. Probably part of the research facility. At last she saw another sign directing her to turn right, and spotted what appeared to be the main building at the end of a long driveway. With no obvious area to park, she stopped where her car seemed the least intrusive and shut off the ignition. Home sweet home.

A number of people, mostly men, were walking around the area, not the least bit concerned about a visitor in their midst. Maybe they'd been told to expect her. Carla emerged from the car stiff, sweaty, and coated with a light dusting of potato chip crumbs. She brushed the crumbs from her skirt, instantly aware that her corporate suit and heels wouldn't be seeing the light of day again until she was safely away from this swampy setting. A glance at her watch showed it was just before five. Right on time. *Whew.* Her fist clenched in a quick, victorious pump.

She waited beside her car, assuming whoever the research facility had assigned to meet her would be coming along any minute. But as several people went by without a word to her, she began to wonder if she'd misread the sign. Or that the main research building was located somewhere else on the grounds.

She'd just considered getting back into her car and driving farther along the road when she caught sight of a man approaching her, the slim but strong type who'd probably been a champion swimmer or runner in high school. His six-foot two height gave him a long, loping gait that reminded Carla of a wolf on the hunt. As he neared she could see his disheveled hair was dark brown and on the long side, locks of it brushing across his forehead that he swept back with a gesture both impatient and automatic.

In the same movement he used a finger to push up round, frameless glasses that had slipped down his nose. Behind the glasses were blue, piercing eyes that took in her wind-blown hair, travel-wrinkled suit, and heels sinking into inch-high mud with a single, somewhat disapproving glance.

Carla straightened when she noticed his look and gave him a hard stare right back. So she was a little rumpled, so what? She'd traveled over eight hours to get here and ought to be cut some slack. Maybe she wasn't at her corporate best when it came to appearances, but it didn't mean she wasn't cut out for this assignment. Whatever it was.

"Excuse me, could you tell me where I can find Mr. Jackson's office? I'm supposed to be meeting him today." She punctuated her question with a high-wattage corporate smile and assumed the man would flash one right back.

Instead he looked at her as if she'd spoken ancient Sanskrit, at first giving her nothing more than a grunt and a frown. Then he said, "You must be the new intern."

"That's right."

He grunted again and started walking away, apparently assuming she'd follow him. "Thought you'd be here an hour ago."

"I—" She took a couple of running steps to catch up with him. "I had difficulty finding the place."

Apprehension jerked her nerves tight. Was she starting off on the wrong foot? She knew she was on time, so what's with the attitude? "Wait just a minute."

He stopped walking and swung his glance back over his shoulder, cool eyes assessing her once more.

"Could you let me know where we're going? I'm supposed to be at Mr. Jackson's office by five and I don't want to be late." Despite her anger it did occur to her, as she stared right back at him, that he was actually somewhat good looking. In fact, *very* good looking, despite his lack of manners. He possessed an alarming sensuality, all the more potent because he wasn't even trying. It was just his natural aura, like the way he walked, or spoke, or filled out those jeans she'd been trotting behind. *Nice.*

She wondered if she'd be working with him on this assignment, and a curl of desire clenched in her belly. *Shit, Carla. Calm down.* But damn, he was easy on the eyes, to put it mildly. Downright hot, in fact. Still, she couldn't let her focus stray. Not now. She'd only be reminded it had been a *really* long time since she'd last had sex, and with that grim thought came a whole host of other things to ponder. Like relationships, or men in general, or—

She blinked to clear her head and returned to the matter at hand. "I'll ask you again," she said, her voice remaining firm, "to tell me where we're going."

"You said you needed to get to Jackson's office."

"Yes."

"Well." He turned away and resumed walking, expelling an audible sigh. "That's where we're going."

With a couple of quick strides, she caught up. "Thank you."

He gave her another grunt that she interpreted as "you're welcome" as they wove through a path littered with rocks, leaves, and sticks. Eventually the path gave way to a clearing, and in the distance Carla spotted some sort of rustic yet curiously cozy house. The place was good-sized considering its location in the middle of deep bayou country. The wooden clapboard siding was gray and faded, and a small porch lined with vertical columns jutted out front. Old wooden stairs led up to the door, looking like they wouldn't object to a new coat of paint.

Without hesitation Mr. Grunter, as she'd secretly deemed him, climbed the stairs and opened the front door. As she entered, her gaze fell on a plaque mounted to the wall just inside. *Welcome to The Snake Pit!*

The hairs on the back of her neck shot up and she nearly tripped over her own feet. *Snake pit?!* Where exactly was he taking her? She let loose a slow, steadying breath and followed him to the end of a long hallway near a staircase. A door leading to an office stood open.

Grunter stopped just shy of entering and actually held out an arm, indicating Carla should step inside first. She would have noted that small miracle of manners were she not so intent upon making a good first impression on Mr. Jackson who, she presumed, awaited inside. But when she entered the room, it was empty.

Grunter walked in behind her and rounded a modest desk. "Have a seat," he said, nodding toward a chair in front of the desk.

Carla stepped over to it but stopped short of sitting. "Will Mr. Jackson be joining us soon?"

"There's no *Mr.* Jackson." Grunter took a seat behind the desk as he repeated his instructions for her to do the same, this time with a clear touch of impatience in his voice. Carla sat, confusion wrinkling her face.

"I don't understand." She pulled the assignment sheet from her purse and glanced over it once more. "My instructions clearly state I'm to meet a Mr. Jackson upon my arrival. But you're telling me he's not here?" She sat back in her chair, considering. "This *is* Rivard Research, isn't it?"

"That's right."

"Well, then what—"

"I'm Jackson."

"*You're...*" She stole a glance at her paper and then looked back at him. "...Mr. Jackson?"

Grunter folded his arms across his chest, leaned back in his chair, and propped his feet up on the desk. He gave her a curt nod, as if Carla had tried his patience one too many times.

"I'm Jackson Rivard. Owner of Rivard Research." His cool eyes flicked along the length of her, judgmental, dismissive, like a potential cattle buyer assessing stock. "And you're apparently this month's eager beaver executive intern."

A rush of anger shot through her blood and her face flamed red. He'd mocked her before seeing even a single minute of her work, falling just short of rolling his eyes at her existence. *Not cool.* Her heartbeat raced to triple time and she tightened her folded hands. With feet firmly planted on the floor, she leaned forward and stared at him through narrowed eyes.

"I apologize if I've kept you waiting," she said in a steely voice, "but the fact that you were expecting me an hour ago appears to be your fault, not mine. My instructions say to arrive by five o'clock, and I've done so. The fact sheet states I'm to meet a Mr. Jackson." She held it up so he could see for himself if he wished.

He declined.

"I've done that as well. What I'd now like to know is whether there's something I *haven't* done. Or whether I did something incorrectly. Because from where I sit, your behavior is completely rude and inappropriate and I'd like to know what I did to deserve it."

She punctuated her statement with an outward huff of air, her face awash in indignation. She crossed her arms, awaiting his reply, shielding herself from the onslaught she felt was sure to come. What she received, instead, was silence.

****

Jackson Rivard sat in his chair for a good long minute, considering what Ms. Corporate just said. He removed his glasses and set them on the desk, then rubbed his eyes with forefinger and thumb. Bone tired didn't even begin to describe how he felt, and the day was far from over. Tests needed to be run, he had reports and analysis to review. And where the hell was the contractor for the new lab they were building? Last week there'd been that problem with the plumbing. *Merde*. He had so much to do and not enough hours in the day to do it, and on top of everything he had to deal with this new intern. An intern he didn't even want. Still…

He stopped rubbing his eyes and let his gaze drift over her, more carefully this time. He took for granted that she'd be like every other young corporate executive he'd had the misfortune to meet: self-indulgent, MBA-waving narcissists who assumed their degrees entitled them to advise him on everything from operational efficiencies to best hiring practices.

But this one seemed a little different. Her fiery spark of annoyance was definitely interesting. Pretty ballsy calling him rude, but she was probably right. Manners weren't always his strong suit. Anyway, her gumption gave him hope that she'd be able to last for a month around here. And from the way she spoke and carried herself, the lady clearly had a brain in her head. Exactly how she intended on using that brain, and whether she'd be like the others in advising him on corporate bull was still to be determined. But he could see the potential.

She remained sitting pencil straight in her chair, cheeks flushed, sparks shooting from her eyes. Her dusky pink lips parted to let out an impatient sigh, and an unexpected spear of lust shot straight to his cock. *Damn.* He hadn't realized before now that this gal—he had a folder somewhere with her name on it—was dead-on gorgeous. Not in a swimsuit model kind of way, which he disdained, but as a real woman. She was a little on the short side, with a pretty face and a truly beautiful smile. And how refreshing to look at a woman with actual curves, instead of a size 0 who would fly away in a stiff breeze. And those legs…nice.

Unable to help himself, he let his eyes travel down the length of them, savoring the journey, like a voyage over cream. He could imagine parting those thighs and running his tongue along the length of them, kissing the silky skin. He hadn't seen legs like those in a long time.

Well, not that it mattered. He needed to stop his

train of thought this second and tamp down the tent in his jeans. He had zero time for it. Besides, he was no more interested in meeting a woman than flying to the moon. Only one woman in his life deserved his care, one woman to whom he devoted his time and energy every single day. That woman was his sister. Amy. He had no room for anyone else.

"You didn't do anything," he finally said with weary resignation. "Let's forget it and start over."

Not exactly an apology, but with the resolved glint in his eye and the crossed boots twitching atop his desk, Carla decided she'd get no better. She nodded and straightened in her chair, awaiting instructions on her assignment for the next month.

"How much do you know about what we do here?" Jackson asked.

"Very little," Carla replied. "On purpose. We're specifically advised not to do any research about the place we're sent to or the people with whom we'll be working." She declined to mention that, contrary to the instructions, she actually *had* tried to find out something about this place, but had come up empty. Nothing on the web, not a book to be found. Strange.

He frowned. "Why?"

"Because this is an aptitude adventure. Commonly referred to as a fear assignment."

"A what?"

"A fear assignment." Despite his obnoxious snort of skepticism, she soldiered on. "High potential employees on the fast track in my company are given a series of assessments designed to extrapolate indicators of their personality as they relate to decision making abilities. As part of the assessment we have to reveal our fears, and then we're given an assignment in which we face one of those fears head on. We don't know which one it'll be—the company makes that determination. But how well we complete the assignment while dealing with the fear measures factors in our personality. The company uses the results to determine who's worthy of advancement."

"So if you do well here you get a promotion, and if you don't, then you get…"

"Well, I…I don't get anything. My personality metrics will be deemed substandard."

"Substandard? Your career could take a dive after one assignment?" He grimaced, as if personally offended. "Sounds like a bunch of psychobabble hogwash to me."

"Well, maybe because…" She hesitated. Jackson's reaction surprised her. Not because he'd spoken so plainly but because, deep down inside, she'd wondered the same thing herself.

Not comfortable with sharing those thoughts, instead she defended Bartlett Silver. "Maybe that's because you haven't had any experience with personality assessments," she said. "But my company has been successfully using them for years. It's a first-rate technique."

"And your company is…" He swung his boots off the desk and straightened in his chair, then thumbed through a thin manila folder on his desk. Carla caught a glance at the tab and saw her name scrawled on it.

"Bartlett Silver Management Consulting."

"I see." His eyes skimmed across a piece of paper. Carla smiled, assuming she'd finally get a little sense of him being impressed. Bartlett's name often caused that reaction.

Instead what she received from him was a frown. Or perhaps more of a scowl. "What exactly does the company do?"

His lack of recognition surprised her so much that for a second her mind went blank and all she could do was stare at him, blinking like an owl. When she finally found her voice, she said, "We're a management consulting firm." When no response came, she added, "We advise companies."

"On what?"

"Well…on everything. Organizational structure, operational efficiencies, best practices, cost savings—"

"They can't figure that out for themselves?"

"Not as well as we can." Carla couldn't control her defensive tone. "It's our expertise, after all. We use a variety of analytics to assess current state and project growth. Then we compile a…" His glazed look made it difficult to go on, especially when his only response was a grunt. Apparently, his go-to reaction.

"This is a medical research facility," Jackson finally said. "I don't do metrics testing or put people on the fast track. I also don't use personality profiles or test anyone's decision making abilities. I've got no use for that crap. If people can't make good decisions they don't work here. Simple as that."

He picked up his glasses from the desk and put them back on. Then he leaned toward Carla and pinned her with intense blue eyes, both intimidating and sexy as hell. "What I do is attract the best damn researchers in the country to work for me. They believe in the mission here as much as I do, which is important 'cause I can't pay them everything they're worth. They come here with a passion as strong as mine for the research we do here."

As he spoke she noticed a slight lilt in his voice, an accent as light as it was elusive. Where did he come from, this intense, sexy, cerebral, rather rude man? And what exactly was the mission he was so passionate about? Suddenly, despite the awkward start, she found herself intrigued by Jackson Rivard and his business.

"What research are you conducting?"

"A cure for MS." His voice held undeniable conviction.

"Why are you focusing specifically on multiple sclerosis?" she probed.

"The reasons don't matter." His clipped tone made it clear the subject was closed.

"Okay, sure. Then maybe you could let me know what exactly you'll be having me do?"

"Just observe, to begin with. I don't want you touching anything until I can trust you."

"Excuse me?" Her face burned. He acted as if she were ten years old. "Just exactly what makes you think—"

"I trust no one until I know them. That's just the way it is. You're not being singled out."

She nodded, mollified he'd picked up on her thoughts.

"Once I'm sure, then I'll assign you some preliminary lab assistant work. My researchers will let you know what they need."

"Fine." She tapped some notes into her phone, launching into work mode. "What else?"

"Sterilizing equipment, transcribing notes, maybe feeding the snakes. Although I'm still not sure—"

Jackson stopped abruptly, likely noticing the expression on Carla's face. "You all right?"

In a micro second her skin had gone deathly white, as if every drop of blood she possessed had drained to her feet. Her jaw went slack, her eyes felt as round as dinner plates. "Wh—what…did you say about…"

"Snakes?" He finished for her. "You're asking about the snakes?" For the first time since Carla had met him, the man actually cracked a smile. "I take it snakes are your fear." Once more he leaned back in his chair, having the audacity to chuckle. "In that case, this is going to be quite a month for you."

Black spots danced in front of her eyes and, with a sickening lurch, the room started spinning. "What kind of place *is* this?" she asked, her voice barely above a whisper.

"I told you, we're a medical research facility. We conduct research on the properties of snake venom and how the proteins in the venom could be used to cure sickness and disease." Jackson held out his arms in a sweeping gesture, as if to encompass the entire area. "I've got over a hundred king cobras on this property and caring for them takes a lot of effort. That's where you can help me the most."

Luckily for Carla, her impression about Jackson being a former sprinter held true, for he needed every drop of speed he possessed in order to catch her before she hit the floor in a dead faint.

Chapter Two

Carla opened her eyes to the sight of Jackson staring intently into her face while his deceptively powerful arms, like steel bands surrounded by rippling muscle, carefully cradled her. Hot, male heat burned into her right arm where it rested against the solid wall of his chest. She closed her eyes again. *Mmm...nice.* She could get used to this. It had been way too long since a man had last held her.

This particular man, however, wore a dark frown on his face and was definitely not demonstrating any romantic tendencies toward her. Then she remembered what had happened, and wished she could faint dead away again. Or at least crawl into a very large hole. Instead, she reluctantly shifted out of his arms and attempted to stand up.

"Go slowly. You don't want to get dizzy." Jackson helped her to her feet. She made it up okay, although her legs felt as wobbly as a newborn foal's.

"Sit." He eased her into the chair. Once she sat, he crouched down to bring his face level with hers. He reached behind him to the desk and handed her a glass of water. "Drink."

She did as ordered, taking small sips before giving him back the glass. He returned it to the desk and then peered into her eyes. To her surprise, he reached up and cupped his hand against her forehead so his thumb pointed down. Then he very gently used the pad of his thumb to touch her eyelashes and pull up first her right eyelid and then her left. He looked intently, his face a study in fixed concentration. The warmth of his breathing drifted across her cheeks. A light dusting of stubble shadowed his jaw and the scent of soap still lingered on his skin. Her pulse rate jumped, and she suddenly had an overwhelming urge to lean into him, lay her cheek on his shoulder, and close her eyes. So strong was the urge—and so hugely inappropriate—she straightened like a shot and pulled away.

Jackson frowned, surprised when Carla jerked back, but then he realized being inches away from a man she'd just met must've made her uncomfortable. He thought to apologize, in fact opened his mouth to do so, but at the same moment the tip of her tongue nervously brushed along her lips, and a surge of hot lust shot straight to his groin.

Mon Dieu. He needed to get a grip. Five minutes in his office and this girl had him hard as a horny teen. He hadn't meant for them to get this close, but she'd fainted and he'd responded, relying on his medical training to make sure she was all right. Only problem, they were still really close to each other. He just had to lean forward and her lips were his. And he wanted to do it…

Overcome by the unexpected, he stood. What the hell. One minute this high-flying corporate over achiever sat in his office talking about psychometric testing and other bullshit, and the next he's hit in the gut with an overwhelming urge to kiss her. Or more. Shit. His research was on the verge of a major discovery, and all of it for Amy. No one else. The best way to deal with a distraction like Carla Saunders was to stay the hell away.

He leaned back against the desk and shoved his hands in the pocket of his jeans.

"You all right?"

"I'm fine." She drew in a deep breath and then her words came out in a rush. "I'm really sorry about what just happened here. I wasn't expecting—"

"Forget about it. You were caught by surprise."

Carla shrugged, apparently still uncomfortable about her reaction.

"As I was saying, this is a research facility. We're involved in learning about the potential medicinal benefits that can be derived from snake venom, specifically the king cobra's." He felt himself relax as he entered the familiar terrain of his scientific world.

"Our objective is to isolate and identify the various proteins in snake venom, and then conduct tests on the proteins to determine their efficacy in the development and possible cure of multiple sclerosis.

"Apparently you have a fear of snakes, which I guess is why your company specifically sent you here to do whatever operational efficiency bulls— Ah...thing you're supposed to be doing."

Carla nodded. "This place would definitely fit the bill for a 'fear assignment.' "

"I'm sure it would." He shook his head, wondering what exactly he was doing. He sorely needed the help, so occasionally he took on interns. Generally they were veterinarian students interested in specializing their field of study in exotic animals rather than the usual dogs and cats expertise.

But every once in a while he agreed to take on

someone from the corporate world, and more often than not regretted it. They all came armed with nothing but jargon-laden corporate speak, going on at length about how he needed to "leverage his assets" and "think outside the box" to come up with "integrated solutions" for his business. He had zero interest in what they were talking about, but they could be useful in assisting the researchers. And, their deep-pocketed companies paid him well for the incalculable experience he provided their employees. He supposed it was his version of an "integrated solution."

He hadn't worked with Carla's company before, but the fee they'd agreed on was exorbitant. Cash like that—funding research, supplies, and salaries for his staff—just couldn't be passed up. The way he figured it, why the hell should he? For that kind of dough, he could put up with her "consulting" him.

He expelled a weary sigh. "Look," he began, "you're going to have to deal with your fear or you won't last a day, much less a month." Despite his gruff exterior, he wasn't insensitive to people's fears. God knew, he had his own just like anyone else, the biggest one being Amy not having enough time.

He swung out of his chair. "I need to get back to work. Let me show you your room. If you want a tour of the place you'll need to change your clothes. There's no use for a suit and heels here. I hope you brought more casual stuff."

Carla nodded. "Don't worry, I came prepared. I didn't know where I was going, but my instructions told me what kind of clothes to pack. I assume jeans are okay?"

"They're fine. Let's go."

With the ease of a trained athlete, Jackson lifted himself from his chair and walked out of the room. Carla trailed behind. She hadn't meant to linger, but as she followed him out the door she couldn't help noticing once again how *very* nicely he fit into his jeans. Not wanting to give up that hot rear view, she just naturally fell into place behind him. He had that lean body and wolf-like gait, and *damn* the view back here was fine and—

She looked up, realizing he'd glanced behind to see what was keeping her and she'd been caught staring like some lecherous peeping tom. *Shoot me now.* The unmistakable heat of a blush crept up her cheeks.

Thinking fast, she feigned a stumble and cursed her inappropriate footwear as she hurried to his side. "Sorry," she muttered. "I really do have the wrong shoes. I'm having a bit of a hard time keeping up."

He stared for a moment, saying nothing but making it pretty obvious he didn't believe a word she'd said. His response was his usual grunt, but Carla thought she might have seen a whisper of a grin touch the corner of his mouth. Could it be…was he flattered? He looked straight ahead so she couldn't be sure. At least he wasn't scowling.

They walked down the long main hallway and up a set of back stairs leading to the second floor.

"A lot of my researchers have rooms here." Jackson gestured toward the closed doors on either side of the hall.

"You mean offices?"

"Offices and bedrooms. They write reports and analyze test results in the quiet of their private rooms. They're fully equipped with laptops, printers, fax machines, etc. Anything they need."

"They don't go home at night?"

"Some do. I'm sure you noticed it's pretty remote out here. Most of the researchers only return home at the end of the week. This facility is too far away for them to drive back and forth every day. Besides, a lot of work is done at off hours. This is no nine-to-five job, and Saturday and Sunday are like any other workday. My researchers are often here for two weeks or more at a stretch before taking a couple of days off."

They slowed in front of one of the doors and Jackson cocked a thumb toward it. "That's my room." They continued along the hallway, passing a couple more doors and then turning a corner to the end of the wing. "This one's yours."

The very last door, Carla noted, but just down the hall from Jackson's. Not that it mattered, of course.

He fished a key ring from his pocket and quickly flipped through it, finding the correct key in seconds. He took it off the ring, stuck it in the door and turned the lock. Then he pulled it out and handed it to Carla.

"Don't lose it; it's the only one there is."

She raised a surprised eyebrow. "You don't keep copies of your keys?"

"I do, but another intern who used this room took the key and never returned it to me. I've meant to get a copy made but haven't gotten around to it." He reached a hand to the door knob and gave it a swift turn. "I've got better things to do. Besides, if I need to get in this room badly enough I will. A key's not going to matter."

Deciding not to comment on that rather ominous sounding statement, Carla nodded and stepped inside the room. A pleasant surprise greeted her.

The space was almost like a suite, with the living area and desk in the front and the bedroom toward the back. Jackson hadn't lied when he said the rooms contained all the latest equipment. A laptop, phone, headset, digital tablet, laser jet printer, and a set of reference books including several different dictionaries were all placed neatly atop a large desk. Carla noticed numerous medical books and recalled Jackson's comment about the large number of medical students who came for internships. To no surprise, there wasn't a single book on business to be found.

Jackson pointed out the closets within the suite and the door to the bathroom, then nodded in the direction of the bedroom.

"I'll wait outside while you change." He turned and left without another word.

When she heard the click of the door behind him, Carla expelled a sigh of relief. Was she really going to spend an entire month with this man? He of the grunts and few words and clear dislike for the corporate world didn't exactly make her feel all warm and fuzzy. Then again, that wasn't his role. His job provided Carla with a setting where she could face her fears and perform her work and then leave at the end of the month without a backward glance. Mr. Jackson Rivard and his gruff demeanor but mighty fine ass would be naught but a distant memory once she was through. She never had to see him again. The faint haze of disappointment around that thought didn't matter. Not one bit.

Carla heaved her duffel onto the bed and unzipped it. She'd bring her suitcase in later, but she'd packed a change of clothes and shoes in the duffel bag she could use for now. She pulled out what she needed and peeled off the sweaty skirt, blouse, and blazer. Standing in only her bra and panties, she looked longingly toward the bathroom. Dare she risk an extra five minutes for a jump in the shower? She knew Jackson stood out in the hallway, expecting her just to change her clothes and come right out. She chewed her lower lip, deciding. Then she made up her mind and took off everything.

Screw it. I'm hot, I'm sweaty, I've been traveling the entire day and I deserve a shower. He can wait five extra minutes.

Twenty minutes later, she emerged from her room. The shower had been heavenly and she just hadn't been able to pull herself out. She felt a little guilty, but it couldn't be helped. Unfortunately, a deserted hallway greeted her when she stepped out the door. *Damn.*

She walked back the way they'd come, assuming Jackson had gone to his room to wait for her. But which one was it? Three doors down, or four? She ambled down the hallway, gut churning with indecision. Knowing these rooms were not just offices but more like private apartments held her back from knocking. She didn't know a soul apart from Jackson and she didn't want to disturb anyone. Still, she had to find her host. Taking her best shot at the door she thought most likely his, she gave it a few raps.

She waited, listening intently for any type of sound. Was there someone inside? She thought she may have heard something but couldn't be a hundred percent sure. She knocked again.

"Coming," a female voice called out.

Carla cringed. *Shit.* She'd either gotten the wrong door completely, or she'd gotten Jackson's door but had disturbed his…wife? Girlfriend?

Steeling herself, Carla waited for the door to open. But when it did, instead of being berated by an irate girlfriend, a beautiful young girl in her early twenties greeted her. She sat in a wheelchair.

"Hello." She had a smile as warm and welcome as the sun. "Can I help you?"

"Ahh…" Carla halted, momentarily at a loss for words. She sensed a familiarity from the way the woman spoke, but couldn't quite figure why. "My apologies. I was looking for—"

At that moment, the adjacent door opened and Jackson stepped out into the hallway, his face glowering and eyes icy cold. In seconds he was beside the girl and his angry face became transformed into one of concern. "Amy? Is everything all right?"

"Of course, Jackson," she assured him. Amy looked up at Carla. "I think this lady may be lost."

As if noticing her for the first time, Jackson turned to look at Carla. "What are you doing?" She could not mistake the irritation in his voice.

"She's right, I lost my way. You didn't say where you were going. I did my best to guess where that might be."

"You guessed wrong."

"For that I apologize." Carla bristled. "Not to you, but to the young lady." She directed her gaze to Amy. "I'm really sorry, I didn't meant to disturb you. Mr. Rivard left no instructions where to meet him so I was trying to do my best on my own."

"No harm done." Amy smiled at Carla and looked up at Jackson. "I'm fine, really. You'd better see to your guest."

He leaned down to be at the same level with her

and then murmured something in her ear, clearly meant for Amy alone to hear. Carla backed away, giving them privacy. Obviously Jackson was in love with this woman. Carla did her best to ignore the burn of jealousy flashing through her veins. He could be incredibly rude, but the man couldn't be faulted for ignoring his loved ones.

Amy rolled her chair back inside and Jackson gently shut the door behind her. He turned to Carla.

"Let's go." He set out toward the stairway.

His sharp tone irked her and she wanted to say something. *Hold off, Carla.* She sighed. Her conscience was right. The traveling had tired her, and she didn't want to blurt out something she'd regret.

As they stepped outside, she noticed it hadn't gotten much cooler. At least the breeze had picked up. She paused and slipped a hand beneath her hair to raise it, allowing the air to cool the back of her neck. She noticed Jackson glaring at her before quickly turning away. Shoot, was he annoyed she stalled? Is that what he thought?

He headed toward the main group of buildings at a fast pace. At least she had no trouble keeping up since she wasn't sinking into the ground on spiky stilettos. The practical walking shoes she now wore, though boring, couldn't be faulted for impeding her progress.

"These buildings are mainly labs," he said, indicating the small, white, wooden structures dotting either side of the walkway. "You'll find anywhere from five to twenty researchers in any given one, depending on what they're doing."

He pointed toward a building directly on his right. "This one serves as long-term storage for extracted raw venom. It needs to be kept at a constant temperature in a sterile environment so the tests aren't altered by potential contamination. There are only two people on the entire grounds, not including myself, who I allow in there. I don't want to take the chance of ruining the samples."

"The fewer people allowed in, the lesser the chance of foreign substances entering the lab."

"That's right." He sounded impressed. "You catch on fast."

"Yes, I do." She didn't mince words. She needed Jackson to know she hadn't ended up here by accident. She still smarted over her embarrassing pass-out in his office and wanted him to see her, the *real* Carla Saunders, rising exec, not some swooning, weak-willed idiot.

He showed her where various tests were conducted, where they sterilized equipment, where they tended after king cobra hatchlings. Once more she felt the hairs on her arms rise, as if one of those very snakes were crawling across her skin. She tried to repress a shudder but it slithered down her body. She chanced a quick look to see if Jackson had noticed, but his attention was directed the other way so she might've dodged that bullet.

"What kind of research is done there?" she asked, nodding toward the largest building.

"Gastronomic." A rare grin touched Jackson's lips. He sniffed the air with gusto. "And if smell is any indication, our 'researcher' Jean Auber is making *boeuf bourguignon*." He turned to Carla. "I hope you're hungry."

"I am, actually. I haven't eaten for hours."

26

"Chef Jean'll take care of that." He placed a light hand at the small of her back, guiding her toward the door. Her body reacted as if he'd stroked a finger across her breast, her pulse kick-starting into overdrive, sending tiny beats of pleasure flowing through her body. *Silly, silly girl. Calm down right now and remember: for the next month, this man is your boss.*

They entered a rectangular room lined with long tables where around twenty-five people were eating dinner. "Food's included for everyone so there's no need to pay. But let me show you the kitchen first," Jackson said. "You can meet our Cajun cook."

Through a set of double swinging doors was a kitchen similar to a full-service restaurant but on a smaller scale. Three people busily prepared food. One of the men, presumably Jean, stopped working and crossed the room to shake hands with Jackson.

"Salut, mon ami!" Jean called out. *"Ça va?"*

"Très bien." The two men shook hands. The conversation continued in French. Jackson nodded from time to time, looking toward Carla, before switching back to English.

"Jean asked me to welcome you to his kitchen."

"Merci," she replied.

"If you have any special requests feel free to let him know. You can do so through me, as Jean doesn't speak any English. For which," Jackson gestured toward the chef, "he apologies."

Jean nodded, probably guessing what Jackson said.

Carla smiled back, then took a stab at her response. *"Chef Jean...ah, c'est ma...plaisir...manger tous que tu..."* She paused, suddenly not remembering the verb for "to cook." She was trying to say it would be her pleasure to eat whatever he cooked. Her French was only at the beginner's level, although she hoped to get better before her transfer. She bit her lower lip. The word had vanished from her mind. Shoot, what was it? She saw Jackson and Jean waiting, patiently, wondering if she was going to continue. Then, suddenly, she had it.

"*Que tu te fais sauter.*"

Dead silence filled the air. Chef Jean's face grew pink as he strangled over a cough before he excused himself and turned away. Carla's gaze whipped to Jackson, whose lips were screwed tightly shut, but didn't entirely contain a wicked grin. She groaned.

"What did I say?"

Jackson took her arm and led her toward the dining area. "Your message came across."

"*What* message?" She stopped walking and turned toward him. "Jackson, please. Tell me what I said."

"Well, here's the thing. You were fine at first. But you ended up telling him it's your pleasure to eat everything when he got laid."

"I...what?" Her face flamed red. "How can that be? I thought *sauter* is the verb for to cook. You know, like, 'I sauté mushrooms.' "

They reached the buffet table and Jackson handed her a plate. "That's a good guess," he said. "But *cuire* is what you were after. It means 'to cook.' *Se faire sauter* is slang for 'to get laid.'"

Where was a gigantic hole when a girl needed one? She shook her head, spooning rice onto her plate. "I can't ever eat here again."

"Of course you can." Jackson grinned. "In fact, I'm sure Jean's cooking will get even better whenever he sees you. He'll be inspired."

As they walked along the food bar, taking what they wanted, she looked at Jackson. "I take it French is your native language?"

"One of them," he clarified. "I was raised bilingually, French and English."

That would explain the sexy ass accent. *French.* She nearly sighed aloud. What could be more perfect?

As they made their way to the dining area, she noticed how everyone nodded hello to Jackson. She was greeted just as warmly even though she didn't know a soul. Obviously association with the boss had its perks.

They found seats close to a group of four researchers, and Jackson made introductions. "This is Quinn O'Hara, our top researcher. He's been with me for over ten years."

"And have every gray hair on my head to prove it." Quinn chuckled. He stuck out his hand. "Pleased to meet you, Carla."

"You as well."

"Quinn will show you the ropes tomorrow." Jackson turned to Quinn. "Start her out in the data room."

"Will do."

He pointed out the other three people: a man in his thirties named Phil Spencer who was a herpetologist; a biology student on sabbatical from the University of Mumbai named Bhajan Singh; and a girl named Lisa Martin who looked to be in her late twenties and who'd recently obtained her Ph.D. in zoology. She had an open, friendly smile and gave Carla a warm welcome.

"It'll be nice to have another girl around here," Lisa said.

Carla lifted a surprised eyebrow. "Am I the only other one?"

"There are two other female researchers besides Lisa," Quinn said.

She thought back to the woman in the wheelchair. "What about Amy?"

"Amy isn't one of the researchers. She's a nurse," Jackson explained. His calm voice hesitated, as if weighing whether to say more. After a breath, he added, "She's also my sister."

Carla waited for him to elaborate, but he stayed silent. She knew this couldn't be the entire story and wondered whether there was something else about Amy he chose not to reveal. If so, he wouldn't be sharing anytime soon. She had the distinct impression he preferred keeping personal matters to himself.

"Okay. Good to know." She let it go and turned to Quinn, asking him questions about his work and life. As the researcher spoke, she noticed out of the corner of her eye that Jackson relaxed once the questions about Amy had passed.

By the time she and Jackson finished eating and went back outside, darkness had fallen and stars filled the sky. They fell into step together, headed back toward his house. Sweetly scented night-blooming jasmine perfumed the air, and nocturnal creatures of the bayou like cicadas, bullfrogs, and screech owls infused the darkness with a symphony of sound.

"Toto, I have a feeling we're not in Manhattan anymore," she joked, enchanted by her surroundings.

"I'd guess the noises there are more honking horns than bullfrogs."

"Definitely. Cars, cabs, garbage trucks, music,

people. New York is a city of sound."

Jackson whistled low in the dark. "I don't know how anyone lives there."

"It's the energy. There's no other place like it."

"Sounds like it works for you."

"Yeah, definitely." She looked around, her gaze catching the feathery fronds of Spanish moss swaying gently in the light evening breeze. "This area is great, too. The nature is beautiful for sure, but I couldn't imagine living here the way you do."

"What do you mean?"

"You've got no one for company but a handful of work colleagues and lots of snakes." She couldn't repress a shudder. "You even live in a place called The Snake Pit."

Jackson shrugged relaxed shoulders and chuckled. "One of our biochemistry doctoral students dubbed it that years ago. When he was appointed to the head board position at the Karolinska Institute in Sweden, we made that plaque in his honor." He glanced over at her. "I didn't realize you'd noticed it."

"Oh, I noticed it all right. Almost turned around and ran when I spotted the sign."

"But you didn't."

His quiet words were coated with something that almost sounded like admiration. Could it be? A surge of pride had her straightening her spine as she walked.

"So in addition to the aptly named living quarters, what other benefits could I get here that I couldn't in the Big Apple?"

"Huge amounts of space," he said emphatically. "Air and land you'll find nowhere else. I couldn't imagine living in a congested city, far from nature, and stuck in a closet-sized apartment surrounded by people every square inch around me."

"It can be tough sometimes," she conceded. "But what about the convenience of having everything you need right at your fingertips?"

"Everything I need is right here."

Was it? Really? They turned down the path leading to "The Pit." She took another opportunity to look around but the inky darkness made it difficult, like trying to spot a lump of coal on a tar road.

"But there's nothing here. Aside from work buildings, I mean. And the, uh, snakes."

"Like I said, everything I need."

"What about services?"

He glanced over at her, brow furrowed with curiosity. "Services?"

"You know, like an ATM. Or the gym. Grocery store, dry cleaners, doctor's office? You've got none of that anywhere around here."

The crunch of their shoes on the path mingled with the shrill whir of cicadas. As Carla turned to look at Jackson, he shook his head.

"We don't need that stuff down here. No one wears clothes that have to be dry cleaned. If we want exercise we go for a run. There's tons of space for that. And Jean takes care of the food. He's got delivery set up with a grocery store that drives out once a month with a big load."

"Doctors?"

"Pretty much everyone here has medical training. We get by fine."

Simple. Uncomplicated. She liked that. Life in Louisiana bayou country seemed to be the polar opposite of Manhattan insanity. It was comforting. But, she quickly reminded herself, probably also really boring.

"I guess I'm not going to have to rely on my Girl Scout survival training out here after all."

Jackson's unexpected quiet laughter rumbled through the night. Such a soft, sexy sound. Carla thought about how nice it would be to hear more of it when she kicked a small rock and stumbled on the path.

"Ow!" She stopped walking and rubbed her foot, wincing. "Night vision goggles would come in handy around here."

"Is it too dark?"

"Well, given the fact that the only light out here comes from the buildings, I'd say yeah, it's pretty dark."

"Huh." He looked around. "Guess I never thought about it."

"You don't find it...I don't know...lonely like this? With no lights and so few people around?"

"No," he responded. "Not at all. I guess..." For a moment she didn't think he was going to finish. But then he said, quietly, "I guess the solitude suits me." His admission seemed to catch him by surprise as he fell quiet after that.

Carla itched to probe, to find out more about him. To learn how he can be so isolated and so content. If that, in fact, was true. She frowned in the darkness. From the little she'd observed so far, Jackson seemed to keep distance between himself and others, even among those who seemed to know him best.

Except for Amy, that is.

"Well," she said as the walk ended at the porch

stairs outside Jackson's house, "at least we both have what we want."

He paused, frowning, as if considering what she'd just said. From the light of his porch she could see his eyes glitter, and he gave her a look of intense depth, as if trying to catch a glimpse of her soul. He took a breath, about to say something, but then apparently changed his mind and let the moment pass.

They stood together that way as a quietness, like mist, filled the air between them. She sensed Jackson's presence even more strongly now then she had when she came to in his arms. Maybe his moment of honesty had caused it. A peek of the real man behind the gruff façade.

Whatever the reason, her heartbeat quickened as unexpected desire grabbed hold. She could feel it surrounding her, sultry as the night. Jackson continued to study her, but then she noticed his gaze slip downward, lingering on her lips. His breath hitched as his eyes slid lower still, burning her breasts with his heated look. Her nipples hardened, readying for touch. The pull she felt nearly caused her to take a step toward Jackson. Her weight shifted to her left leg as her right foot began to lift when the unexpected sound of his voice shattered the silence.

"This is where I say goodnight," he said quietly. "I'll see you in the morning."

The comment so surprised her that for a moment she was speechless. Obviously he hadn't felt the same urging toward her as she had to him. She couldn't deny the letdown. His unexpected "good-night" left her sputtering for something to say and without thinking she blurted out, "Aren't you coming to bed?"

Flames, inferno hot and ablaze with life, licked their way up her neck and cheeks and flushed her skin pomegranate red. She would have given her life savings for the ability to disappear from her horrendously embarrassing slip of the tongue. Her only saving grace was the pitch dark of night masking her furious blush.

"I mean…I was trying to say…"

"I know what you meant." The steady calmness of his voice acted like a balm. "I'm not turning in for a while yet. There's a lot left for me to do before it's lights out." He looked away from Carla and nodded toward the stairs. "But you go on inside. You'll be busy tomorrow so you'll want your sleep."

Just then her mind returned to the one element of her fear assignment living up to its name. "Will I…be seeing the snakes?"

She hadn't meant it, but her voice crept up on the last word. *Damn.* She hadn't wanted Jackson to hear her trepidation.

"Not yet. But you'll at least see where they are tomorrow."

"Great!" she replied. Too quickly.

Jackson frowned and took a step toward her, his slim-muscled frame suddenly within a foot of her much shorter, fuller self.

He leaned in, studying her face, a woodsy scent drifting off his skin. "Are you going to be all right?"

"Of course." *Please, please, let me stay. I have to succeed here. Paris is riding on it.*

"Because if you're not, you might want to request a different assignment. You *will* be dealing with snakes in some way. They're the whole point of why we're here."

35

"Yep, I know. And I'm looking forward to learning about them."

Jackson stared a moment longer, his gaze hard and intense. He studied her carefully, skepticism etched on his face. Except as he stood there, Carla couldn't help but notice his breathing become just a bit more shallow. His lips parted, and the tip of his tongue darted out to lick them. The doubt of a minute ago seemed to ease. Jackson relaxed his rigid stance and shifted his weight, tightening the distance between them. He said nothing, but starlight reflected in his eyes revealed irises that were becoming smoky dark. Maybe he wasn't as immune to the rising heat between them as she'd first thought.

Out of the corner of her eye she saw him lift a hand. He made a move toward her, his face leaning in fractionally closer. She inhaled that woodsy, sexy smell and sucked in a breath, anticipating his approach. Her pulse jumped and her heart banged out a few quick somersaults in her chest.

As if changing his mind from whatever he'd been thinking, he stepped back and straightened, his posture firm with resolve. "All right, then. Good night."

Disappointment crushed her like a balloon jammed with a pin. She was also infused with a strong sense of rejection, as if Jackson had considered kissing her but changed his mind because he found her lacking. Still, she refused to let him see her stung. Making her way toward the stairs, she mustered up a casual voice. "See you in the morning," she called out over her shoulder. She entered the house and shut the door behind her.

****

Jackson watched her through the windows until he

saw her heading down the hallway toward the back stairway, the one leading to the bedrooms. He let out a breath he'd been unaware of holding and swore softly into the night. *Merde*. After only a few short hours, he knew this girl was trouble. And he had an entire month left to go.

He turned and began walking the way they'd come, toward the cobra enclosure. He had researchers whose sole jobs were to look after the snakes, but he couldn't rest before he checked on them himself. The snakes were the reason he got up every morning. They were the fuel keeping him going. He knew, in the depths of his heart, the cobras he raised and studied were going to lead to one of the biggest scientific breakthroughs since the polio vaccine.

He reached the king cobra enclosure and walked inside the nondescript, low white building, similar to others on the property. He spent most of his time here. One of the doors in the building gave direct access to the enclosure where the snakes were kept. The area spanned several acres, though no one dared walk there at night. He absolutely forbid it. His requirement was for the safety of both the staff and the snakes. Although the cobras were primarily diurnal, they would sometimes emerge at night. Jackson would not risk someone accidentally stepping on or kicking a snake while walking around in the dark enclosure. On this he didn't bend. Breaking the rule meant immediate termination, no questions asked. So far, he'd not had a single violation.

He went now to another room within the building, one that could almost be mistaken for a television newsroom. Over a dozen large flat-paneled monitor screens were mounted on one wall. The screens showed various views from the multiple closed-circuit cameras fixed inside the cobra enclosure. Low-density lighting allowed for the ability to see the enclosure without disturbing the snakes. With the cameras in place the researchers could keep an eye on the property at night without being inside the enclosure. Having someone watch the monitors twenty-four hours a day was one of his requirements. Each of the researchers took various shifts throughout the week. A Taiwanese Ph.D. candidate named Cheng Li currently manned the desk.

"Hey, Cheng." Jackson sat down at the control desk. "How's it going?"

"Very well, Mr. Jackson. I recorded something in the log that may interest you."

He signed on to the computer in front of him and clicked on the shared drive where everyone with access to the database recorded notes from the day's observations. He read over what Cheng had noted thus far during his shift. In seconds his eyebrows raised with happy surprise. He looked at Cheng.

"How certain are you?"

"Your timing calculations are accurate, Mr. Jackson. Two weeks left before she delivers."

Jackson clapped his hands together and smiled. "That's the best news I've heard all day."

A gravid, or pregnant, female king cobra lays between twenty and forty eggs in a nest she makes out of sticks, twigs, and leaves. The incubation period is approximately sixty days. Jackson had run calculations to determine the conception date. Although he had a one hundred percent accuracy rate in predicting the birthing time frame, he insisted on having his staff double check the work.

"That means we'll be seeing the hatchlings toward the end of the month," he remarked. "Which will make our case for the Atlantis grant money even stronger."

"I will make certain Mr. Quinn includes the information in our proposal."

Jackson swung his chair around to face Cheng. "Do you know if he's finished yet?"

"Yes," Cheng confirmed with a nod. "He told me so this afternoon."

"Excellent." After reading through the rest of the notes in the log, Jackson checked the monitors one last time and then rose.

"Good night, Cheng."

"Good night, Mr. Jackson."

He left the monitor building and walked back the way he'd come, toward home. He remembered what Carla had said about it being dark here. For the first time as he looked around he had to admit she had a point. He knew these grounds so well it had never occurred to him to spend money he could use for research on outdoor lighting. As he stepped over rocks and sticks littering the path, he realized not all his researchers knew the area as well as he. For all practical purposes, this area was their home as well as his.

In the darkness, his lips dipped downward. A few hours on his property and Carla Saunders had him seeing his world differently. The next month couldn't go by fast enough. He didn't want her here, making changes to his life. He didn't want her or any woman doing that to him.

But *damn.* There was no mistaking the heat between them. When she'd nibbled at her lip as she mangled French he practically groaned aloud, thinking of those very lips doing some nibbling on him. Even now he could feel himself go hard.

The intensity of his reaction caught him off guard. Just the thought of her had him panting like a dog. Her neck...*mon dieu.* He could trace a finger, or the tip of his tongue, along its creamy length, then slide on down to the sweet swell of her breasts.

He stopped walking, his cock too hard. For just a minute he stood there and let his mind drift, fantasizing about taking her nipple between his lips and sucking just so, enough to make her arch her back and demand he take more. He wanted her to moan and let him know she enjoyed it as much as he. He'd caress her breast with one hand while skating the other across her stomach, dipping between her legs...

Blood shot straight to his cock and he stifled a groan. His balls throbbed, ready to explode. Fuck. He did not need this. Not now. Not ever. He'd sworn off women ever since... No. He wasn't going to start thinking of that shit now, too.

He angrily ordered his lust to take a hike, kicking at a rock as he stomped home. Carla was a distraction he didn't need. Only thing was, if he was so determined not to think about her, why the hell couldn't he stop himself from doing it?

Chapter Three

Carla awoke with a jolt and looked around in a sleepy daze. She'd had the oddest dream, something about a bare-chested man on a horse, riding toward her. A man with olive skin and piercing eyes. She awaited him wearing a long, flowing dress, standing on a rocky beach where he was about to rescue her from vicious hissing snakes slithering all around her feet. She shivered as she thought back on it, but then groaned aloud. *Seriously, Carla?* The man on the horse had been Jackson. *Crap.* One day and he was already starring in her dreams.

She shook her head. The dream had seemed so *real.* It even had a film score accompanying it. Except... She looked over at the night table, where she'd left her cell phone. The light flashed while it rang. That was no film score she'd been hearing, but the William Tell Overture. She cleared her throat and snatched up the phone.

"Hello?"

"Carla?" Ice rattled and she heard a faint sucking sound, that of someone finishing the last drops of a soda through a straw. "Is that you?"

"Bryce?" She brushed a hand across her eye, swiping away the sleep. "What time is it?"

"Oh, it's early. I wanted to catch you before I left for the office."

She sighed and glanced at the bedside clock. Five forty-five. *Hell*. She was *not* a morning person. "Well, I guess you've done that. I was still sleeping."

"You should be up. Today's the first day and you don't want to be late."

No apology, no sympathy, no inquiry as to how she was doing. Just a bit of scolding before breakfast. Lovely.

"I'm hardly going to be late. I've got three alarms set."

"Why didn't you call me yesterday?" She heard the faint sucking sound again. No surprise. Bryce was a voracious diet soda drinker. Like an addict, the first thing he did upon waking was to crack open a can, and he took his last sip of the day right before turning out the lights.

Carla felt her body tense with irritation, a frequent occurrence whenever she spoke to Bryce. She'd never particularly liked him, but played nice because his mother and hers had been best friends since childhood. Her mother had told her, about a thousand times, how much it would mean to both her and Bryce's mother, Joan, if their children were to marry. Carla would be like the daughter Joan never had.

Problem was, Bryce was an avaricious narcissist with a grotesque capacity for ambition, aligning himself with Carla so he could wallow like a hog in her family's wealth. It was that very ambition that made Carla's mother believe Bryce would be an enormous asset in Carla's life. His zealous drive for success could help steer her career ever upward, lending a guiding hand in navigating treacherous corporate waters. He'd even fooled her parents into believing he was crazy about her and waiting only for the right time to propose. To her, he had all the personality of a leech, attaching himself strictly for the purpose of sucking the life out of her.

"I've been busy," she said. "And I'm busy now. I need to get ready."

"You can't expect me to believe you need to swing into action when sixty seconds ago you were sleeping." Suck, suck. "So tell me what's going on."

She took a deep breath, filling her lungs to maximum capacity, and then slowly, slowly, pushing the air out. She'd learned the relaxation technique years ago in a yoga class. Turned out to be useful in preventing her from verbally tearing Bryce's head off. "There's nothing to tell so far. I just got here. I met Jackson and several of his researchers and had a tour of the grounds. That's about it."

"Huh." She could hear the boredom in his voice already, but then he seemed struck by a thought. "Who's Jackson?"

"Jackson Rivard. He owns the research facility."

"Yeah?" Suck. "What do they research?"

"Ah…" The mere thought of the purpose here had the effect of someone slamming defibrillator paddles on her heart, with the once steady beats roaring into triple time.

"They research…um…king cobras."

"Snakes?" He sputtered, as if ejecting the diet soda from his nose. "That's what they're researching?" She heard his scoff of evil scientist laughter. "Good luck with that."

Jerk. "It'll be fine." Just hearing his laughter, as if he were a mean little school boy scaring a girl with a lizard, put determination in Carla's backbone and made her straighten in bed. Bryce was such a creep, offering zero support and laughing at her fears. Time to ditch him and get to work. "In fact, I'm looking forward to it." Her resolve came through loud and clear.

She could sense Bryce's surprise. "Well, I'm not sure I believe—"

"Believe it." She flipped back the covers and rose from the bed. "And now I have to go. I'll call you."

"Don't forget. I'm speaking to your mother later today. She'll want to know we touched base."

"Later." She hung up before he could get in another word. How like Bryce, to think he could manipulate her actions through her mother. She padded across the room to the shower. What a spineless, deceitful—

She cut off the thoughts with a twist of the shower knob. She refused to poison her mind with rage and begin her fear assignment out of focus and distracted. In fact, she thought, stepping into the water and letting it cascade down her face and body, she was no longer even going to think of this as a *fear* assignment.

From now on, it would be a *fantastic* assignment, one filled with learning, opportunity, and—admit it, you're by yourself—a bit of eye candy to boot. From now on she would have a month of fun, not fear. She squirted shampoo in her hair and gave her head a vigorous scrub, getting rid of bad thoughts and bad Bryce.

Minutes later she dressed in jeans and a long sleeved blouse and slipped on flat sensible shoes. She swung her long, auburn hair into a ponytail and applied just a bit of mascara and lip gloss. She was ready to face the day, at least she would be after she'd had breakfast. As if on cue, her stomach growled. Last night's *boeuf bourguignon* seemed like a lifetime ago.

She arrived in the caf and looked around. So far, no Jackson. She did, however, spot the researcher, Lisa. Grabbing scrambled eggs, bacon, toast, and coffee from the breakfast line, Carla walked over to the table where Lisa sat. Before she could ask to join her, Lisa looked up and a smile lit her face.

"Morning, Carla! Come join me."

So enthusiastic was her greeting that already Carla felt like she'd found a good friend. She sat down on the bench across from her. "Morning."

"Did you sleep okay?"

She nodded as she took her first sip of coffee. Hot and strong, just as she liked it. "Actually I did. I thought maybe I'd have trouble on the first night, you know, being in a new place and everything. But I didn't at all."

"Jackson really takes pains to keep the facility nice for us," Lisa agreed. "The bed in the room I sleep in here is better than the one in my own home."

Carla smiled and forked up some eggs. "Where's home?"

"I'm originally from northern California, but I've been here in Louisiana for the past four years." Lisa paused to take a bite of her own food. A hearty fare of pancakes and bacon, Carla noticed. A breakfast soul mate. "How about you?"

"Upstate New York originally," Carla replied. "Although I've lived in Manhattan for going on ten years. I went to college there, both undergrad and graduate school, and now I work there, too."

"I take it you like the Big Apple."

"It can get a little hectic," she admitted. "But yeah, I like it." She took another sip of coffee and considered. "I guess maybe I just like cities. After this assignment I'm getting transferred to Paris."

"Paris?! Ooh, la la!"

"I'm super excited."

"I guess you truly are a city girl."

"Definitely. I could never live in a place like this, here in the country."

Lisa gave her a grin. "Never say never." She took a last swallow of her coffee and rose from the bench. "I'll see you later, Carla. I ran some tests yesterday and I want to check the results."

As Lisa stepped away, Carla noticed someone coming to take her place. Someone tall, and dark, and...well truthfully, a bit rumpled on this particular morning.

"Morning." Jackson took the seat Lisa had just vacated.

"Good morning," she replied, although she wondered if it was in fact a good one for Jackson. Even through his rimless round glasses she could see his eyes were a little bloodshot, as if he hadn't gotten a very good night's rest.

"How was the rest of your evening?" he asked.

"Fine. I went to bed shortly after you dropped me off at the house. I guess I was pretty tired."

"You had a long trip to get here."

Carla noticed Jackson had no breakfast plate in front of him. "You don't eat breakfast?"

"A couple of hours ago."

Suddenly she felt guilty, as if she were already late

before the day began. She glanced at her watch, but it showed only seven thirty. "I'm sorry, I wonder if my instruction sheet is wrong. It said I should be ready to go by eight o'clock."

"Eight's fine. But I start at dawn."

"Oh." She'd always thought of herself as a hard worker, but his energy made her feel like a slug. Her breakfast began settling like lead shot in her stomach and she set down her fork. "I'm ready to go. What should I be doing?"

"Today you'll be working with Quinn in the data room."

Now that he said it, she recalled his instructions to Quinn the night before. So what's going on with the little twinge of disappointment because she wouldn't be spending the day with him? *Nothing, that's what.*

She plastered a smile on her face. "I can't wait."

"Then let's get started. Come on, I'll take you over there."

They rose together and left the cafeteria via a back door Jackson said led to the area farthest from where the snakes were kept.

"Figured it'd be a good place for you to start."

"I'm fine to start with the snakes."

He frowned and gave her a look clearly indicating he assumed she'd lost her mind. "You'll just be observing and on light duty at first," he reminded her. "Besides, yesterday you passed out cold when you found out we research cobra venom."

"Yeah, well…" The pass-out still embarrassed her, but the reminder of waking up in his arms left her momentarily speechless. Those muscled guns of his were one of the better places in which she'd lately found herself. She cast a side-long glance in Jackson's direction, noticing he wore a sleeveless shirt offering her a generous view of his sculpted, bronze biceps. Then she also realized his sleeveless shirt revealed a tattoo on his left arm, a band of some sort circling the bicep. She looked for another moment and realized, to no surprise, the band was in fact a snake biting its own tail.

"It's the Ourobouros," Jackson said in response to her unasked question.

"I've seen it before, though I can't say where. It's mythological, isn't it?"

"That's right. It's the symbol for life's eternal cycle of renewal."

"Makes sense why you'd have that kind of tattoo," she said as they turned off the path toward one of the research buildings. "It goes along with your mission here of finding cures for sickness. Renewing life, so to speak."

They had reached the front of the building. She set her foot upon the first step but halted when she noticed Jackson had stopped. Thinking maybe he had to fish a key out of his pocket to get in the door, she was startled when he did nothing. Instead he just looked at her, the expression on his face a curious mixture of annoyance and admiration.

Suddenly self-conscious, she looked down at her blouse to see if maybe she'd spilled something from breakfast. No, nothing there. Did she have something stuck in her teeth? A smudge on her face? She lifted her hands and wiped them lightly across her cheeks, but without a mirror she couldn't be certain she'd gotten it. Still he said nothing.

"What?" she finally asked. "Did I do something wrong?"

He frowned. "Why would you think that?"

"Well, because...I don't know. Maybe because you're just standing there looking at me as if I've grown a second head."

"Sorry." He shrugged his shoulders. "You just...surprise me is all."

"Oh. Well..." Wait, did he just compliment her? A curious tingle heated her cheeks. "I hope that's a good thing?"

He paused before answering, as if considering her question. Then at last he said quietly, "I'm not sure."

Abruptly he turned toward the stairs and went up. Carla dutifully followed behind, shaking her head. The man confounded her like no one she'd ever met.

Quinn greeted her inside and immediately made her feel welcome. His burly frame, solid as a sea captain's, offered sharp contrast to Jackson's athletic physique. Quinn had pale blue eyes that twinkled as he greeted her, and a cloud of unruly salt and pepper hair swirling about his head. His warm smile came quickly and often. Something else, Carla noted, very different from Jackson.

"Come on in here," Quinn said, after Jackson had left. He directed her to an area chock full of humming computers. "This is the data room," he explained. "It's where our main frame computers are housed. In the back we have storage cabinets where there are actual hard copies of original documents. Of course we also have them scanned and stored on the mainframe, but Jackson likes keeping the originals as well."

Quinn held out an arm, indicting the direction they

were headed. "For all of his extensive education and intelligence, I personally think Jackson harbors a slight suspicion about the reliability of computers. He knows everything is backed up and stored but, for some things, nothing less than a hard copy will do." Quinn opened a door and indicated Carla should step inside. Lining both walls in every available inch of space were rows and rows of storage cabinets.

"I take it this is the filing area," Carla said.

"Right you are. Everything is labeled and in its exact place. Jackson demands perfection when it comes to these files. As he points out, it's worthless to keep anything if you can't find it when you need it."

"True enough."

"At the end of this room is a desk and some stacks of papers," Quinn said, walking toward the area he meant. "I'm afraid this is where you're going to get started. Filing papers."

Carla looked around. "That's no problem." She felt oddly compelled to reassure Quinn she didn't mind her assignment. He seemed so apologetic. "I've spent plenty of time doing that in my own office."

The desk was a basic, utilitarian office desk with drawers on either side and a chair in the middle. But stacked all across the top of it, in several tall but neat piles, were the papers to be filed. Now she understood why Quinn had seemed so sheepish. There must have been over a thousand pieces of paper atop the desk.

"We've fallen a little behind in our filing," Quinn said.

"Just a little."

"Well, we do have a lot—"

Carla stopped with him a smile and a wave of her

hand. "I'm only teasing. I know you all have more important things to do than file papers." She pulled out the chair and sat down. "Besides, at least this keeps me away from the snakes."

Quinn's forehead wrinkled with surprise. "You don't like snakes?"

"I'm afraid of them. That's actually why I'm here. This month-long assignment is supposed to force me to deal with something I'm afraid of. And snakes are it."

At that Quinn let out a hearty belly laugh. "Shoot," he said, when he'd recovered enough from his mirth in order to talk. "If I were you, I'd turn around and ask for a different assignment. You're not going to get away from snakes around here."

"Unfortunately, that's the point."

"Well, okay then. Let's get started."

Quinn showed her what to do and she got to work. Five hours later, with stomach growling and back aching, she'd made a significant dent in the pile. A glance at her watch showed the time as just after one. No wonder she was starving.

Stepping outside felt like entering an oven, and the humidity had skyrocketed. She blew at stray pieces of hair prying themselves loose from her ponytail and hanging limp against her forehead. She regretted today's outfit, especially knowing she'd packed shorts and light skirts. But an old nemesis—vanity—had steered her toward the flattering black jeans.

Slapping at a horse fly buzzing around her face as she walked to the caf, Carla let out a small breath of exasperation. The truth was, she felt self-conscious around Jackson and was very aware what she wore today had a slimming effect on her hips. And the long-sleeved blouse? Well, the jiggly bits of her underarms were concealed a little better, that's all. She rolled her eyes. *Keep your focus on Paris, you dope, not on your new boss.* Still, the outfit made her feel good, and maybe that's what really mattered.

She reached the doors to the caf, greeted by the heavenly smell of cayenne pepper and garlic. Her stomach let out a hearty growl in response.

She looked around the caf, but it had mostly cleared out. It seemed as if nearly everyone had already eaten lunch. Everyone, that is, aside from Jackson. She spotted him sitting alone at an empty table, digging into a bowl of shrimp *étouffée*. He had a large stack of papers before him he appeared to be reviewing, managing at the same time to look downright gorgeous.

Helpless to do anything for a moment but stare, Carla soaked up the sight. Jackson sported the same gruff, bedraggled yet sexy scientist look he'd had in the morning, with light afternoon stubble now adding to the mix. His shirt was damp with sweat and clung to his skin like the male version of a wet T-shirt contest, emphasizing the firm muscled chest beneath. His bronzed forearms rested atop the table, and she could see the snake tattoo wrapped around his left bicep. He leaned forward as he ate, bowl in front of him, taking spoonfuls of *étouffée* as he read the papers. Amazing that a snake scientist could look so hot.

She stepped lightly as she approached, but nevertheless he looked up as soon as she was in hearing distance. She noticed he didn't exactly smile when he saw her, but his eyes were welcoming as she neared the table.

"You just taking a break now?"

"I think I lost track of time," she replied. "There's a lot of filing in that room, and before I knew it, I felt my stomach growling."

He actually had the decency to look apologetic. "It's not the greatest challenge, I know. But it seems to be our default starting point for all of the interns."

"Good to know I'm not special," she joked, a little thrill of victory shooting through her as she noticed a small grin lifting the corner of Jackson's lips.

"Food's over there," he said, nodding toward the long table that, like last night, was set up buffet style with the day's offerings.

"Great. I'll be right back."

The shrimp *étouffée* smelled terrific, and simply lowering her face toward the chafing dish and letting herself be surrounded by the heady aroma of roasted shrimp, garlic, cayenne pepper, and Cajun spices sent her senses into overdrive. She took a heaping bowl of it, then walked carefully back to where Jackson sat. The last thing she needed was to lose her footing and go flying to the floor, landing in a slippery heap of shrimp *étouffée*. The thought was at once so terrifying and hilarious she choked back giggles as she approached the table.

"Something funny about the food?"

"No." She shook her head as she took a place across from him. "Not really. I was just thinking—" Her pocket buzzed. She reached in and pulled out her phone, glancing at the number as she did so. *Damn.* Her mother.

She debated whether to answer it or press silence when Jackson gave a nod of assent. "Go ahead. Might be important."

"Well, I…" Another buzz, this one seeming more impatient, as if mimicking the feelings her mother undoubtedly had about Carla not answering the call. She sighed and pressed answer.

"Hi, Mom."

"Carla?" Some papers rustling in the background and the sounds of rapid-fire instructions directed to her assistant. Then, "I'm sorry, honey. Too many things going on at once."

"Like always."

"Listen, I have to make this quick but I wanted to let you know I heard from Bryce this morning."

Whooppee. "Oh?"

"He sounded a little put off. I— No, I have to stop in Lisbon first. I can't go straight to Paris, Betheny. I'll need an overnight in Lisbon and then into Charles de Gaulle by noon the next day. Carla?"

"Still here." She bit back a weary sigh, wishing for once her mother would call her without doing ten other things at the same time.

"Anyway, apparently you forgot to call him yesterday."

"I didn't forget, Mom, I just—"

"Remember, honey, we've gone over this. Men are very impatient and they don't like to be kept waiting."

"I know, Mom. You've mentioned it before." *About fifty times.*

"Bryce is concerned about you, Carla. I think you may have hurt his feelings."

Whoa! Was this conversation for real? "I'm busy here, Mom, and I can't know my exact schedule."

"No, I won't be checking any luggage. They charge those ridiculous fees nowadays and anyway, I don't have time to stand around collecting my bags. Carla?"

This conversation needed to end. Now. "I'm here, Mom, but I have to go. Anyway, sounds like you're off on another trip."

"I am. There's a dynamite new Portuguese player who's going to give LeBron a run for his money. But we've got to get him here, first. Apparently he wants more money. Athletes!" Carla could hear the exasperation in her mother's voice, but there was no mistaking the excitement a new challenge brought her. Linda Saunders absolutely loved her job.

"Anyway, I just wanted to let you know about Bryce. He's keeping an eye on you for us, after all."

Carla barely contained the groan rising in her throat. Leave it to Bryce to convince her parents she needed looking after and he was the one to do it. His ambition knew no limit. As far as he was concerned, he was practically a member of her family without ever having proposed to Carla.

She ended the call and set the phone down with a sigh of disgust. Jackson looked up from his papers.

"Something wrong?"

Damn. He must've heard her sigh. "Oh, I…nothing." She shrugged. "My mother called." When Jackson made no reply, Carla felt compelled to fill in the silence. "She can sometimes be frustrating."

He nodded, his dark eyes seeming to fill with understanding. She wondered if he had the same experiences with his family but knowing how he clammed up on the personal stuff, she held back on asking him.

The rest of the afternoon passed by uneventfully, as

did the next two days. Carla saw so little of Jackson during that time she began questioning if he avoided her on purpose. She'd seen him a few times talking with colleagues, and she knew he'd seen her, but she hadn't been invited to join the conversation. Not that she could've exactly contributed to the snake chat. Still. She had to reassure herself that his absence was merely coincidental. She could hardly have given off such a bad impression, at least not in a single day. Right?

Her internal dialogue played itself out in her mind with alarming frequency. She did her best to stay positive but his curious absence made her wonder. It also made her think about him way more than she should. Needing a distraction, she decided to propose a project for herself in the data room.

"You want to what?" Quinn scratched his head when she first brought up the idea.

"Overhaul your database."

"Overhaul how?"

Carla tapped a few keys to bring up the program they were using. "This was a good system in its day, but it's really old," she explained. "If you continue to use this you'll pretty soon find yourselves without tech support. You're also vulnerable to viruses. I'd love to get you set up with cloud computing."

"Cloud? Hmm. I, ah…" She could tell by Quinn's muddled expression he had no idea what she was talking about. Not wanting him to feel foolish, she quickly covered.

"You guys are so busy here I know you haven't had time to think about this, but it's part of what I do. My company specializes in advising companies on operational efficiency. Being as updated as possible with your systems is part of it. I happen to be kind of a tech geek so I know a little more about cloud computing than others. I'd be happy to do some preliminary work for you just as an introduction. What do you say?"

Quinn chuckled as he gathered papers on his desk, preparing to leave for the day. "I say you know a whole heck of a lot more about this stuff than I do, Carla. And if you think this is something we need, I'm not one to argue. I'll run it past Jackson to be sure, but I say go ahead. Make our day."

She smiled at his movie reference. "Great. I'll type up some notes so you and Jackson know exactly what I'm doing."

He glanced backward from where he'd been headed toward the door. "Aren't you coming to dinner?"

"Yeah, but probably later. I'm eager to get started." *And get my mind off your boss.*

"Suit yourself. See you later, Carla."

She sighed and returned her attention to work. Far from being hungry, her stomach clenched like a sailor's knot. She wanted to succeed in this assignment— correction, *had* to succeed—but with Jackson AWOL she really had no idea if she was on the right track or not. His absence distracted her like ants at a picnic, but she refused to let it jeopardize her purpose. She'd prove her usefulness and get herself one step closer to Paris.

Hours later, the click of a door provided the first interruption of the night. She glanced up from the monitor to the clock on the wall, shocked to realize it was nearly midnight.

"You're still here?"

She didn't have to see the face to recognize the voice. She tamped down her smile and turned around, ignoring the cloud of butterflies swirling about her tummy.

Jackson strolled across the room and took a seat beside her. His jaw was shadowed with stubble. Stray locks from his unruly dark hair draped across his forehead. He wore a white sleeveless T-shirt, areas of which clung to his chest, damp with sweat from the relentless humidity.

"I saw the light as I walked past on my way home," he said. "Thought maybe someone had forgotten to turn it off. I didn't expect anyone to still be here."

"Time flies when you're having fun."

His eyes flicked over to the monitor. A hint of his woodsy scent drifted toward her, and she wrestled against the urge to close her eyes and breathe him in. "Quinn says you're getting us into the twenty-first century."

"I hope you don't mind. I mean, I know you don't like this consultant stuff. I just thought—"

"It's good, Carla." He cut her off but his voice was soft. "I like it."

He rolled his chair over to get a better look at the monitor. With him so close she could feel the hot surge of body heat rolling off his skin, like shimmering waves rising from a desert road. She dropped her hands in her lap, striving for calm. She needed to be as indifferent to his presence as he seemed to be to hers.

His slim, strong fingers skated across the computer's touchpad as he reviewed her work, saying nothing for several minutes. At last he sat back and looked over at her. "Tell me about this."

"Okay. Well, for starters, what do you know about cloud computing?"

"Heard of it, but not much beyond that."

"Essentially it's a way to store and manage your data via remote servers, like the Internet, rather than on a local server or personal computer."

His cocked his head, gaze focused and intense. A thrill shot through her, pleased she had his attention. "What's the advantage?"

"You can access your data from all different kinds of places without having to use a specific computer or computing device tied to a local network like you do now. With the cloud, all your data is stored remotely. It's secure, easy to set up, and can also save you money." She returned her attention to the monitor. "Let me show you."

Again he shifted closer to her, but she stayed focused on the project, managing to ignore her jacked-up heartbeat even as she spied a trickle of sweat tracking its way along his collarbone.

"Right now you have to be in this room, sitting at these monitors, in order to access your data."

"It's worked fine so far."

"I know. But let's say you need to go on a business trip to meet with clients."

He raised an eyebrow at her.

"Okay, okay. You don't go on business trips."

"Or meet with clients."

She expelled a breath of frustration. "Could you work with me for just a minute?"

His lips twitched with a faint smile and she nearly gasped aloud as she realized he was teasing her. "All right," he agreed, maintaining a straight face. "I'll go along."

"Thank you."

"So I'm on this hypothetical business trip to meet with…clients, did you say?"

"Or vendors, if that's what they are in your world."

"Suppliers."

"Fine. You're on a trip to southern Florida, let's say, because your supplier of live mice to feed your snakes wants to introduce you to a new breed of mice that might…um…you know, be more nutritious for your snakes."

This time he could not contain a chuckle. "I can't wait to hear how you're going to tie a new supply of mice with having my data in the cloud."

"Then you, *Mr. Jackson*, should prepare to be impressed." She shot him a smug grin and pulled up the home screen for his data.

"Anything you need to access starts here. These buttons across the top give you menu options for what you want to see." She clicked on one and opened up breeding history statistics on all of his cobras. "I started with this because it's the most organized of the databases on your local server. By switching over to the cloud, you could now access this on your hypothetical trip to inspect those new mice. You look at the breeding history of your female cobras and make a decision about which mice will be right for which snakes because you have all your data right where you are."

She risked a glance at him to see if she was making sense. He said nothing, brows furrowed as he scrolled through the screens. Her hopes of impressing him jumped off a cliff.

"Is anything wrong?"

He looked at the monitor for a few minutes more then sat back in his chair, studying her through narrowed eyes.

"For the first time ever someone from the business world has done something for me that makes sense."

She couldn't hold back the elated smile dancing on her lips. "Happy to be of service."

"You said this works on all devices?"

"Wherever you have Internet access."

"So I could pull up the data on a tablet. Or smart phone."

"Sure. If you wake up in the middle of the night and can't sleep, you feel like checking on the cobras, just fire up your tablet and pull up the data. Saves you from stumbling through the dark to the data room."

He shifted away from her in his chair and she wondered if she'd touched a nerve about the pathway being so poorly lit. "I'm sorry, Jackson. I didn't mean to harp on the lights. I was just making a joke. A bad one, obviously."

"I wasn't thinking about that at all."

"Oh. Well, what?"

At first he grunted, his typical "no response" response, sitting back in his chair as if weighing whether or not to answer her at all. Then at last he said, "I have frequent insomnia. I wake up a lot in the middle of the night."

She nodded but kept silent. He seemed to have more to say.

He shook his head, a combination of disbelief and wonder etched on his face. "You couldn't have known that."

"No."

"It's just an odd coincidence you picked that example."

"I…" She hadn't been told about his insomnia, but for some reason a part of her had felt as if she'd known. She chanced a direct response. "I get the feeling you think about what you do all the time. This place is beyond just your work; it's your life. And if that's true, it means your thoughts about everything here interfere with your sleep. You'd be the kind of person who wakes up a lot. Assuming you can even get to sleep in the first place."

A wry grin touched the corner of his mouth. "You read me right. Sounds like you can relate."

"Yeah. Unfortunately, I can. I get so caught up in what I'm doing, or nervous about something…" She finished with a shrug. "Sleep becomes impossible."

The conversation stilled and ticks from the wall clock filled the silence. Ironically enough, given their discussion, for the first time that evening she began feeling tired. She noticed Jackson looking up at the clock. He rose from his chair.

"Even for a couple of night owls, we should probably hit the hay."

"All right." She began shutting down. "I can show you more later. There's still a lot to do, assuming you're okay with me finishing it?"

"It's more than okay. It's—"

She looked up at him, wondering why he'd stopped, but the guarded expression on his face yielded no clue. He stood inches away from her, his lithe, powerful physique seeming almost to hover, like a shadow cast from the sun. He watched her with heated intensity and suddenly the mundane task of closing down programs became a challenge as she tapped at the keyboard with trembling fingers. She willed herself to look away from him, focus back on the work. Above her, Jackson's breathing changed, becoming shallower and more pronounced. Finally the programs finished closing. She stood up, facing Jackson, and the atmosphere shifted.

Without warning, a spark of desire lit and unfurled, encircling them like a cat weaving through its owner's legs. Her mouth went dry as her heartbeat jacked into overdrive. Tiny pulses throbbed low in her groin, steadily building, and her nipples pebbled and strained against her lace bra.

She knew Jackson was affected as well by the unmistakable stain of arousal darkening his eyes. He swallowed but said nothing. Instead, he took a step toward her, standing so close now that their legs nearly touched. His scent surrounded her. She thought he would lean forward, closing the space with his kiss, and her stomach clutched with eager anticipation. Heat from his body drifted toward her. A trickle of sweat slid between her breasts. Her breath hitched in her throat and the tip of her tongue darted out to lick her lips.

But then, out of the corner of her eye, she noticed him clench his fists. The muscles in the back of his jaw twitched and he turned away. "It's beyond what you need to do here," he finally said, his voice a dry whisper.

She sensed hesitation, as if he wanted to say more, but she already knew from experience he would not. The silent grunter from day one had re-emerged. Her gaze flashed to the ground and she looked away, not wanting Jackson to see her disappointment.

They walked out of the building, Jackson shutting off lights as they left, and started down the path toward his home. He said nothing more and they likely would have walked the whole way back in silence when Carla's stomach suddenly let out a hearty growl.

He glanced down at her. "You didn't eat?"

"I got so caught up in the work back there I forgot." They passed by the silent and dark cafeteria building. "No chance for a midnight snack at this point," she laughed. "Guess I'll be waiting until breakfast."

"No, you won't." They turned down the bend toward home.

"Is there a secret stash of food I don't know about?"

"I don't rely on the caf for *every* meal. I've got granola bars, dried fruit, and nuts at home."

"Just to make sure your interns don't starve?"

She sensed a brief smile from him, although couldn't quite see it in the darkness.

"Just to make sure *I* don't starve," he said. "I do what you did tonight all the time, so I've learned the hard way to keep an emergency supply."

"Guess we're a lot alike."

He didn't respond at first and she assumed he wasn't going to. They reached the door of The Pit and he dug out his key. But as he stuck the key in the lock he looked at Carla and gave her a brief nod. "Yes," he said, a note of surprise in his voice. "I guess we are."

He walked down the hallway to his office. Once inside, he opened a desk drawer crammed full of food. She grinned when she saw it.

"You definitely don't go hungry."

"And neither will you. Here." He held out a hand with two granola bars and a plastic baggie filled with dried cherries and almonds.

As she took the bag from him, his fingers brushed against hers. He didn't do that deliberately, did he? Her skin prickled all the way up her arm from the brief contact, but when she looked up and caught Jackson's gaze his guarded expression revealed nothing. She could only conclude it must have been an accident and reminded herself to stay focused on the job. And Paris. *The sparks you sense are one-sided, Carla, and only because it's been way too long time since you last had sex.*

"Thanks," she said. "This'll be a nice snack."

"No problem." He shut the desk drawer and they left the office, Jackson pulling the door closed behind him. They walked upstairs and then headed down the hallway, toward their rooms. When they reached Jackson's door Carla raised a hand and wished him a good night, intending to keep walking.

"Carla…" His quiet voice stopped her.

She turned back around, assuming he'd continue, but he stayed silent, watching her. She held back a breath of frustration. *I'm dealing with the most perplexing man on the planet.* "Is there something you needed?"

"No, I…" He ran a distracted hand through his hair. "I just wanted to…ah…thank you for all the work you did. On the data."

"Probably changed your mind about how valuable we consultants are, right?" She couldn't help but tease.

One side of his mouth curved upward. "I wouldn't go that far. But you—" He cleared his throat. "I appreciate what you did. Good night." Without another word he stuck his key in the lock and went into his room, shutting the door behind him.

Carla stared after him, making sure her jaw didn't hit the floor. What was that about? On one hand he thanked her for the effort, on the other he was shutting the door in her face. Despite the hot body and breathtaking looks, Jackson Rivard began to revise her description of the mad scientist. Shaking her head, she walked to the end of the hallway to her room, wondering how in the world she'd get through the month.

****

She spent the next day walled up in the data room. Getting Jackson's research facility fully set up with the cloud had gone well, helped along by several calls to IT back at her office to assist with the stuff she didn't know how to do. She felt a great sense of accomplishment from helping Jackson out, but talking with the office also reminded her of the heavy expectations on her head for this assignment.

She sat back in her chair, thinking about the conversation she'd just had with her boss, Justin Carey. His first comment after picking up the call had been to express disappointment she hadn't checked in sooner. "We're expecting to hear from you several times a week, Carla. In case that wasn't made clear."

"No, it's clear. It's just difficult. It's remote out here and signal strength isn't good in every building. I—"

"Has Rivard signed on as a client?"

"Not yet. It's only been a few days and he's skeptical."

"This won't be considered successful if you don't get him."

"I realize that." *You jerk.*

"Have you come up with demonstration analytics? He may not understand the complexity and breadth of our portfolio offerings."

"He understands just fine, Justin. The man's not an idiot. He's a research scientist with a Ph.D."

"Yeah, well. He researches snakes, let's not forget that. Just get him signed on."

Click.

What a horse's ass! She'd wanted to throw her phone against the wall but she kept her cool. *Remember Paris. That'll get you through this.* It should, anyway, although it didn't seem to be doing the trick at the moment.

The time slid toward noon. She knew people would start heading over to the caf, stomachs growling for lunch, but food was the last thing on her mind. She could thank Justin for ruining her appetite as well as her mood. Deciding to work off her irritation with a vigorous walk, she grabbed a sparkling water from the small fridge and headed out.

The temperature had soared since the morning, but the lush vegetation around the facility provided decent shade. She headed down a path she knew led to the bayou, enjoying the chirps and whistles of bird calls and the low drone of insects. She smiled, imagining herself on an exotic trek through the Amazon jungle.

Her illusion shattered with the buzz of her cell phone. She pulled it out of her pocket and glanced at the screen. A text from her mother.

Have u called Bryce yet?

Crap. She bit back a growl of frustration. The day just went from bad to worse. She jabbed "reply" on the screen and started pounding out a text back, fingers flying over the keypad as she explained how time consuming the assignment was, leaving her no time to focus on everything she had to accomplish *and* keep Bryce uppermost in her mind, when the crack of a branch interrupted her agitated opus.

She looked up and took in the loping wolf gait of Jackson heading her way. His hair was in wind-blown disarray as always, probably due more to him forgetting to get it cut rather than trying to achieve any type of look. He wore dark green cargo pants very nicely outlining his long, muscular legs, and a white T-shirt that clung like a lover to his sweaty chest. Just like that, the sun came out. Her breath hitched in her throat.

"Sorry. Didn't mean to disturb you." He glanced at the phone in her hand. "Looks like you're busy."

"I— No. This can wait. I'm just going for a short walk. I hope it's not a problem?"

He raised a questioning eyebrow. "Why would it be?"

"Well, I'm on company time. I shouldn't be wasting it."

"This isn't an office, Carla. We don't keep schedules around here." He nodded in the direction she'd been headed. "I'll join you on that walk if you like."

Yeah, she liked. "Definitely. Thanks."

They turned onto the path, for a time strolling in companionable silence. Then Jackson asked, "You were headed to the bayou?"

"Yeah." She nodded. "I thought it might relax me.

Water usually does."

"Same for me." He paused, then added, "There's something about the stillness of the water. It's soothing, and takes away my stress. I walk down here a lot."

"That's too bad."

His brows furrowed. "What?"

"Well, you said you walk here to get rid of anxiety and you come here a lot. If that's the case, it must mean you're pretty stressed."

His eyes twinkled as he grinned. "They teach you that logic in business school?"

"No, I actually came up with it on my own."

He let out a low whistle. "Impressive."

"I thought so."

Wow, his teasing was pretty darn impressive, too. She felt her heart stand up and do a back flip.

Her pocket buzzed again and she yanked the phone out, glancing at the screen. Her very impatient mother, likely wondering why Carla hadn't yet replied to her text. She stuffed the phone back into her pocket.

"I'm guessing that phone is contributing to your need to walk?"

"It is," she admitted. "But how—"

"You've got stress lines around your mouth that weren't there a minute ago."

"Hmm." She nodded her approval. "You're pretty good at reaching conclusions yourself."

"And I didn't even go to business school."

She couldn't help but laugh. It felt good being with him, so surprisingly easy.

They reached the edge of the bayou, greeted by a chorus of insects and the site of a white ibis plucking through the water as it searched for lunch. Jackson pointed to a grey lump in the water some distance away. "You see that?"

"The log in the water?"

He shook his head. "Not a log, it's an alligator."

"Shit!" She jumped back, arms swinging to catch her balance.

"Don't worry," Jackson assured her, his expression serious, although she swore she heard amusement in his voice. "He's not interested in you at the moment. When he gets hungry he'll come closer to the water's edge. But you should know these guys are out here and what to look for so you stay safe. Bayous can be dangerous for a city girl."

"Oh yeah?" she shot back. "Well, never fear. This city girl can handle 'gators. Just try snatching a cab out from under me and you'll see how tough I am."

He held up his hands in mock surrender. "I wouldn't dare."

They slipped into an easy stroll while making their way alongside the water, and Carla tried ignoring the warm tingles of pleasure darting through her blood. Beautiful summer day, hot guy by her side…not a bad way to spend an afternoon.

"Seriously, I'll be okay," she continued. "I might not know about creepy-crawlies, but I can take care of myself."

"Living where you do, I don't doubt it. No wildlife in that concrete jungle you call home, but I imagine there are still plenty of sharks around."

"Definitely." An unwelcome image of her boss, snarling like a rabid dog, popped into her mind. She smothered it. "And those sharks can be tough."

"But you still like big city living?"

"My family's there. I like being able to see them."

"So you're close?"

"Close?" She paused, considering the question. Her family could be frustrating, exasperating, challenging, but couldn't that be said about most families? Her classic over-achiever parents put the same expectations on their children as they did on themselves. It could be tough sometimes, but Carla knew her success thus far in life owed a lot to her parents' love and encouragement. "We are, yeah," she said. "I'm especially close to my brother, Carl. He's my fraternal twin."

"Your twin? So there are two of you?"

She nodded. "And two more on top of that; three brothers altogether. My twin, Carl, and then Mike and Adam, who everyone calls Butch. They're all older than I am, although Carl only by a couple of minutes."

"Any sisters?"

"No. I wish. It'd be nice to have another female in the house to ward off all the men."

"Aside from your mother, you mean."

She took a sip of her water. "Mmm-hmm. My mom can fend for herself just fine. She used to be a professional basketball player."

Jackson raised an eyebrow in surprise. "No kidding?"

"Yeah. A good one, too. But then she broke her leg and it didn't heal quite right, so there went her sports career."

"*Ça, c'est dommage.* It must have been a real setback for her."

Carla emphatically shook her head. "Not my mother. She immediately signed up for law school and started classes six months after her injury. Graduated a year later."

"A *year*?"

"Yeah. She threw herself into it, taking on a massive class load and continuing right through summer. Now instead of being an athlete, she represents them."

"Wow."

"Yeah. Wow."

She managed a weak smile, but trying to follow in her mother's high-flier footsteps could sometimes be a tough gig.

"What about your father?"

"He's the CEO of an aviation company brokering the sales of private executive jets."

"So your parents are pretty classic under-achievers, then?"

Carla glanced over, thinking for one second he was serious. But then she saw his eyes, sparkling as they teased her, and her stomach twisted into a gigantic knot. Just when she'd thought Jackson Rivard had not a funny bone to be found, his gentle teasing shredded all doubt. And *oh*, that smile. He could light a city with it.

She smiled back at him, her insides melting. "My brothers are just as lazy and sluggish as my parents."

"*Mais oui.*" Jackson plucked a small stone from the ground and sent it flying to the water, skipping over the tranquil bayou before it sank. "I have no doubt. So let me guess. One of them for sure has to be an attorney."

"Check. That would be my oldest brother, Mike."

"As I suspected. Which would mean another of your brothers is a business executive, even a CEO maybe?"

"Butch is a Vice President of Marketing, so I

suppose that's close since he theoretically could work his way up to CEO if he wanted to."

"What about Carl?"

The mere thought of her twin brought a smile to her lips, like thinking fondly of an old friend. "Carl's the publisher of *Downhill.*"

"The ski magazine?"

"Yep."

"Interesting. So he followed your mother in the sports world, at least peripherally."

"He also skis. Not professionally, but he's really good." She took another sip of water. "Actually, my whole family, except for me, is athletically gifted. My dad's a runner, Mike and Butch played football and wrestled, and Carl's the skier."

"But you?"

"Hopeless. I trip over my own feet. I have no knack for sports."

"Not everyone does. But you're a rising executive like the rest of your family."

Carla shrugged. "Well, yeah, I guess I am."

"Why the hesitation?" Jackson studied her closely.

"I didn't hesitate."

"Sure you did." His assertion, as if stating a fact, was tough to disagree with.

"Well, I…I guess I just don't think of myself in the same way," she admitted.

"Why not?"

"Because I—" *Because I don't really like my job.* Wait, where had *that* come from? Why had she even thought it? She worked so hard on getting to the top. How could she think she didn't like her job?

Her parents and brothers were proud of her.

Friends from grade school often spoke of how high and how far Carla had come in the years after school. Why would she have spent all that time and energy and effort on doing something she didn't like?

She sat down on a fallen log, energy suddenly zapped. She was tired, that was all. Tired of the intense long hours, the pressure of getting promoted, succeeding in this assignment, and the dreams of Paris that sometimes seemed so very elusive. Combine all that with having to spend an entire month working with snakes, and no wonder she had doubts.

Brushing all troublesome thoughts aside, she smiled brightly at Jackson. "Because I just focus on the present," she said, "and doing the best job I can right here, right now. I don't want to dream all the time of the future and what might be out there for me. I'm different from my parents and brothers. That's what I meant."

He made no reply, but still held her gaze. From the expression on his face, having a difficult time believing her. *Well,* she thought, *so be it.* She wasn't here to convince Jackson Rivard or anyone else of her plans for the future. She needed to get through this month and then be on her way to Paris. Any thoughts outside of that were pointless.

She finished the last of her water and stood up.

"Better get back to the data room," she said, ignoring the desperate tone of forced happiness she heard in her own voice.

She began walking away, moving several steps ahead of Jackson when his quiet voice stopped her.

"Have dinner with me tonight."

Chapter Four

Beneath the branches of a cypress tree, a brown pelican rose up from the water and flapped its wings against the lazy bayou, its splashes rippling the calm, still air. Carla stared at the water, feeling like she, too, had just been smacked with pelican wings.

Her breath caught in her throat, and she paused before turning around. Had she heard right? Dinner? With Jackson? Did he mean just the two of them, or did he mean why doesn't she sit at his table with him in the caf, or did he mean—

Her thoughts were spinning so quickly she didn't have time to process them. She turned, facing him, not exactly sure what would come out of her mouth.

"I—" She cleared her throat, tried again. Damned if she'd let him hear the tremor in her voice. She pressed her suddenly sweaty palms against the sides of her jeans, covertly trying to blot them dry. "Dinner?"

His eyes narrowed as he studied her. "Yeah." He nodded. "Dinner." When she didn't immediately reply, he added, "You don't eat it?"

"Yeah. I mean, of course I do."

"Good. 7:30?"

"Yeah, 7:30 works."

"*Bon.* See you then." He turned and looked out at the water, his behavior as calm as if they'd just discussed the weather. She checked herself. He *had* asked her out on a date, right? And if that was the case, she had things to consider. Like where they were going, where she should meet him, or—biggest question of all—what she should wear. As she pondered these thoughts she remained standing in front of him, as if bolted to the ground.

He frowned. "Something wrong?"

"No, I…I'm just wondering where I should meet you?"

"At the house. My car is parked in back, but I'll bring it around. It can get swampy back there."

"Okay, will do."

He returned his attention to the bayou and she knew she'd look ludicrous asking more questions. He'd only invited her to dinner, after all. It's not as if he'd said, "Hey, why don't you sleep with me tonight?" A ridiculous heat crept into her cheeks at that thought, and she rushed to turn away, walking fast as if she were late for an appointment.

The data room was quiet as a tomb, but she welcomed the privacy. Finishing the big filing project from her first day gave her a chance to think without interruption, something she needed right now. There were so many questions running through her mind, the most prevalent one being why Jackson had asked her to dinner.

She considered several possibilities. Maybe he welcomed all his new interns this way. Or maybe he already had the reservations and whoever he'd originally been going with had to cancel. Perhaps she was just a fill-in. She didn't love the idea, but supposed she had to think about it. Besides, better that over another scenario popping into her mind, one that planted a ball of nausea in her stomach.

Maybe he felt sorry for her.

She paused in her filing, the very thought making her ill. Could that be it? With all her talk of her over-achieving parents and her super star brothers, had she painted a gigantic "L" for "Loser" on her forehead? Poor, poor Carla. Short, slightly overweight, no good at sports, a junior executive at best who's even afraid of snakes. Is that how he saw her? She cringed at the thought.

For the next several hours she filed without stopping, taking no breaks, not even a moment for the ladies' room. She wanted nothing more than to block the anxiety from her mind. Diving into a project had always worked in the past. Until Quinn stuck his head in the door to tell her to knock off for the day, it worked this time, too.

"We're not running a forced labor camp," he teased at nearly half past six. "Come on, Carla. You can stop for the day. If anything, you must be hungry."

That did it. With the reminder of her upcoming dinner looming before her, no way could she could file another piece of paper. Besides, she was hot and sweaty and needed to get ready.

"Thanks, Quinn," she said as she walked toward the door. "I guess I'll see you tomorrow."

Quinn frowned. "He's keeping you in here?"

"Well, I'm not really sure, to tell you the truth. He hasn't said anything."

"If I know Jackson, he'll put you somewhere else tomorrow. He does his best to make these assignments meaningful, and being stuck all day in the file room doesn't exactly qualify."

Carla grinned. "I'm going to agree with you there. But he hasn't said anything to me yet."

"I'm sure you'll run into him in the caf. You can ask him then."

She waved good-night to him as she walked out the door, realizing Quinn had inadvertently answered one of her questions. Apparently Jackson did not have a habit of taking all his interns out to dinner, so that scratched one possibility off her list. It remained to be seen why he'd asked her.

The time neared quarter to seven once she got back to her room. She knew she'd have to kick it into gear to be ready on time. After all, she still had no idea what to wear.

She jumped into the shower and quickly rinsed off, deciding not to bother washing her hair for a second time that day. She'd just put it up into a simple bun. All dried off, she wrapped the towel around herself and opened the closet door. Decision time.

It very likely wasn't any place ultra-fancy, so she ruled out the cute little black dress she'd brought along. She really didn't anticipate ever wearing it this month, but didn't want to be caught unprepared just in case. She had a denim skirt she liked, but would it be too casual? With a sigh of impatience and a glance toward the clock, she thumbed through her options. Silk pantsuit, no. Business suit, no. Her fingers lit upon a red and black cotton skirt she liked. She pulled it out and held it in front of her as she stepped over to the full-length mirror. She sorted through her blouses and spotted a black top. She had a belt that would work with it and complement her waist. This might be it. Only thing is…

She looked at it again. The blouse had a v-shaped neckline that would show some skin. Not a lot, but undeniably there. Hmmm. She thought about it and was surprised to realize how much she wanted to wear it. How she wanted to entice Jackson and have him get a glimpse of her sexy side. So what if she could stand to lose a few pounds? She also had a pretty face, a great smile, and damn it, nice cleavage. That sealed the deal. She set the outfit on the bed. She'd pair it with sandals and call it a day. Or a night, as the case may be.

She returned to the bathroom and glanced once more at the clock. Ten past the hour. She'd better hurry. She wound her hair into a loose bun, swept powder on her face, blush on her cheeks, added mascara to bring out her eyes. Lastly she dabbed a touch of lavender scent behind her ears, on her wrists, between her breasts. She gave herself a critical look and decided she'd do.

Ten minutes later, with a couple of minutes to spare, she was ready. She went downstairs to wait for Jackson, who already stood in the hallway. She took one look at him, and her pulse shot to the moon.

Gone were the sleeveless T-shirt and cargo pants he'd worn earlier in the day, replaced with nice jeans and a long-sleeved white linen shirt that looked striking against his olive skin. He had the sleeves rolled up to the middle of his forearms. There was something outrageously sexy about the casual exposure of that skin, as if not wearing the sleeves as they were meant to be turned him into a bit of a bad boy, the kind of guy parents warned against but to whom women were drawn like moths to flame.

His hair looked darker than usual, and as she drew

close to him, Carla realized it was because it was still damp from a recent shower. But what she noticed the most were his gorgeous dark blue eyes unobstructed by glasses.

"Very nice," he said, low, as she approached.

"Thanks. You look pretty great yourself." Her gaze swept over his face. "You're not wearing glasses."

"Occasionally I bother to put in contacts." He held out his arm, directing her toward the front of the house. "Why don't you wait on the porch? I'll pull the car around."

As she stepped outside, the hot humid air wrapped itself around her like a damp blanket and in only seconds she could feel a trickle of sweat rolling between her breasts. She blew out a breath of air, silently admiring the people who could stand to live in this weather year-round.

Seconds later, Jackson's car came around the corner. To her surprise, he drove a hybrid SUV, new car smell still lingering inside.

"Nice car," she said as she climbed aboard.

"Thanks." He waited until she buckled up and then they were off. "I only got it a couple of months ago. I needed carrying room in the back."

For one wild second Carla's heart sank. Why did he refer to needing car seat space? Were there little ones in his life she'd not known about?

As if reading her mind, Jackson continued. "We transport the snakes from time to time, and it's tough getting the cages into the back seat of a car. So I traded it in for this."

Her head whipped around to the back seat, heartbeat pounding in her chest. *Snakes?* Here? Her eyes darted to and fro like a frightened mouse, but she saw no evidence of snakes or cages. "Are there any back there now?" she squeaked. *Damn.*

Jackson chuckled. "Don't worry, the coast is clear. I wouldn't do that to you."

"Thank you." Carla gave him a grateful smile, ordering herself to enjoy the ride and not jump around like a skittish cat. *I wouldn't do that to you.* Words casually said, yet sexy as hell.

She sank back in her seat, letting the conditioned air cool both her skin and her thoughts. "So where are we going?"

He gave her an enigmatic shrug. "You'll see."

"I'll see? When? You're making me a little nervous here." At his raised eyebrow she added, "You work with snakes for a living, after all."

His white teeth flashed in the waning light. "No snakes where we're going. Just relax. We'll be there in about half an hour."

It was clear he'd elaborate no further, so she had no choice but to trust the sexy snake man and enjoy the ride. After cruising along some of the darkest roadways she'd ever been on, Carla finally saw lights in the distance. Not many, but enough to indicate signs of life. As they drew nearer, she realized that the lights belonged to a single restaurant, seemingly in the middle of nowhere, like a lone lighthouse perched atop a cliff. The place was lit up like a Christmas tree with hordes of cars parked haphazardly around the unpaved, gravelly lot.

Jackson navigated the bumpy terrain, looking for a place to park. There appeared to be no designated spaces; people simply left their cars wherever they found room. Once he'd gotten a spot, Carla opened her door to get out and could hear the pulse of music coming from the restaurant. She looked around for a sign indicating the name of the place, but there was none to be had.

"Where are we?" she asked Jackson as he came around the car to join her.

"Les's Place. Been here for years."

"Really?" She began climbing the short set of stairs leading to the front door, with Jackson close behind.

"Does that surprise you?"

"Well, they don't appear to do any marketing. At least, I didn't see this advertised in the 'Welcome to Louisiana bayou country' brochure I picked up at the tourist information booth at the airport. And I also didn't see any website links when I researched this area."

Jackson kept a straight face, but Carla looked up at him when he opened the door for her, certain she detected amusement in his eyes.

Still, he appeared to take her comments seriously when he said, "No marketing, eh? You think that's a problem?"

Whatever response she might have given was swallowed up by the boisterous noises greeting them as Jackson opened the door and they stepped inside. The joint was jumpin'. A six-piece band filled the back of the room. The fiddle player, who doubled as lead singer, was a petite blonde with spiky hair. She was accompanied by the accordion, guitar, bass, drums, and something that looked like a washboard. The blonde sang about life on the bayou with infectious energy.

All around the packed room people smiled and

clapped, strutting their stuff on the makeshift dance floor in front of the band. Matching the style of the parking lot, wooden tables were scattered throughout the restaurant in no particular order but wherever room allowed. Hungry diners occupied nearly every one of them, downing heaps of jambalaya, *étouffée*, rice and beans. Carla's mouth watered.

"C'mon," Jackson said, "there's room over there."

He slid his hand into hers as he led her across the rustic wooden floor toward an empty table. His touch was warm, strong, the grip of a man used to handling powerful snakes. Her knees trembled from the rush of excitement brought on by the feel of him. And suddenly she was seized by a sudden crazy urge to hold his hand forever.

As they made their way through the crowd she wondered, just for a moment, whether people in the restaurant assumed they were a couple. She knew she did when she spotted a pair holding hands. She also knew she liked that thought about her and Jackson, probably a little too much.

They reached the empty table and sat down. Jackson held up two fingers to someone unseen behind Carla's back, and then turned his attention back to her.

"You were saying something about marketing," he said, straight faced but with eyes sparkling. "To get people in here?"

"Okay, so maybe they don't need it right now," she conceded, shrugging off the empty feeling she'd gotten when he released her hand. "But that doesn't mean they shouldn't think about it. What about the future? Companies should always have a strategic business plan to map out their vision. They ought to be thinking five, ten years down the road." She realized this was the perfect segue to talk about Rivard Research. She was supposed to be getting him to sign on as a Bartlett client, after all. "Your company, for example. Do you have a strategic business plan?"

He frowned. "What do you think?"

"Well, okay. But you need one." She warmed to her topic. Strategic business plans were something she knew a lot about. "Take the restaurant business as an example. It's a volatile industry. Today's hotspot is tomorrow's dud. If they want to keep the kind of crowd level they have tonight, they've got to have a plan."

"And you think a research lab needs that, too?"

"Of course."

"Did you learn that in grad school?" His fingers idly toyed with the salt shaker but he kept his gaze focused on her.

"Among other things."

"Such as?"

She thought back to her course curriculum. She'd gotten her MBA three years ago, but the classes remained fresh in her mind. Her 4.0 GPA had been hard earned. "Well, such as financial accounting, managerial statistics, operational management, marketing management."

"How about psychology? Is that on the curriculum?"

"Psychology?" She shook her head. "No, why would it be?"

Jackson leaned forward in his seat, facing her with the studied, intent look that was beginning to give her some trepidation. "This place has been here for three generations. Les's grandfather started it, a French

Creole whose family has been in this parish since the nineteenth century. Les's father took over from his father, then passed it down to Les. They've never done any marketing, or promotions, or hired a public relations firm because they don't have to. Because what matters is this is a great place. It's got the right music, food, and ambiance that keeps people coming back."

Jackson looked around the room, taking it in with a sweep of his head. "The crowd level here tonight is no fluke and it doesn't matter that it's Friday night. It's packed like this every night. Les and his family understand what it takes to make a restaurant right, and it's what you have here. That's what I mean about psychology. Understand what makes people tick. It doesn't matter if you do all the marketing in the world. If the place isn't good, people won't come."

At that moment, the unseen waitress to whom Jackson had signaled moments ago arrived with drinks. She set them down and handed them menus, saying she'd return in a minute to take their orders.

Carla looked down at the glass before her. The liquid inside was blue.

"A blue bayou," Jackson explained. "It's made with blue Curaçao and vodka." He lifted his glass and tilted it toward her. "*À votre santé.*"

"Cheers." They clinked glasses and she tasted the drink. It was actually quite good, both sweet and tart. And strong.

"Better not have too many of these or I'll be under the table."

"I limit it to one myself," Jackson agreed. "Especially since I'm driving."

Carla opened her menu to study the options but

85

noticed Jackson ignoring his.

"I take it you know what there is to eat here."

"There's nothing I haven't tried," he admitted.

She closed her own menu and laid it aside. "In that case, why don't you order for both of us? That way I'm sure to get the right thing."

"You trust me that much, do you?"

"Well," she laughed, "I'm out here in the middle of nowhere, on a pitch black night, with absolutely no idea how to get back to the facility. If not for you, I may be lost forever. So yeah, I think I'll trust you to get me some good grub."

Her humor made him smile, his soft lips curving upward, eyes sparkling in the light, and Carla had the same reaction to it now as she did before. He left her breathless.

The waitress came back and Jackson ordered for them both, speaking in French too rapid for Carla to keep up. She had no idea what he ordered. For all she knew, she could end up with a plate full of braised intestines and boiled cow brain. Or—she shuddered at the thought—rattlesnake stew.

Once she left, Jackson apologized to Carla for speaking French, explaining he hadn't meant to exclude her but it had been a necessary precaution.

"Our waitress," he cocked his head toward where the girl had walked away, "has slipped up when I've ordered in English. She knows a bit, but we've got a better chance for success when you tell her what you want in French."

"I don't mind," Carla assured him, "but I'm trusting you weren't doing it because you were secretly ordering me haggis."

Jackson raised an eyebrow. "In a French Creole restaurant?"

"I know, I know. But still. The thought of eating sheep's organs doesn't do much for my appetite."

"I promise you, haggis is not among tonight's fare."

She took another sip of her drink. The alcohol buzzed through her veins, making her feel wonderfully mellow. She sat back in her chair, grabbed hold by the relaxed feeling settling in her blood, caused in part by the drink, in part by the surroundings—the music, the aromas, and the smokin' hot scientist sitting across the table.

They talked casually, about nothing in particular, and the minutes flew by. Before she knew it their waitress was back, weighed down by a gigantic platter of food.

"*Bon appétit,*" she said, setting it before them. The most incredible aromas Carla had ever smelled filled the air between them. She closed her eyes and inhaled, suddenly immersed in the scent of garlic, onions, cayenne pepper, sweet basil, and oregano.

"This looks and smells fantastic," she said, unable to conceal the smile from her face.

"I hope you're hungry, because we've got food for an army. I wanted you to have a real sample of authentic Louisiana cooking."

Carla set her napkin in her lap, listening to Jackson as he pointed to each item and explained what they were. "Over here is deep fried okra. This is boiled crawfish accompanied by *maque choux*. Then we have pork boudin, bite-sized muffalettas, red beans, rice, Creole jambalaya, and boiled shrimp with *remoulade*."

Elizabeth Shore

She looked over everything, mouth watering. "I don't know where to begin. Some of this stuff I've never heard of."

"Think of it as part of your fear assignment. Venturing into unknown food territory."

"Unfortunately for me, eating food is never a problem. Or never very scary," she commented casually, not thinking much about it since her mind lingered on the choices before her.

Jackson surprised her when he looked away from the food and straight at her. "Why do you cut yourself down?" he asked.

She looked up from the platter, fork held in mid-air. "Cut myself down? I'm not." She put the crawfish on her plate and shrugged. "At the same time I'm a realist, and I'm aware I could stand to lose a few pounds."

"According to whom?"

"Well…I guess, according to TV and movies. And fashion magazines. Pictures of skinny celebrities are everywhere. Thin is in, at least for women. That's the look celebrated and admired."

Jackson speared some okra and shook his head. "I'm surprised you're such a follower. Especially with your background."

She set her fork down and frowned. "What do you mean?"

He rested his arms across the table top and leaned in to her. "You've got a former pro basketball player for a mother, a father who runs marathons for fun, brothers who excel in every sport they've ever tried, and then there's you, who admits she's not cut out for sports at all and seems perfectly comfortable with it. I

88

didn't detect either embarrassment or envy when you were telling me about your family. But yet you compare yourself to unknown stick-like movie actresses and indicate you don't quite measure up." He paused for a moment, letting his words sink in, while he slowly chewed some okra. "I just didn't expect to hear something like that from you."

Carla sat back, startled. Was there truth in what he said? Was she secretly embarrassed about her weight, to the point of not even admitting the feeling to herself?

"I'm not sure what to say," she finally responded. "Maybe you're right. I guess I never realized it."

He gave her that stare of intensity like a scientist analyzing data. "You're a beautiful woman, Carla. It would be a shame if you weren't aware of it."

A rush of heat washed over her body, like stepping before the flames of a roaring bonfire. Except this heat came flooded with desire, a flash so sudden and unexpected it consumed her. Her imagination kicked into high gear and she had a movie-like image running through her mind, the camera panning over items of clothing strewn about in the hallway, a bra, a sock, pair of trousers, like a trail of breadcrumbs leading the viewer farther down the hallway toward a room at the end where sounds could be heard, whispers and moans, and then over to the bed, the rumpled sheets a precursor to the activity atop it, where she and Jackson were as tangled as the sheets, each of them naked, and kissing, until he adjusted his position to begin slowly moving down her body, taking her hardened nipple in his mouth—

Her inner policeman busted in on the fantasy. *Step away from the scene with your hands high!*

"Thank you," she managed, trying to douse the heat. "That was a nice thing to say."

"I didn't say it to make you feel better."

"Then why did you?"

He shrugged, served himself crawfish. "Because it's the truth."

"And you always speak the truth?"

"Yes."

She polished off her drink, feeling a courage born from the alcohol easing through her veins like the bayou named after it. She leaned forward in her chair, not minding that her position might just offer Jackson a glimpse of her ample cleavage. That's why she'd selected this blouse in the first place. Maybe later, and sober, she'd regret it, but not now.

"In that case, how about a few truths about yourself?" She picked up a piece of crawfish and ate slowly as she watched his expression. It went from neutral to guarded in about half a second.

"You see?" she said to him, before he'd had time to respond.

"See what?"

"Your face."

"I can't exactly see my own face."

"I know you can't, but you know yourself, and you know how you feel. And right now, you're not very comfortable. I want to know why."

He said nothing for a long time, as if considering her question. Or, Carla thought, whether he wanted to answer it.

As if confirming her guess, he sighed and set down his fork. "I didn't bring you here to play Twenty Questions."

Carla smiled. "Interesting," she said, taking a bit of *maque choux.*

"What?"

"How fast you became defensive before I said anything. You're warding off questions before they're even asked."

He locked gazes with her and sat in his chair as silently as a statue, the twitch of muscle at the back of his jaw the only indication he'd heard her.

"Let me prove you wrong," he finally said.

She looked at him through narrowed eyes, clearly not believing him. "What do you mean?"

"Ask your questions."

"And you'll answer them?" An excited thrill skittered down her spine.

"Yeah. I'll answer them." His shoulders slumped and he slowly exhaled, casting his eyes to the ground as if bracing himself for an unpleasant conversation.

The thought of having caused him to feel that way killed her earlier excitement and put an odd ache in Carla's heart, like she'd disappointed a new friend.

"Jackson, I'm sorry. Let's forget it, really. Your personal business is yours alone. I overstepped my boundaries."

To her surprise, he adamantly shook his head. "No, you didn't. You were right. Sometimes it takes a stranger to point out something you should have known for years. I'm not comfortable talking about myself, but maybe I should learn to get over it."

"There's nothing wrong with being private."

"No, there isn't," he agreed, swallowing the last of his drink. "But it's tough to know me if I clam up on your questions." He saw her glass was empty. "Can I

91

get you another drink?"

"No." She shook her head, definite on that point. "One of these is plenty."

"Doesn't have to be alcoholic. I'm having sweet tea."

"Oh, well in that case. Tea sounds good."

At that moment their waitress passed by and Jackson held up two fingers. "*Deux thés*," he said as she picked up their empty glasses.

Once she'd left, Carla decided his French background was the perfect place to begin. "Okay, let's start with your parents. Are they French?"

He nodded tightly. "Yes."

"But you were born here?"

"Yes. Amy and I both."

"And I assume you learned French from your parents and English from school?"

A shadow of a smile crept across Jackson's lips. "I would say I learned English more from watching TV."

"Really?"

"When you're a kid, you're a sponge. You soak up knowledge. So I'd describe my English as primarily Saturday morning cartoons with a dash of after school specials thrown in for good measure."

He said it with a straight face, but she could see the twinkle of humor in his eyes as he spoke.

"I thought I detected a Saturday morning cartoons accent."

Jackson snapped his fingers and shook his head. "Busted again."

Carla laughed aloud, just at the moment when their teas were brought. The waitress smiled as well.

"You are 'aving a good time, *non*?"

"Yes," Carla answered sincerely, catching Jackson's easy grin out of the corner of her eye. "A wonderful time." She lifted her glass and tilted it toward him. "Cheers."

"*Santé.*"

He kept eye contact with her while they drank, his gaze so direct it bordered on rude, but she realized with a start she was beginning to like it. It showed an honesty in him. He didn't try to be anyone except himself, and he played no games. His intensity was also sexy as hell. He focused solely on her, as if for this moment no one else even existed.

"Yo, Jackson!"

A guy across the room waved a hand and walked over. Tall and rugged, his disheveled brown hair hung long, like an '80's rock star's. He wore faded jeans that nicely traced the contours of his muscled thighs and a sleeveless black T-shirt revealing biceps the size of mountains. His gaze swept the table as he approached, sea green eyes not bothering to hide his curiosity about Carla's identity.

He and Jackson exchanged a manly hand slap when he reached their table. "Good to see you out here, man," he said. "It's been awhile." His focus shifted to Carla, a silent but clear indication he'd like an introduction.

"Ah, Chase, this is Carla Saunders," Jackson said. "Carla, Chase Durand."

She extended her hand to him. "Nice to meet you, Chase."

"*Enchanté,* Carla," Chase said with exaggerated interest, taking her hand and actually kissing the back of it. He waggled his eyebrows as he did so and said, as if only she could hear him, "Don't let Jackson know I'm making a move on his date. The guy gets very jealous."

"It'll be our secret," she laughed, liking him already. She also didn't mind being referred to as Jackson's date. It had a nice ring to it.

"How've you been, Chase?" Jackson asked.

"Cool, man. Like always. Been busy, too."

"Glad to hear it."

"You and me both. Rough patch for a while, but we're good." He nodded toward Jackson and Carla.

"Take it easy, Jackson. I'll see you around. And nice to meet you, Carla." He gave them a salute and sauntered back over to his table where he joined a boisterous group of friends. Carla noticed Jackson smiling after him.

"A friend of yours, I trust?"

"Yeah," he nodded. "A good one."

"Have you known each other long?"

He took his tea and downed a long swallow. "Since we were kids. We went to school together."

"It's great you still have a childhood friend. It's unusual these days."

"I actually have a couple of them, but Chase and I are probably the closest."

She sat back in her chair, thinking. "I have friends from college, but even those tend to drift apart."

"Could be a different culture down here. Families know each other for generations and people don't tend to move as much as they do in New York. Least I'd guess that's how it is."

"I think you're right," she agreed. "The strong family bonds down here are really nice."

"Yeah, they are."

"What does Chase do? Is he in science as well?"

Jackson grinned. "No, not at all. Chase is more of a free spirit, I guess you could say. He's an artist."

"Yeah? What kind of art?"

"Glass. Really cool and unusual sculptures. He's finally started to get something of a following, which he should have because he's extremely talented." Jackson paused to drink the last of his tea. Then he added, "There's something crazy and unpredictable about Chase. I think it's why we're friends. I see features of myself in him."

"You do?" Disciplined, well-ordered Jackson has a wild side? *Interesting.*

"That surprises you?"

"Well…kind of…"

He wagged a scolding finger. "Never judge a book by its cover, Carla."

He kept his face serious but she could see by the press of his lips, as if holding back a grin, that he teased. Then, unexpectedly, he winked at her.

A slow burn of desire started low in her groin and made her belly flutter as if millions of hummingbirds suddenly took flight. Her heartbeat thumped like a drum in her chest, pulses building and growing steadily faster. Super hot snake scientist was turning her to jelly.

A beautiful, lyrical ballad filled the room. Couples took to the dance floor at once, swept along by the music. The soft shuffle of boots scraped across the wooden floor as the petite blond crooned about losing her heart on a lonely bayou night.

She watched the couples as they swayed around the room, admiring the ease with which they all seemed to know the dance. She turned back to Jackson, thinking to ask him more about Chase.

Jackson held out a hand before her. "Dance with me."

Her jaw nearly fell open with surprise—and excitement—never thinking for a minute that Jackson Rivard was a man who would dance. Maybe he'd been right about that unpredictable thing. Her gaze took in the sight of his strong, muscular arms and she imagined them wrapped around her, holding her tight as he guided her across the floor. His body would be pressed up against hers, and she'd feel the scorching rock hard wall of his chest…

Oh, but this was a bad idea on so many levels. Right?

She shrugged, embarrassed warmth creeping up from her neck to her cheeks. "I don't know how."

"I'll teach you. Come." He stood, apparently not accepting no for an answer. Carla's heartbeat knocked against her chest, nervous anticipation fueling its speed. As discreetly as possible, she swiped her damp palms along the sides of her skirt before accepting Jackson's outstretched hand and rising from the table, allowing him to lead. They made their way across the room and onto the dance floor, where Jackson found them room.

"The Cajun waltz is very similar to other kinds of waltzes," he said, "except we tend to hold our women closer, and the music can be a lot slower than a Strauss waltz, for example."

Carla shook her head. "I don't know how to dance *any* kind of waltz, so it's a waste of your time to explain the difference."

Jackson smiled. "Then just follow me."

"I'm going to make a fool of myself," she said, trying to ignore the swirling butterflies in her stomach as Jackson placed his right hand against the small of her back.

"Think of it as part of your fear assignment," he whispered in her ear. Carla's heart leapt as the caress of his breath drifted against her skin.

"It's three steps," Jackson explained as he resumed proper posture. "Long, short short; long, short short. Let me lead you. You'll be fine."

With him as her guide, she believed him. The warmth of his body flowed to her through his hands, his strength and sureness like a beacon, guiding her way. She made a couple of missteps in the beginning, but Jackson turned out to be such a competent teacher he neatly covered for her.

"Relax," he said. "And enjoy."

She did her best. The music captivated her, its mournful beauty striking a chord in her heart. She opened her mind to everything around her: the band, the other dancers, the heat of their bodies, the aromas of the food. But mostly she embraced the man who held her, who led her around the room, making sure she looked like she belonged there.

"Don't look at your feet," he whispered into her ear. "Look at me."

She did as he asked, raising her chin to look into Jackson's blue eyes, and then she was lost. Her breath whooshed out as he trapped her in his gaze, like an insect in a spider's web. Except unlike the insect, Carla never wanted out. She felt as if she could drown in him. Helpless, her mind drifted to thoughts of what he could do to her. His lips on hers, fingers skating across her naked skin, his body flush against hers on the bed while he held her down, sucking her breasts, his rock hard cock pressed against her thigh. She could reach down between their bodies and take him in her hands, stroking him, teasing, making him even harder. She would hear the ragged panting of his breaths against her skin, ready for her. His fingers would drift downward to slip between the wet folds of her pussy, mercilessly stroking until her hips arched up, so hot for him, and then he would enter—

The music stopped, dousing her fantasy like a bucket of cold water. Jackson stepped back to look down at her, smiling.

"Did you like it?"

Ooooh yeah. "Definitely. A lot." She prayed like mad that she bore no telltale red face from her little mental visit to his bedroom and plastered on a giant smile. She needed to pull herself together and pay no attention to her trembling knees or the throbbing pulses between her legs. Jackson Rivard was dangerous—to her career, her fear assignment, her sanity. She had to remember that.

"Thanks for the dance," she said. "It was great."

"Glad you enjoyed it."

The lively sounds of zydeco kicked in and had people stomping their boots all around them as Jackson led her back to their table.

"There's still a lot of food left," he said, noting the platter wasn't more than half empty.

"Good, because I'm still hungry," she replied with gusto, pushing aside all earlier thoughts of mind-blowing sex with Jackson. Since he'd earlier accused her of being a "follower" of the skinny-woman mentality, she wanted to prove him wrong. More than that, she wanted him to know her: a woman who didn't necessarily fit the public perception of a perfect body, but rather a woman who's fun, and pretty, and who liked to enjoy herself. Part of the enjoyment came from the visceral experience of a good meal, and she intended to take full advantage of it now.

For the next hour they ate and drank tea and talked like old friends. Relaxed and at ease, Jackson opened up and shared details about himself. She learned he'd earned his Ph.D. in microbiology before he turned thirty. He focused on studying the causes and effects of multiple sclerosis with an eye toward finding a permanent cure. He believed strongly king cobra venom held healing properties that could be part of the cure. His research facility was among the world's largest specifically dealing with king cobras, and his research partner, a brilliant scientist in his own right, was his father. She'd also learned he did indeed love to dance and had learned everything he knew from his mother.

"She must have been a great teacher," Carla noted, "because you're an excellent student."

"She was," Jackson said, but that short, simple response changed the mood in a microsecond. She heard the tension in his voice and with it came a strong sense of dread. Her skin prickled and her stomach clenched tight.

"She's no longer alive, is she?"

He looked at her for a moment, then his eyes dropped to the table. "No."

Way to keep the party lively, Carla. She struggled for the right words to offer an apology.

"Neither is my father," he said. "So we can get that

out of the way, too."

Her cheeks grew warm. "Jackson, I'm so sorry. I never meant—"

"I know. There's no way you could have known. But you can understand I don't like to talk about it."

"Of course."

"They died…" The traumatic memory seemed to rob him of speech. She saw his eyes go dark and fill with sorrow, his earlier ease vanishing like mist. He balled his hands into fists, tight with anxiety. After swallowing several times he expelled deep breaths of air, fighting for calm. "They died in a car accident," he uttered, in a dry, cracked voice. "Two years ago while on a vacation in England. The night was dark and rainy, and my father lost control of the car. They slammed headfirst into a tree and died upon impact. Simple as that."

"And it changed your whole life."

He gave a brief, almost imperceptible nod. "Yes."

Carla became aware of the buoyant music, the stomping feet of the dancers, the pungent smell of grease beginning to overwhelm her. Suddenly she wanted nothing more than to get out of there. She leaned forward in her chair to be heard above the music. "Maybe we should go?"

"Sure." He paid the check and they left, the lively Cajun music fading into the distance as they walked toward Jackson's SUV. If anything, the parking lot was more crowded now than it had been when they arrived, but Jackson deftly steered them out and in minutes they were back on the road. The night remained dark as ever, but as Carla craned her head around to look up, she was astounded by the sky.

"Wow." She whistled under her breath. "I don't think I've ever seen so many stars in my life. It's amazing."

Jackson nodded. "You can really see them out here because it's so dark. No light pollution to dim your view. And it's clear tonight."

"Could we stop? Please? I'd love to see this view just for a minute. This is definitely something you can't get in Manhattan."

"Sure. Let me find a place where there's a shoulder." They drove for another mile or so and found a place where the road widened so Jackson could pull over. He stopped the car and killed the lights, plunging the road into inky darkness.

Carla jumped out and looked up, letting out a gasp. Billions of stars flooded the sky, so densely packed they were like a carpet of light, stretching toward infinity. She recalled as a kid learning about constellations; now for the first time she could clearly see them. Orion, Aquarius, the Big Dipper, all right there, twinkling above her head.

"It's just incredible," she breathed, feeling a curious need to keep her voice low, as if they were in a church. "I've never seen anything like this. The stars are overwhelming me."

Jackson's boots crunched the gravel as he walked around the SUV to stand beside her. "It's a moving sight, isn't it?"

To her surprise, the hot wetness of a tear trickled down her cheek. She nodded, looking at Jackson, who gazed intently at her. "I don't know why this affects me so much. I didn't anticipate it. I just...I don't know. It's a beauty so pure and so powerful all at the same time."

She gave him a shaky, slightly embarrassed smile and lifted her hand to brush away another tear that threatened to spill. But before she could do it, Jackson reached out and grasped her wrist, stilling the movement. Then with his free hand he wiped her cheek.

Carla's pulse jumped at the sweep of his finger against her face, and a rush of desire, just like at the restaurant only a hundred times more powerful, crashed into her with the force of a boulder. The faintest sigh escaped her lips, so soft as to almost be unheard, except here, in the middle of an empty road, a sigh was as loud as a shout.

Jackson's finger stilled against her cheek and, with his palm, gently cupped her face. He stepped forward and slid his hand against the small of her back, guiding her toward him, and then he bent down and captured her lips.

Carla groaned as Jackson's warm mouth fit against hers. He lifted his free hand to weave his fingers through her hair, tilting her head back and then cradling it in his palm while caressing her with the side of his thumb. The kiss deepened as he nibbled her lips, first the top one, then a gentle tug on the bottom before softly licking at the seam. She opened her mouth to the sensual slide of his tongue against hers and fire ignited her blood when she heard him groan.

He guided her backward, slowly, step by step, until she felt the warm metal of the SUV against her rear and the delicious press of Jackson's hard cock against her front. She sighed into his mouth while her hands explored, skating over his ribs, the dip in his waist, and then around to his back, sliding over tight bunches of muscle and the firm sloping curve of his ass. Heat radiated from him in torrid waves and she felt through her fingertips his damp shirt clinging to his skin.

His scent surrounded her—a heady, male mixture of soap, sweat, and raw desire. The hard strain of his erection pressed like sensual torture against her abdomen, causing her pussy to ache with need. Jackson trailed the backs of his fingers against her neck, easing downward, until he reached the swell of her breast. Keeping his touch agonizingly light, he caressed the bare skin of her cleavage, giving her prickly goose bumps all over. She hadn't been touched intimately in a long—really long—time, and Jackson's feather light caress was like lighting a fuse on a rocket. She longed for him to dip his fingers beneath her bra and tease her aching nipples or, better still, to take them in his mouth and suck. A hungry groan escaped her lips.

Her senses went soaring skyward and she shivered with delight. Hot, relentless pulses of need sent moisture throbbing through her pussy. She angled her pelvis forward and teasingly rubbed against his bulging cock, thrilled by his sudden, sharp intake of breath. Jackson's hand slipped inside her blouse and underneath her bra. His palm circled her breast, gliding over the skin, until at last he began lightly pinching her nipple.

She groaned as his teasing fingers rocked an ache straight from her nipples to her clit, wishing his hands would drift lower. Her head dropped back against the SUV as she closed her eyes and gave herself up to his touch. She arched her back, filling his hand with her breast. His breath caught, and then his lips and tongue pressed against her throat, branding her with his kiss.

Grabbing fistfuls of his shirt, she pulled it out of

his pants and slid her hands under to settle against the hard, rippled plane of his stomach. His skin was hot, lightly coated with sweat. Her hands traveled higher, toward his chest. She found the small, hard beads of his nipples and began teasing them, filling the sultry night air with his soft groans.

Jackson pulled her blouse higher, exposing her, taking her nipple in his mouth and sucking. His tongue swirled around the tight bud, turning it to stone before pulling away and licking along the side of her breast. Rocked with pleasure, she arched her pelvis hard against the bulge of his cock as her hands traveled south and began to caress the swell of his ass. She whispered, "Jackson."

His head snapped up and he released her nipple from his lips.

For a second he stood, immobile, as if gaining control of his senses. Then he stepped back, away from her, and released a slow, shaky breath. As he did so, a wave of disappointment washed over her.

"We should go." His tense words broke the still air.

"But—"

"Before it gets too late." He was already walking around to his side of the car, opening the door, climbing inside. She jerked her blouse down, having no choice but to follow.

He had the SUV started before she'd even shut the door, and the second her seatbelt clicked into place they were off. What had happened? She was dying to ask, dying to know where the sultry, smokin' scientist had gone. But when she glanced over at Jackson, she saw the cool, guarded man she'd first met.

The ride back to the facility was as silent as the

night. Jackson was clearly caught up in his own thoughts and not interested in talking. It made her sad, because the evening otherwise had been so nice. But sometimes there was just no figuring out a man. Least not this one.

It was nearly midnight when they pulled up to the house. The grounds were quiet, with most of the lights out in the lodging buildings. Carla could hear the cicadas, crickets, and other night creatures as she walked with a silent Jackson to the front door. Finally she decided she'd had enough.

When he went to open the door, she stopped him with her hand. "I want to talk about what happened back there."

He shook his head. "It won't happen again." He once more tried to open the door, but she was firm. She stepped in front of him, blocking the way.

"I'm not the one who stopped," she reminded him. "You were. Why?"

His face clouded with annoyance and something else—she couldn't quite be certain—that looked like pain.

"We were standing on a public road. I assumed voyeurism wasn't your thing." He turned away, but not before she saw his gaze flicker hungrily over her breasts.

She didn't buy his sarcasm for a minute and vestiges of her arousal mere minutes ago had her still aching for his touch. "Really? Was that the reason? Well, in that case…" She trailed her fingers down his forearm. "We're not in public anymore, and your bedroom's just up the staircase…"

He shook her hand away. "Stop. I'm not doing

this."

"Why?" His emotions fed her anger like kindle to a fire. "You're lying to me, Jackson. You didn't stop me because you didn't want it. There's something else going on, something you're not telling me. I just want to know what it is."

He shook his head, refusing to say more. With a quick dart of his hand, he reached out and twisted the front door knob. Exhaling a long breath, he held the door open, an obvious signal for her to step indoors. "*Bon soir*, Carla. I'll see you tomorrow."

"You can't just brush me aside."

He shut the door behind them and tossed his keys in a basket he kept in the foyer. "Report to building eight tomorrow morning."

"Building eight?" She frowned. "Have I been there yet?"

"No," he said, already walking down the hallway toward the back staircase. As he began climbing the stairs he gave her one last bit of information. "It's where we keep the snakes."

****

Jackass.

Jackson leaned against the door and heaved an irritated sigh, feeling like a total jerk. *Merde*. What the fuck was the matter with him?

Making his way to the bathroom, he began stripping off his sweaty clothes, dumping them on the floor as he walked. He wasn't normally a slob, but right now he had other things to think about besides dirty laundry. Like getting his mind off of Carla Saunders.

He stepped into the shower and turned the water on full blast but icy cold, letting out a grunt as the frigid spray hit him. Damn it, he'd get rid of this wood one way or the other. He briefly considered relieving himself the easy way and jerking off, but chucked the idea. It meant he'd fantasize about Carla while doing it, and that's exactly what he was trying like hell not to do. Still, shit. She made it tough.

He grabbed a washcloth, soaped up, and scrubbed his body hard as he tried not to think about her—about her legs, or her breasts, or the smooth creaminess of her skin. That kiss had set him on fire. He shouldn't have started it—he knew he shouldn't have—but it'd be easier to freeze hell than keep saying no to her irresistible body. Damn, she'd looked so *hot* tonight. Her shapely ass, the hint of cleavage behind her blouse. His cock had practically stood up and saluted when she first came down the stairs.

Still, he might have been able to keep his hands to himself if not for that stop to look at the stars. When he saw the tear on her cheek and she admitted how overcome she was with the natural beauty around them, his resistance took a dive. At that moment he'd felt a connection with her. She got him. She understood the beauty of the bayou and why someone would want to be here. He hadn't felt that kind of connection with a woman in a hell of a long time.

And that kiss...*damn*. It nearly made him explode in his jeans. He'd wanted to bury his face between those gorgeous breasts, suck her nipples and wallow in the amazing lavender scent drifting off her skin. She turned him on like a hound in heat, but he thought he'd been hiding it pretty well. Until tonight, that is. When he'd looked over and saw that tear...

He groaned and scrubbed harder. He knew he

Elizabeth Shore

shouldn't torture himself, but he had this sexy-as-hell, smart, energetic, and beautifully uninhibited intern living here day and night, who he sensed was as turned on by him as he was by her. It'd be so easy just to let go, to let them both have what they so obviously wanted.

He'd avoided her for the past few days because he didn't want to lose focus. He'd made a promise and he couldn't—wouldn't—break it. He would find that cure and fulfill the pledge he'd made—to his parents, to himself, and especially to Amy. Carla Saunders, with her smoking hot body and intriguing personality could mess with his head big time. He only had to think for two seconds about Katherine to remind himself of what a beautiful woman could do to a guy. It's why he'd pulled away from Carla tonight, despite how hot he burned for her.

But, seriously. A month? It went by so fast she'd be gone before he knew it and then he'd be able to stop thinking about her. And it was just sex, nothing more. No feelings or emotions, none of that shit that just messes things up. And man, oh man, could he ever imagine how good it would be. He heard his subconscious start to get pissed. *C'mon, dude. Look in the mirror. You want her, she wants you. Stop holding back. You can do this without fucking up your goals and have some fun along the way. It's only a month. Go for it!*

He took a breath, looked down. Still hard as a rock. Yeah, he could do this.

Chapter Five

Carla patted on one final sweep of powder and gave herself a critical look in the mirror. Not bad for someone who'd skipped a night of sleep. A few eye drops to remove the red, concealer to remove the dark circles and *voilà*! Fresh as a daisy. At least, that's what the outside world would think.

She left her room early, intending to get breakfast before she reported to building eight. But as she walked on the pathway toward the caf she remembered the purpose of building eight and felt a surge of dread, thick and hot like lava, oozing into her stomach and taking with it any remnant of an appetite. She swallowed back a rush of bile and sat down on a nearby bench. She was flushed with heat and sent a silent prayer of thanks heavenward that she hadn't forgotten her deodorant. She sat for several minutes, getting her breathing under control, when Lisa Martin walked by.

"Carla?" She stopped and leaned down, peering intently at her. "Are you all right?" She frowned with concern, shoving wavy brown hair behind her ears as she took a place on the bench. "You don't look well at all."

Carla gave her a weak smile. "I'm fine."

"You're white as a sheet. Should I get you some water?"

"No, it's okay." She shook her head. "If you could

just sit here for a minute I'd really appreciate it."

"Of course!" Lisa sat back on the bench and eased Carla back as well. "Just rest here for a minute. You look kind of like you've had a scare."

"Well, I have, in a way." Carla let out another breath, feeling once more under control. "Listen, I don't want to make you late. If you could just point me in the right direction to get where I'm going, I'll be fine."

"It's no problem for me to walk you there, Carla," Lisa said as they both rose. "It's not exactly like we're on the clock around here. Where are you headed, anyway?"

"Building eight."

"That's where I'm going! C'mon, I'll show you." Lisa's enthusiastic smile reached all the way to her warm brown eyes.

They turned onto a path toward the building. "So you're seeing the snakes today. Wow. I'm impressed."

"Impressed?"

"Definitely." Lisa let out a whistle. "Jackson usually makes interns wait a lot longer and do more beyond what you've done before they're allowed anywhere near the cobras."

"Guess I'm lucky," Carla replied. Was Jackson giving her some weird kind of punishment for last night, secretly blaming her for what happened? He knew her deep fear of snakes. It seemed far-fetched, but she couldn't help but wonder.

Carla took a deep breath; let it out. "Actually, the snakes are what caused my reaction back there."

"The snakes? What do you mean?"

"I'm afraid of them."

"You are?"

"Yes. Very."

Lisa stopped walking. "Then what in the world are you doing here?"

She explained the purpose of the fear assignment, not surprised to see confusion washing over Lisa's face.

"Huh." Lisa frowned. "Well, I'll be. So what happens if you can't control your fear?"

"Nothing good."

"Wow, so this is a big deal, then?"

"You could say that."

They resumed walking, Lisa turning them off the main path and toward a low, white building nestled among soaring live oaks.

"That's building eight. The enclosure for the snakes is behind it; you can't really see it from here. But the main entrance for the enclosure is through the building. There are other entrances around the perimeter, but those are generally used just for emergencies."

They walked up the few steps to reach the front door and stepped inside. The room they entered was filled with row after row of computers and printers, an enormous server room off to the side, and countless large monitors, like in a TV newsroom, mounted to the walls.

"Very high tech," Carla commented as they found seats in front of a couple of monitors.

"It's the best in the country," Lisa said as she began studying the data on the screen. "Jackson's invested a fortune in this facility, and it shows. We all feel really lucky to work here."

"He told me all of you believe in his cause, finding a cure for MS."

"Absolutely." Lisa nodded with enthusiasm. "There's so much research showing king cobra snake venom's unique properties could be used toward a cure. We just have to find it."

Her energy and unshakeable conviction were catching, and for the first time since she arrived, Carla found herself having some curiosity about the snakes instead of just pure dread.

"So how does this all work?" she asked Lisa. "Can you show me?"

"That's what I'm here for," Lisa said with a bright smile. "We rotate shifts in this facility and I'm here all day today, so I'm all yours. Come on, let me give you a tour of what we do."

For the next two hours, Carla was rapt with awe as Lisa took her through the monitoring system, record keeping, and data analysis that happened in building eight. She pointed out the sterile room where they kept some of the venom samples, how they needed to be stored at a certain cold temperature and kept in specific containers. She also showed her the vessel the handlers used to extract venom and the room where they did it.

"It's open right now," Lisa explained, "because we're not extracting until this afternoon, so come on in."

They entered the room. A stainless steel table dominated the middle of it. Hanging on the wall, like pool cues, were a number of long metal instruments.

"These are used by the handlers to carry the snakes from their containers over to the table, or to hold them down when they're on the table. Every extraction involves two people. You ought to watch it sometime."

"I..." She swallowed, stomach churning as a wave

of terror engulfed her. "I don't know. Just the thought of a snake being on this table is giving me goose bumps."

"Honestly, nothing will help you overcome your fear better than to confront it. And isn't that the point of your fear assignment? To test you in an actual situation you're afraid of?"

Carla gave her a wan smile. "You sound like my boss. Or my mother."

"Ouch!" Lisa laughed. "I'm guessing that's not a good thing." They turned to walk out the door and go back to the main room.

"Actually, it is a good thing," Carla said once they'd taken their seats in front of the monitors again. "My mom's great, but she can be demanding."

"Mine, too." Lisa glanced at the monitor and typed at the keyboard. "Well, there you are!" Carla couldn't see what she looked at, but whatever it was caused her new friend to smile.

"Come over here." Lisa motioned to Carla. "I want you to see something."

Carla rose from her chair and walked over to where Lisa sat.

"All of these monitors," Lisa gestured to the one in front of her as well as the myriad ones mounted on the wall, "show different areas of the snake enclosure behind this building. We've got all kinds of cameras installed within the enclosure so we can find our snakes when we need them. Through the computer we can click on any camera and control it remotely. So it allows us to turn the camera in several different directions to capture as wide an area as possible."

Carla stood behind Lisa and peered at the monitor.

When she saw what was on it, she gasped, heart pounding like a herd of stampeding elephants. She whipped her head sideways and shot her gaze to the floor, the chairs, anywhere but the monitors.

"C'mon, Carla. Conquer that fear and look at her. She's beautiful."

"I can't. She's a snake."

"She's a pregnant snake." She glanced at Carla who still stared at the floor. "Allow me to introduce you to Mariah."

Carla's head turned fractionally to look over at Lisa. "Mariah?"

"Sure. We love to name our snakes, and that one seemed to fit. Here, I'll put the view of our girl up on one of the large wall monitors. Have a look."

She could hear the slight hint of a command in Lisa's voice and knew she was right. She was behaving like a little girl and not the high-powered rising executive she fancied herself to be. She let out a deep breath and looked up.

The female king cobra was coiled in what looked to be a nest. Surrounded by bits of grass, leaves, and twigs, she'd made a secure place in which to gestate and await the birth of her hatchlings.

"She's lying atop her eggs," Lisa explained, "and she'll stay that way until they hatch. If we look around with another camera—" She tapped a few keys and another view came up. This time they spotted a larger snake, coiled as well, fairly close to the female's nest. "That's her mate, Drew. He'll guard the nest until the eggs hatch. It's an unusual arrangement within the snake world, this complex nesting and rearing behavior."

"How long until they hatch?"

"Gestation period is sixty to eighty days. Then, once they hatch, both Mariah and Drew will leave the young hatchlings."

Carla leaned forward for a closer look at the monitor. Despite her fears, she found herself fascinated by what Lisa told her, but she frowned at this latest bit. "Leave them? Why?"

"To make sure they don't eat them."

"Eww. Eat their own young?"

"It's more common than you might think in the animal kingdom. But instinct makes the mother leave the nest. Same thing with the father. It's really pretty fascinating when you think about it. Once the babies hatch, they've already got the same amount of potent venom as their parents. And they know instinctively how to raise themselves and how to hunt. It's amazing."

Carla returned to her chair, considering what Lisa had just said. Now that she was getting used to seeing the snakes on the monitor and her roaring heartbeat had settled, she could appreciate a researcher's passion for all the crazy dynamics found in nature. Lisa's enthusiasm was slowly—slowly—catching on.

"So, when the handlers extract the venom, I take it they first have to enter the enclosure to get the snakes out?"

"They do, yes. That's why we have this complex set of cameras, so we can find the snakes. We'll keep them in glass cages for a week at a time while we extract, then we put those snakes back in the enclosure and bring in different ones. Jackson insists on this rotational method so as not to stress the snakes through excessive extraction. He believes allowing the snakes to be in a natural setting will give us the purest venom samples. I have no cause to question him. He's a brilliant scientist and he's also the one who had the vision for this place." Lisa looked around. "I feel really lucky to be working here."

The respect Lisa had for her employer could not be mistaken. When she spoke about Jackson her face lit up, as if she were describing a rock star. *Maybe*, Carla thought, *within the world of king cobra research, that's what Jackson is*.

"How long have you been here?" she asked.

"Well…" Lisa looked away from her monitor and sat back in her chair, thoughtfully sipping coffee from the travel mug she'd brought along. "I actually first came here to conduct coursework related to my doctorate. Once I completed it I stayed on as a research assistant to earn some money while I wrote my dissertation. The research I did here went into my thesis. That was three years ago. Jackson made me a full-time staff member once I'd defended my dissertation and was awarded the degree."

"So once you first came here you never left?"

"I guess I just fell in love with the snakes."

But hopefully not with their owner, Carla thought, embarrassed by the spear of jealousy piercing her heart. She didn't know whether Lisa and Jackson had ever had a relationship; in fact, for all she knew they could be having one now. But that was none of her business. It shouldn't matter. It definitely shouldn't.

"You like him, don't you?"

Carla jumped out of her thoughts like a thief who'd been caught in the blinding glare of a police flashlight. And just like the thief, she was guilty.

"Well, sure," she answered in a rush. "I like him just fine. He's smart and seems nice and I appreciate his willingness to help me on this assignment and—"

"That's not what I meant." Lisa leaned forward in her chair, hands resting on her knees. "Look, Carla. I happened to be walking past The Snake Pit last night and saw you and Jackson getting out of his car. Where you went, what you were doing, that's none of my business. But I don't want secrets between us, so I thought you should know."

"Oh. Ah, okay. Thanks for telling me." Though Lisa hadn't asked, she felt oddly compelled to fill in the details. "We went, um, he took me to dinner. At Les's Place."

"That's nice. Les's is fun."

A wall of silence sprung up between them. Carla looked away, trying to decide what to do, what more to say, when at last she simply shrugged and threw in the towel. "It doesn't make any sense, I just got here, but there's—"

Lisa's eyes filled with understanding. "I know. There's just something about him."

"Are you and he...I mean..." Her cheeks burned.

"Are we seeing each other?" Lisa let out a small laugh, but without jest. "No, I'm not screwing the boss, don't worry."

"I'm not worried, I just—"

"Look, Carla, you don't have to explain anything to me. Whatever's going on between you and Jackson—*if* there's anything going on between you and Jackson—is none of my business and frankly, not something I care about. I'm here for my career, that's all. And besides, as far as the home front's concerned,

117

I've got it covered. My boyfriend, Brad, and I got engaged three months ago, so I'm in the middle of planning a wedding."

"Oh, that's great!" Carla's eye automatically dropped to Lisa's left hand, but it was bare. Lisa quickly noticed.

"I don't ever wear my ring to work. Jewelry of any kind can be a hazard around here. It can get stuck in equipment, have chemicals spilled on it, or just plain get in the way when we're conducting research. So I leave it at home."

"Sounds smart."

Lisa rose from her chair. "Listen, I'm going to get myself another cup of coffee and then we'd better get to work. If you want some, come with me. There's a little pantry room back here where we keep a pot going pretty much all day long."

"Coffee would be good."

They walked toward a hallway off the main room leading to the pantry. While they were fixing their coffee, Lisa stopped and looked at Carla. "Like I said, this is none of my business and I really don't care what's between you and Jackson. But could I give you a piece of advice?"

Carla halted her stirring and looked up. Lisa sounded serious. "Of course."

Lisa nodded and then paused, as if not sure where to begin. "Jackson's parents died in a bad car accident a couple of years ago."

"Yeah, he told me. Last night, in fact."

"It's good you know because it really affected him. Kinda messed with his head, actually. For a long time after it happened he didn't talk to anyone about anything, and certainly not about the accident."

Her heart twisted as she imagined Jackson's pain. "I'm sure he was grieving."

"Of course." Lisa nodded. "We all understood and gave him space. But about six months after it happened, we found out Jackson blamed himself for it. And no matter what anyone says to him, no one's ever been able to convince him otherwise."

"But that's crazy. His father lost control of the car on a rainy night. Jackson told me so himself. He couldn't have caused that to happen."

They picked up their cups and walked back toward the main room. Her mind spun as she digested what Lisa had told her. She felt as if she'd been shown a window to Jackson's heart only to have it slammed shut in her face, leaving behind more questions than answers. How could he possibly blame himself for a car accident that happened an ocean away? Was the hurt he still carried what kept him so guarded? She shook her head, wondering if she'd ever know the answer.

"There's more to the story than that, but I'll leave it for Jackson to tell you. I just thought you should know because...well..." She shrugged. "It sounds silly, but I guess I wanted you to know he's been through a lot and what he doesn't need, on top of everything, is getting his heart broken."

"His heart broken?" Carla tried to toss off the idea as crazy, but even to her own ears, the effort sounded hollow. She could only imagine what Lisa thought. "C'mon. It was only dinner."

"Yeah, well." Lisa resumed her seat in front of the monitor. After clicking around a few times, she turned back toward Carla. "You wouldn't guess it from the outside, but Jackson's heart is more fragile than most."

Brusque, brooding, no-nonsense Mr. Grunter has a fragile heart? It made no sense. Yet the sincerity and seriousness in Lisa's voice forced Carla to take note.

"Thanks for letting me know."

"No problem." Lisa grabbed her coffee and stood up. "Now, why don't we get started? Come over this way. I'll show you the data room where you'll be working."

The rest of the day passed by in a flash. Once Lisa had shown Carla what she wanted her to do, she spent the rest of the day archiving records and synching them with the central databases she'd already created. The information she came across was fascinating. She found data related to the snakes themselves, such as their care and feeding, extraction analyses, and reams and reams of test results. Rivard Research was a very busy lab and the scientists wasted no time in testing the venom once they'd extracted it.

As she entered the information, Carla was surprised to feel a sense of pride surging through her, even though her association with the lab was superficial and short-term. Nonetheless, what happened here was meaningful. It mattered. No one in this lab discussed "pushing the envelope" or creating a "value-added proposition." No, what they did here was try to improve lives, simple as that. It wasn't a matter of going after the "low hanging fruit." It was a matter of making sick people better. *And you could help them.*

She scolded her rash inner voice and ordered it to pipe down, even while knowing the thought was true. She definitely could help them. Operational efficiency, cash flow generation, optimal staff management.

Jackson hated all of that, but she knew she could convince him he needed her. *You mean he needs Bartlett Silver. Geez, Carla. Are you forgetting the point of the assignment?*

Of course she wasn't. She'd just...well, kind of thought of her and Bartlett Silver as one and the same. That was all.

She glanced up at the clock, amazed to see the time well after six. She got up and walked into the main room. Lisa was gone; sitting in her place was the young Indian biology student whom she'd met in the cafeteria. She gave him a friendly wave as she left the building, noticing he studied on his monitor the same gestating cobra Lisa had been looking at this morning. Carla found herself wondering if there was a problem, and then actually chuckled aloud as she walked down the stairs. Never in a million years would she have guessed she'd ever be concerned about a snake.

She heard the crunch of gravel behind her as she walked but didn't need to turn around to identify the source of the sound. Jackson's presence was easily felt, like the inexplicable sense of knowing when someone is staring at you from behind. With him, however, it was more than just sensation; he emitted an aura as strong as a touch...and just as powerful. He said something to her, though he was still far enough away she couldn't make out the words. She knew the voice, though. Low. Soft. Intense. She turned and saw him walking toward her.

"I didn't catch what you said," she replied when he came close enough.

"I wanted to know if you'd survived the cobras." His smooth low voice contained no trace of tension from the night before. He stopped only steps away from her and hitched his thumbs in the pocket of his jeans. The movement drew her gaze down his legs and over to territory it had no business visiting. Immediate heat rushed to her cheeks as memories of last night surfaced, his hot kisses on her skin, her breasts. She mentally kicked herself, willing those thoughts aside, even as she felt her panties dampen.

Determined to focus, she smiled up at him. "I more than survived. In fact, I found it interesting."

"Not terrifying?"

They headed toward the cafeteria. "Well, since I didn't actually see any real snakes, just those on the monitors, it kept the terror at bay."

He chuckled. "That's good."

"It's really impressive," she added. They approached the cafeteria building, but rather than walking up the steps to the entrance, Jackson stopped and turned to look at her.

"What is?"

"Everything." She spread her hands, palms up, as if to encompass her surroundings. "What you do, these facilities, the research, the mission, your staff…"

He pierced her again, those blue eyes studying her so keenly as if he could see her soul. The look was penetrating, intimidating, and sexy as hell. It so distracted her she lost her train of thought.

"I'm glad you like it," he said, his voice low.

Jackson glanced sideways, as if to ensure they were alone. When he returned his gaze, she was startled to see an ink black taint of desire reflected back at her. Suddenly she sensed an unexpected change in the air. It was as if an undercurrent of energy, not there minutes before, suddenly came to life. Her heartbeat skittered against her chest.

He eased his way closer, narrowing the gap between them. She shivered as he lifted a finger and trailed it down her arm, leaving a sizzle of heat in its wake. Her reaction was immediate, nipples pebbling beneath her blouse.

She licked dry lips. "Jackson, what—"

"What am I doing? Is that what you want to know?"

She nodded. He took another step toward her.

"It's pretty simple. I've been thinking about last night." He stood so close his thighs brushed hers. She was suffused by his heat and his intoxicating woodsy smell. A slow, throbbing ache began building in her core.

"You made me lose sleep, you know?" He caressed her arm and along the side of her neck. He slipped his hand into her hair. "I couldn't get you out of my mind."

With the tips of his fingers he lightly stroked along her collarbone and the base of her throat. His eyes glittered as he looked down at her. She heard a change in his breathing as it grew heavier, more pronounced. "You're a very bad girl, Carla."

Her voice was little more than a whisper. "Am I?"

"Oh, yes." He leaned in and brushed soft lips against her neck. "You distract me."

"And that's bad?"

"Of course it is. I have work to do."

She glanced down and saw the rise in his jeans. Emboldened by her effect on him, she put her hand on his chest and felt his thundering heart. A rush of excitement heated her blood. Jackson wanted her.

Badly. Still, her mind clouded with confusion.

"I don't get it. Last night you made it pretty clear that—"

"That we weren't doing this. I know; we shouldn't." He kissed her neck once more. She nearly purred. "I have work to do, you have an internship to complete." He murmured the words against her skin. "But I can't stop thinking about getting you naked."

"Oh really?" She pulled back to look at him, attempting to be stern even while her pussy throbbed with need. "You had your chance last night and didn't take it. What makes you so certain I'm going to let you do that now?"

He stood stock still before her, intensity blazing like fire. "I can be very persuasive when I want something bad enough."

Her pulse shot to the sky. "And you want this bad enough?"

His jaw set as he stepped into her space. "I want *you* bad enough," he said, drawing her into his embrace as he claimed her with lips and tongue that were rough, possessive, his mouth mashing against hers as if driving home the strength of his need. The stubble on his jaw scratched around her lips, branding her.

This isn't like before, Carla thought in a dreamy haze, her clit beginning to pulse. This isn't a soft, whispery kind of kiss. This is a hard, passionate, no-bullshit kind of kiss. The kind preceding an endless evening of loud, sweaty sex. The kind of sex she hadn't had in a *long* time.

She moaned and slipped her arms around his neck as his free hand caressed her face. He's a face kind of guy, she thought. Nice. She liked that.

Heat poured from Jackson's body like a furnace. She slid her hands over his shoulders and down along his back, tracing the outline of his linen shirt where it stuck fast against hard, sweaty muscles. Her palms dipped lower, skimming over the tight curves of his ass. Jackson responded with a throaty groan.

She opened her mouth to him, deepening the kiss. The warm exhale of his breath drifted across her cheeks and she heard him let out a quiet groan of desire as he pulled her tighter into his body. Her breasts pressed hard against his chest, her willing hands sliding back up over his shoulders and arms. Sighing, she kneaded the ripple of muscle beneath his shirt.

The intensity of his passion caught her off guard, but she wasn't about to protest. Only problem was, they were outside where anyone walking by could see them. They were also standing. Another problem, because she was aware of the wetness in her panties and the hot throbbing of her clit and knew she was more than ready for him. She couldn't satisfy her need standing up. She moaned in frustration.

Jackson broke the kiss and looked down at her. "My bedroom," he ordered, words coated with lust. "Now."

To drive home his point, he held her gaze while sliding the palm of his hand down a trail from her neck, over the swell of her breasts, against her stomach, and then to the hot core between her legs. Hand open, he ground his palm outside her jeans, his expert touch finding her clit while her knees turned to water.

"Stop," she pleaded in a ragged whisper, not wanting him to but aware they could be seen.

"Only until I get you inside."

He took her hand in his and together they turned, almost racing toward The Snake Pit, neither of them talking. Way too keyed up for conversation, she suspected Jackson felt the same. She only hoped the short walk back to his bedroom didn't slacken his desire enough for cool logic to prevail. After all, she'd only be here for a month and after she left they'd likely never see each other again. Why start something now? On the other hand, her need for him was real and she didn't want to be logical or rational. She wanted to have sex with him, logic be damned.

Once Jackson shut and locked the bedroom door behind him, he turned feral on her. With his wolf-like gait he stalked her, moving toward where she stood by the bed. His eyes sparkled in the gloaming, irises wide and dark, gaze riveted to her face. He pulled her against him and re-fired their earlier kiss, slipping his tongue into her mouth, tangling it with hers as his hands slid everywhere over her body. He fumbled at the buttons on her blouse like a starving man after food. Once he had it off, seconds later her bra was gone, too.

Carla shivered as the soft breeze coming in from the open window touched her bare skin. Jackson kissed and licked her breasts and stomach as he knelt down before her, his tongue leaving behind a trail of moisture. He reached the buttons on her jeans and easily flicked them open, pulling at the zipper, and then pushed them over her hips and down her legs. Her panties were next.

Before she knew it, Carla stood naked in front of him while he retained every bit of clothing. She was about to protest, wanting to rectify the situation, when he rose and stepped back, hand propped beneath his chin, as if to admire a piece of art. His chest rose and fell with his labored breathing, and his gaze, black with lust, slid over her body. She took a step forward, eager to remove his clothes as well, when he halted her with an upheld hand.

"*Pas encore*," he said softly, shaking his head. Not yet. "Let me look at you first."

Normally she would have been considerably more self-conscious, aware of her few extra pounds, knowing she didn't possess the sleek frame of a model. But the stark yearning in Jackson's hungry gaze told a different story. She was a beautiful, desirable woman who made him burn with need. He whistled low beneath his breath, confirming his reaction was real.

She smiled and walked toward him, her earlier desire returned in full force. "Enough with the viewing," she said. "Those clothes of yours are coming off. Now."

He raised an eyebrow. "Demanding woman."

"I can be. When I want something."

She unbuttoned his shirt as quickly as her fingers would allow, impatient to push away the fabric and have his bare skin touching hers. But Jackson didn't cooperate. He bent forward and began kissing her face, soft butterfly kisses that were lovely, but which interfered with her work.

Then his hands were on her breasts, fingers teasing the sensitive skin, lightly pinching her nipples so they flushed beet red and hardened to pebbles. She let out a gasp and tried to push his hands away, but as hers were occupied with trying to unbutton his shirt, the effort proved unsuccessful.

He was a master at teasing, alternating his touches

between light and tender to hard and demanding. He explored every inch of her, skimming across her stomach, her waist, even teasing her belly button. But then they trailed farther down and suddenly she could no longer think.

With the tips of his fingers on his right hand he brushed through the wiry hairs on her mound and then navigated down her slit, using a caress as light as air to stroke her clit and send her senses into orbit.

"Oh, I…" She couldn't remember what she was going to say.

"Something wrong?"

God no. "No, I just…"

"Maybe this is better?" He sank a finger inside her pussy.

Oooooh. So nice. She tried to respond, but the only sounds coming out were deep, throaty groans. He stroked her slick walls, increasing speed, already a master at reading her needs. With his free hand he teased and pinched her hypersensitive nipples, making her gasp in lustful agony.

She pressed her lips against Jackson's chest, bare where she'd gotten the first few buttons undone before he had interfered with her progress. She licked at his skin, tasting the saltiness, panting against him as he slipped a second finger inside her pussy and stroked while continuing to caress her clit with his thumb. She vaguely wondered where he'd perfected that technique but then decided she wasn't going to care. She had other things to think about right now, namely the pending orgasm about to overtake her.

"Don't stop," she begged in a low whisper. "Please."

"Never." He increased his thrusts, making them harder and deeper. His fingers curved inside of her, skimming her G-spot. Every nerve in her body fired around the slick heat of her pussy. She shamelessly ground against his fingers while winding her arms around his shoulders, holding tight for support. His heady male scent surrounded her as she buried her face against his chest. She rocked her clit against his hand, building pressure. Jackson grasped one of her thighs and wrapped it around his waist, opening her further to him while continuing to stroke.

"Come for me, babe."

She sobbed against him, blood roaring through her veins, skin flushed. She was so close. She thrust against him, needing just a little more, and his circling thumb pressed hard against her clit as he sent her over the edge.

"Yes!" She exploded, pulsing waves of orgasm flooding her senses. Her head fell back, eyes shut tight, mouth open, crying out with ecstasy.

When she floated back to Earth she pulled him to her, kissing him deeply. She needed him inside of her. She took hold of his shirt and went back to work.

"I want you naked," she announced, reaching the last button. His shirt fell open, revealing bronzed skin lightly grazed with dark hair, and tight, hard abs. Just the way she liked 'em. Around his left arm was the Ourobouros tattoo, but now the snake winding its way around his bicep was more sexy than scary. She reached up to push the shirt off his shoulders but as she did so, she saw again hesitation in Jackson's eyes, like he fought with himself, desire against control. Carla knew which side she wanted to win.

"You okay?"

He swallowed hard but didn't answer. The inky darkness of his eyes and the severe swell beneath his jeans proved he was still aroused, so…

"Jackson?" She frowned. "Look, if you don't want this, then—"

He stopped her with a finger to her lips. "I do want this," he said. "That's the problem."

"What—"

She got no further. He pushed away his own shirt and quick as lightning undid his jeans. Yanked off his boxers. He pulled her toward him and they fell into bed. He kissed her, hard, almost as if he had something to prove. And his hands roamed everywhere, her face, her breasts, between her thighs. He was rock hard, cock jutting straight out, a drop of pre-cum glistening on the tip. Carla reached down and stroked him, loving the feeling of soft velvet skin sheathed over a marble rod. She stroked her hand up and down, slow, sure movements that had him panting in seconds.

He flipped her onto her back and eased himself on top of her, resting the bulk of his weight on his elbows. For the briefest of moments he looked into her eyes, his gaze searching, needing to confirm Carla wanted this as much as he did. She gave him a brief nod and whispered, "Yes."

With his free arm he stretched out toward the nightstand drawer, felt around inside, and then raised his hips for a moment as he ripped open a condom packet and slipped it on. Reaching down, he angled his cock between her legs, brushing her slit, gathering moisture. He pushed the head of his cock inside her entrance, a sensual tease of what was to come. His fingers gripped her ankles, spreading her legs wide and then burying his full length in her pussy.

She sighed as he entered, and he waited for a moment as she adjusted to the divine, almost painful stretch of his thick cock. Jackson released her ankles and settled on top of her, resting most of his weight on his elbows. He kissed her, soft as air, and then deeper, melting her with his lips and tongue. His thrusts began, slowly, almost exquisitely so, transforming the pleasure to sublime torture.

But she wanted more, wanted to feel him pounding into her. She bucked her hips, tried to draw him in. He didn't respond but instead he broke the kiss and let his head lean forward so his mouth was close to her ear. She heard whispering, very soft. She frowned. Was he talking to her?

"*Seize, quinze, quatorze, treize…*"

"What?"

"*Sept, six, cinq…*"

"Jackson, what are you saying?"

His eyes had been closed. He pushed himself up with his arms and opened them, breathing deeply. "I'm counting backward."

"What? Why?"

"To distract myself."

"I don't—"

"I'm trying not to come, Carla." Another breath. "At least not yet."

"Oh."

He resumed his thrusts, the feel of his cock slowly sliding into her enough to drive her mad.

"I don't care if you come soon," she whispered, "but I can't take this torture."

"Carla, I—"

"Fuck me, Jackson. Hard."

His breath whooshed from his throat as he groaned. "Your wish is my command."

He picked up the pace, pounding against her, giving her exactly what she wanted. His slick cock rammed hard, balls slapping against her ass as he drove into her. Head bent, he took her nipple in his mouth, sucking her, his wet tongue swirling around the sensitive nub and lightly grazing the peak with his teeth.

She arched her back, giving him more, matching every one of his thrusts with needy ones of her own. He filled her completely, the delicious stretch from his thick cock causing tingles of pleasure to race through her body, from her clenching pussy all the way down to her toes.

She slipped her hands behind him, loving the feel of his hard ass muscles bunching as he drove into her. His hips snapped with violent force as he increased his pace. Straightening once more, he wrapped her legs around his waist and gripped her thighs as he thrust.

Seconds later he surrendered control. His shaft thickened inside of her and for a moment he went still, eyes squeezed tightly shut. His jaw went slack as his head dropped back. He held tight to Carla's thighs and let out an unmistakable groan of intense release before he shuddered and then collapsed on top of her.

He lay unmoving, panting, until at last with apparent reluctance he rolled off of her. He got up to dispose of the condom but returned seconds later, drawing her close so she could rest her head on his arm.

Carla closed her eyes, enjoying the salty smell of

Jackson's skin, the heat of his body seeping into hers. Who would have guessed a snake breeder could be so hot in bed? With a stab of jealousy she realized it was probably because he'd had a lot of practice. But if that was the case, why had he been so concerned with coming too soon? Usually that only happened if it had been a long time since he last...

She propped herself up on her elbow, fixing her gaze on him. His eyes were half open, hooded, and his lips pressed tight as if he had all the problems of the world resting on his shoulders. Not a good look for a man she'd just had sex with.

He glanced over at her when he noticed she stared at him. "What?"

"Nothing, I—" Maybe she was off the mark. But no, she had a gut feeling she'd learned long ago to trust.

"Have you...I mean, has it been a long time since you last...you know...had sex?"

He stiffened at her question. She'd touched a nerve. "Was there a problem?"

"God, no." She rushed to explain. "It was amazing. I just—wait, don't go."

But he'd already slipped out of bed and pulled on his jeans. She longed for cover-up as well. She felt more naked and vulnerable now than when she'd stood without clothing before him while he was fully dressed. Likely sensing her discomfort, Jackson tossed her jeans and blouse onto her lap.

She dressed and sat up in bed, adjusting the pillows so she could prop herself against them. Jackson sat in a corner reading chair, his profile tense as he looked out the window. The stubborn thrust of his jaw and narrowed eyes betrayed his anger. His glasses were on the table beside the bed, so she knew he wasn't really seeing whatever he was looking at. From outside the distant symphony of crickets, cicadas, bullfrogs, and birds did nothing to ease the strained silence.

"I don't know what I said, but I didn't mean—"

He waved a hand to stop her. "It's not you. You've done nothing wrong."

"But then, why?"

At last he turned and looked at her, his expression firm. "There are a lot of things you don't know about me, Carla, and I'd prefer to keep it that way. You're only here for a month; let's not complicate things."

He was right; she knew it. So why did his words cut so deeply?

"I'm not going to deny I wanted you," he continued. "From the minute I saw you."

"You did?"

"Of course."

She waited for him to say more but, as was the way with him, nothing further came. Still, knowing he hungered for her soothed the earlier hurt. "Oh."

His brows knit, as if the answer was so obvious he couldn't understand her confusion. "You seem surprised."

"Well, sure I am." She adjusted her position, looking straight at him. "You didn't exactly come on to me like gangbusters, you know. So how's a girl to tell?"

To her surprise, he actually winced, as if she'd thrown him a punch. "I have my reasons," he said quietly, expelling a weary sigh. "But you're right. It's been a long time since I last had sex. Two years, in fact."

She managed just in time to keep her mouth from

falling open. "Two years? Why?"

By the sharp intake of his breath, she knew she'd landed on one of those things he didn't want to talk about.

When he kept silent she finally asked, "You're not going to tell me?"

"No."

His steadfast refusal to answer her questions cut deep, a painful incision dangerously close to her heart, but she also felt the slow burn of anger take hold.

"So where does that leave us?" She crossed her arms, shielding herself. "I'm just your play toy for the month? A friend with benefits?" Hurt took its place alongside the anger, simmering her blood like the toxic brew in a witch's cauldron. She didn't want it to, but couldn't seem to stop it.

"I'm not laying any claims on you, Jackson, because you're right. My time here is short, and then we'll both go our separate ways. But sleeping together, even if it's only for a short time, means something to me. It means respect, and it means trust. And you with all your secrets, blocking me out like you don't trust me. Well," she shrugged. "It makes me feel…used."

"Don't," he said, eyes filling with compassion. "It's not like that. You're not just a quick lay for a month, Carla."

"Then why—"

He shook his head. "I can't talk about it. I wish I could. I wish I could give you what you're asking for because the last thing I want is for you to get hurt. You're smart, you're beautiful. You even make me laugh, which doesn't always come easy. And I'll tell you this: I want you. I think about having you in my bed practically every damn minute of the day. I've wanted you since the minute I laid eyes on you. I've tried like hell to resist it, believe me, but I just can't anymore."

He let out a frustrated breath of air. "*Mon Dieu,* Carla, I want you again now. I haven't been interested in a woman for a long time, but you're turning me into a hormone-raging sex maniac."

Even as he spoke, she could see the rise in his jeans. Her anger began to fade. There was a raw honesty about Jackson, making him different from other men. And he was sexy as hell, no doubt about it. Despite her earlier frustration, she could feel her body readying itself for him again. Her nipples hardened, yearning for his touch. She liked what he said about wanting her. She wanted him, too.

She scooted off the bed and walked toward him. Slowly. Crossing her arms in front of her, she grabbed her blouse, lifting it up and off as she walked, letting her breasts swing free as she neared him. His chest rose and fell with ragged breaths as his hands gripped the arms of his chair. He licked his lips as she approached, as if readying himself for a treat.

She stopped before him and slowly undid her jeans, pushing them down her legs and then kicking them away, teasing him like a stripper. Naked, powerful, she knelt down before him and stroked his bulge. He groaned.

"I need to finish," he breathed, "what I was telling you."

"So go ahead." She continued to caress him with her left hand while her right hand reached out and undid the top button on his jeans, then inch by inch pulled the zipper down.

"Lift your hips," she commanded softly, and she slid his jeans down as he obeyed. He hadn't bothered with his underwear when he'd put his clothes back on, and now his cock sprung free.

"As long as you're here." He groaned as she licked the tip of his cock, swirling her tongue around it. "*Mon Dieu...*"

She looked up just for a moment. "You were saying?"

"I..." She'd distracted him so badly he didn't seem to remember. For a moment he closed his eyes and gave himself up to her torture, small moans of pleasure rumbling in his throat. But then he refocused and looked down at her.

"As long as you're here," he gasped, "I want you. A lot. I understand if sex alone, without a real relationship, won't work for you. But...ahh."

Her lips traveled down the stiffened shaft. She cupped his balls with her hand and gently stroked them.

"I can't think..."

"You don't need to think." She took her lips away from his cock but continued to caress him with her hand. She looked up at him once more as she stroked. "I'd like to know more about you, but I respect how you feel."

Her hand slid up and down his length with tantalizing strokes. His eyes turned coal black as he burned with desire for her. "So as long as I'm here," she continued, "and if you want me... I'm not about to argue."

She used her tongue like a paintbrush, teasing the head of his cock with small strokes, pulling back as he arched his hips in an attempt to bury himself in the hot, wet cavern of her mouth. He uttered a low groan as his eyes fluttered closed.

"Please," he whispered. "More."

She loved hearing him beg, knowing she was the one he wanted. Deciding to end his torment she acquiesced, filling her mouth with his hard shaft, swirling her tongue along his length.

"Oh, babe, yes. Just like that."

Jackson slid back in the chair, bringing his hips forward. He wound his fingers through her hair, caressing her head, cheeks, and even the whorl of her ears as she pleasured him. His tortured groans filled the room. She relaxed and took him deeper as her fingers gently caressed his balls.

"*Mon Dieu,* Carla," he panted. He leaned forward so with one hand he could tease her nipples, the other still tangled in her hair. She loved his soft pinches and she hummed appreciation low in her throat. His balls tightened and she knew he was close. She hollowed her cheeks, increasing the suction, wanting to give him the orgasm of his life.

But then he reached forward and brought his hands beneath her arms, lifting her to her feet. As he did so, he sat up so his face was level with her stomach. He reached a hand behind the small of her back and pulled her forward so he could kiss her stomach. With his hands he caressed her ass, his palms gliding over the smooth skin. He licked a moist trail along her stomach while he slipped his hands between her legs, caressing her thighs before reaching up to finger her pussy.

"You're so wet," he murmured, teasing the engorged bud of her clit with the tip of his finger, slick from her juices. He stroked, softly at first, then quicker as she began to rock against him. His feet lightly kicked at her legs.

"Wider."

She obeyed at once, excited by the dominance of his command. As soon as she did so, Jackson immediately plunged three fingers inside her slick pussy, possessing her.

She burned so hot for him, wanting him more fiercely than before. Her legs shook and she placed her arms atop his shoulders to steady herself. He continued to stroke, sliding in and out, and she ground against his fingers as he brought her closer to release. Her eyes squeezed shut as she spiraled toward climax.

Then, just as she teetered on letting go, he pulled his fingers out. Her eyes popped open and she gasped with frustration. But as she looked down at him, the wicked gleam in his eyes told her she had nothing to worry about.

He nodded toward the nightstand and at once she knew what he wanted. She walked over and retrieved a second condom from the drawer.

"Put it on," Jackson growled as she returned. "And let's go for a ride."

Her pussy gushed with eager anticipation. She'd gladly ride him, anytime. With trembling fingers, she tore open the packet and rolled the condom onto his stiff cock. Then she straddled his legs and lowered on to him, pinching her breasts as she savored every thick, delicious inch. He rested his hands atop her thighs to help guide her down, filling her completely with his deep penetration.

As soon as he was inside her again, Carla let her

self-control slip away. She wrapped her arms around him, bringing his head against her chest. Jackson took her breast into his mouth, licking, teasing, nearly making her come with his tongue as he sucked her swollen nipple. She cried aloud, too crazed with desire to care if anyone outside the window could hear her.

She wove her fingers through his hair, arching her back and thrusting her breasts forward, wanting Jackson to eat her whole. She rode him hard and fast, then agonizingly slow, teasing him to madness. His fingers were wrapped against her ass, holding on. But as she approached orgasm, Jackson again stroked her clit, placing his palm against her tummy while using his middle finger to rub her slick core.

She cried out, grinding her hips against his cock as he caressed her. Her heartbeat thundered in her ears as she rode him, plunging again and again on his scorching shaft as she barreled toward release.

Jackson's palm whisked out to slap her ass, once, twice, and then she exploded, the orgasm consuming her. She clutched his shoulders and shook, her clenching pussy milking his cock as he bucked his hips and thrust. Seconds later, he let out his own guttural growl and she felt the hot pulses of his cock inside of her as he let himself go.

She rested against him in the afterglow, inhaling his scent, feeling the sweat from his chest mingle with hers and the soft exhalations of his breath blowing across her skin. Their breathing was the only sound in the room apart from the evening songs from the birds, though that had begun to grow fainter as darkness approached. At last Carla stood and began picking up her discarded clothing.

She glanced at the digital clock on his nightstand, surprised the readout was nearly eight. They'd been at it for two hours? She chuckled beneath her breath.

"What's so funny?"

Carla turned back to where Jackson still sat in the chair. "Nothing funny, really. But I don't actually remember ever having sex for two straight hours."

"Never?"

"Is two-hour sex nothing out of the ordinary for you?" She tried keeping her tone light and breezy, but despite her best intentions she wasn't quick enough to drive away the clutch of illogical jealousy squeezing her heart. Who, exactly, had he had two-hour sex with?

"It used to not be, anyway," he replied, and then instantly seemed to regret the comment. She waited for him to continue, but knew the effort was futile. Jackson went silent on her. Again.

She expelled a breath of frustration. "Look," she said, pulling on her clothes, "I meant what I said earlier. I respect you and I won't push you to tell me things you don't want to."

He muttered his thanks, but she heard the tension in his voice as he waited for her to continue. She sure wished she knew what the heck was with him.

"Just tell me one thing—how do I keep you from going hot and cold? You make me feel like I'm in danger any given second of saying something completely offensive, except I don't even know what it is that offends you."

"You don't offend me."

"But then why—"

He sighed like a man bone-weary from having the world's grief on his shoulders. "You asked for a level of trust between us. I ask the same from you. You have to trust me there are some things you can't know, but understand it's nothing about you. I think you're..." His voice trailed away and he shrugged, seemingly at a loss for words.

"I'm what?"

"I think you're amazing."

The combination of honesty and vulnerability etched on his face nearly broke Carla's heart. She wished fervently that Jackson wasn't closing himself off to her, that he could tell her about whatever tore him up inside. It had to be something tragic because when she looked into his eyes, she was saddened to see pain.

And not fresh pain, either, but rather one that seemed to have settled in for a good long time. If she were indeed looking through a portal to Jackson's soul, what she saw was a man who suffered in silence. Her own eyes pooled with tears, wishing he'd tell her more but knowing he wouldn't.

She swallowed against the tight lump in her throat.

"Okay. Well, goodnight, Jackson."

With heavy feet she started for the door. As she placed her hand on the knob and twisted, Jackson suddenly stopped her by placing his larger hand atop hers. He stood behind her so she couldn't see him, but the warmth of his body pressed against hers.

"I know I'm not telling you what you want," he said softly. "I hope you can accept that, because I still want you. Badly. There are just some things about me I don't want to talk about."

They stood that way for nearly a minute, Jackson behind her, his chest against her back, his hand atop hers. At last she nodded, accepting what he was able to give.

"I want you, too," she said. "But since it's a guessing game about what you will or won't talk about, how 'bout if you don't go radio silent when I pick the wrong topic. I'm not doing anything intentional, so it's not fair for you to act like I've just... Oh, I don't know...stepped on your snakes or something."

His soft chuckle tickled her ear. At last, a crack in his icy armor. "Ouch. You wouldn't step on a guy's snakes, now would you?"

His teasing was music to her ears, a soothing, comforting sound like a warm blanket wrapped around her heart.

"No, I wouldn't," she admitted. "I love animals and besides, I'd have to get awfully close to a snake to step on it."

His hand dropped away and he stepped back, allowing Carla space to turn around. Her gaze traveled the length of him, gliding over his tight washboard abs, his chest, his chiseled jaw, finally locking in on his beautiful eyes that revealed yet hid so much about him.

"So we have a deal? You don't turn into silent man if I hit a nerve. Just tell me, okay?"

He nodded. "Deal."

Neither of them volunteered to move. They stood together, not speaking, the smoldering beginnings of desire flickering to life once more. Carla placed her palms against Jackson's chest, the heavy thumping of his heart vibrating under her fingers. His eyes turned dark, stained with need. He placed his palms on the wall, on either side of her head, effectively trapping her. He leaned in, his lips inches from hers.

"I don't want you to go," he murmured.

"It's past dinner time. Aren't you hungry?"

"Not for food," he responded, bending down to give her his kiss.

Chapter Six

It turned out dinner wasn't the only thing she missed. Carla walked to building eight the next morning having gotten only a couple hours of sleep. Her eyes burned, she could barely stop yawning, but she wasn't complaining. Jackson had been on fire. He had an insatiable drive, almost as if he were trying to make up for those two years of abstinence in a single evening. He'd given her a night to remember, with his stamina, and creativity, the way he had kissed her right where—

"Heads up, Carla!"

She snapped her gaze into focus just in time to avoid walking straight into a live oak. Behind her, she heard Lisa's footsteps as she ran to catch up.

"Are you okay?" Lisa frowned with concern. "You just about planted your face in the tree."

"I'm fine, fine," Carla laughed it off. "Just had my head in my thoughts, that's all."

"Must have been some pretty good thoughts."

Carla shrugged, cheeks burning.

"Ooh. Those kind of thoughts." Lisa's smile widened as she raised a knowing eyebrow. "Then I can understand walking into a tree."

Carla said nothing, surprised she actually felt her cheeks go warm. Luckily Lisa immediately changed the subject as they headed toward building eight.

"It's your lucky day today," she said.

"Oh?"

She nodded. "Jackson's doing several extractions this morning, so you'll get to see how it's all done."

At that, any lingering thoughts of lust evaporated like a cloud of steam. Carla was regretting the cheesy scrambled eggs she'd had for breakfast. She swallowed, trying to will away the knot in her stomach. "I can't wait," she said faintly.

"Don't worry, there's nothing you have to do," Lisa assured her. "You're just observing. It's fascinating; you'll see."

They reached the building and went inside. Cheng Li sat at the monitors, as well as another woman whom Carla hadn't yet met.

Lisa made introductions. "Kelly, this is Carla Saunders, who's interning with us this month. Carla, this is Kelly Grassle. She's a researcher specializing in venom medicine. She's done a lot of work with bees, but has recently turned her attention to cobras."

"Hey." Kelly barely gave her a glance as she kept her attention glued to the monitors. Clad in skinny jeans just barely grazing her hips and a clingy low-cut top leaving nothing to the imagination, her attire was more siren than scientist. "You're a student?"

"No," Carla said. "I'm actually a management consultant."

"A what?" At that Kelly looked up, eyes flashing annoyance. "Are you here to talk to us about maximizing efficiency or some other bullshit?"

Kelly had an edge, no doubt about it. Carla shook her head. "No bullshit from me," she said, keeping her tone light.

146

"Then what are you doing here?"

"I—"

"She's here at my request."

All eyes turned to the door where Jackson had just walked in. His demeanor was calm, but exuding respect. He stepped forward, moving toward them with that wolf-like gait that always made Carla feel as if she were being stalked. A shivery tingle slid down her spine, remembrances of the night before.

Jackson joined them at the monitors. There were faint dark smudges beneath his eyes, but nothing else betraying his lack of sleep.

"Morning, Jackson," Kelly said, her tone bright as sunshine, entirely different than it had been seconds ago to Carla.

He ignored the greeting. "Let's get to work. Kelly, you've retrieved the cobras?"

"Cheng Li and I brought them in from the enclosure first thing this morning."

"Good." He turned to Carla. "Did Lisa fill you in on what we're doing this morning?"

"You're taking venom samples?"

"Yes. Kelly and I will be in the extraction room, but the adjoining room has an observation window so you can see what we're doing."

He was all business, and Carla took her cues from him despite her knees knocking with fear. "Sounds good. Is there anything you need me to do beforehand, or afterward?"

"I'll have Lisa show you how to sterilize the equipment once we're finished. But for now, just watch." He gave her a nod and turned away but not before Carla saw, just for a moment, a burn of desire in his eyes. Her mouth went dry.

"Come on," Lisa said to Carla. "I'll show you where you can watch." While Jackson and Kelly entered the main extraction room, Lisa showed Carla the door to a smaller adjoining room separated by a large pane of glass through which they could see everything.

"I know snakes aren't your thing," Lisa said as they sat down, "but you still might find this interesting. Jackson's the best extractor around. He makes a really dangerous job look easy."

Carla's skin prickled with alarm. "Dangerous how?"

"Well, of course either one of them could get bit."

"Bit?!"

"Don't worry," Lisa reassured her. "It's a rare occurrence, and we've got antivenin if something does happen."

There was no time for Carla to respond as she noticed Jackson and Kelly were set to begin. From somewhere beyond her vision, Jackson had retrieved one of the cobras and lifted it over to a stainless steel table by way of a pole with a hook at one end holding the body of the long snake.

Cold sweat beaded her forehead and her stomach twisted in sick revulsion. The cobra's eyes, twin dots on either side of its head, gleamed like chips of black ice. Its forked tongue flickered as Jackson brought it to the table. She needed every ounce of will in her body not to run screaming from the room. Instead, she focused on her breathing, slow, steady breaths, forcing herself to maintain calm. But her heart nearly leapt from her chest when Jackson's fingers wrapped at the base of the cobra's head.

She gasped and turned to Lisa. "Won't he get bit doing that?"

"No, not in that way. By holding it as he is, it's impossible for the cobra to twist her head around and bite him."

Jackson set the snake on the stainless steel table where Kelly awaited him, armed with a pole of her own fitted at the end with a rectangular plate covered in soft padding. It almost looked like a wet-dry mop.

"That's for holding the snake's body down on the table," Lisa explained. "King cobras are so long, one person is needed to hold its body against the table while the handler deals with getting the head to the extraction receptacle."

While Kelly held the snake's body down, Jackson brought her head to a funnel-shaped collection vessel. As he held the cobra's head right to the vessel, the snake bit against the side of it and her fangs oozed venom that slid down the inside of the funnel. Slowly the thick, yellowish substance dripped through the bottom of the funnel and into a glass collection jar.

Carla's heartbeat roared in her ears, jackhammer thuds pounding so hard and fast it was difficult to breathe. In a trembling voice she asked, "How does he get the snake to stop biting?"

"He doesn't. She stops when she wants to. If Jackson were to try to force the snake away from it, he risks damaging her fangs. That's something he would never do."

She watched in slowly growing fascination as Jackson waited with laser-focused intensity while the cobra released her venom. When the snake finally let go, Kelly handed him the pole with the hook and he placed it beneath the cobra's body, then carried the snake over to a large glass terrarium where he gently lowered the creature inside.

A nervous trickle of sweat slipped down between Carla's breasts. "Oh, sweet heaven, I feel like I can finally breathe."

"Not so fast," Lisa cautioned her. "Jackson's doing ten extractions today. That was only the first."

At that reminder, the taste of fear coated her tongue. Carla told herself Jackson would be all right, he'd done this hundreds if not thousands of times before. But she knew the anxiety would not leave her until he finished for the day. She was also aware she cared about what happened to him a little too much for her own good. For her own heart. She tried to shrug the thought away, like shaking rain off a coat after coming in from a storm. But it wasn't shaking off quite so easily.

The next several extractions went as smoothly as the first. By the time the last one approached, Carla was shocked to discover she actually enjoyed it. There was something almost dance-like about the orchestrated movements between the snake, the handler, and the assistant, a curious beauty tinged with lurking danger unlike anything she'd seen before.

Just as Jackson had done several times that morning, he retrieved a cobra from the holding tank, keeping the animal's upper body lifted with his hook while both he and Kelly held on to the lower end. He guided the head of the snake toward the extraction vessel while Kelly kept the snake's body on the table by applying gentle pressure with her holding device.

Suddenly, the snake's massive body twisted with violent force against the holding pole, hood flared and black scales flashing as it slipped from Jackson's grip and dropped to the floor.

"Get back!" Jackson held his palm up toward Kelly. His focus never left the cobra as the snake coiled and hissed, its forked tongue flicking angrily in and out of its mouth.

Carla gasped, horrified. Her knees shook, trembling so hard it was almost impossible to stand. She grabbed Lisa's arm, clutching it like a lifeline. Icy fingers of fear skated down her spine as her mouth went bone dry, her jaw slack.

"Stay quiet," Lisa murmured. "He can handle this, but you don't want to distract him."

Carla could only nod, eyes glued to Jackson.

He crept slowly about the room, gaze fixated on the cobra. "Shh. Don't worry, sweetie. We'll get you back home soon. Stay easy, now. Easy."

As the cobra slithered along the floor, Jackson crouched down, positioning himself so that he could approach her a little behind but also to the side. He waved his left hand toward the cobra, getting her to focus on the movement. Then, with his right hand, he struck lightning fast, wrapping his fingers at the base of the cobra's head.

"Get the hook."

Kelly raced to obey Jackson's instruction, returning to pick up the heavy lower body of the cobra while Jackson retained his grip on the head. Together they brought the cobra over to the stainless steel table.

As if nothing had happened, they continued on with the collection process, Jackson guiding the cobra's head to the vessel and waiting patiently while she bit down and excreted the venom. Once finished, they returned her to the holding container and Kelly latched the lid tight.

Little by little Carla released Lisa's arm as her frantic heartbeat settled back to a normal rhythm. She closed her eyes, letting out a heavy sigh as her shoulders slumped.

"Does that happen a lot?"

"Rarely." Lisa shook her head. "And if it does, Jackson knows what to do. As you just saw."

"Yeah." Faint trembles shook her voice. "As I just saw." And hopefully would never have to see again.

Inside the observation room, Jackson spoke to Kelly. The researcher smiled up at him with adoration in her eyes, like a student to a favored teacher. She asked him something and Jackson nodded. Carla wondered what they were talking about, noting with irritation the ugly head of jealously rearing up. She turned away from the window.

"What's next?" she asked Lisa, forcing enthusiasm.

"I'll show you what we do with the venom, and then go over sterilization procedures with you. We need to prepare the room and equipment for the next extraction."

Lisa led Carla out of the adjoining room and into the larger one. Kelly and Jackson were both already gone, having exited the room via a separate door.

"They're taking the cobras back into the enclosure," Lisa explained. "They won't extract from those ten for at least a week. Jackson doesn't like to overtax them."

She led Carla over to where the collection vessel

was still mounted on the table and picked up a glass test tube filled with a viscous yellow substance.

"This is the raw venom," Lisa said, holding the container before Carla. "Take a look."

Carla flinched but peered at the tube nevertheless, balling her hands into fists by her side to stop the shaking. "It doesn't look like there's very much of it. I thought there'd be more, especially since he extracted from ten snakes."

"Actually, for the amount of venom delivered in a single discharge," Lisa said, leading Carla out of the room and back into the main lab, "the king cobra is among the leaders. Take this statistic: we store the venom in sterile fifty milliliter containers. Care to take a guess how many extractions it takes to get fifty milliliters of raw venom?"

Carla thought for a moment. Fifty milliliters. That wasn't much. She thought back to one of the favorite times of her life, when her parents had taken them all to Paris. She'd fallen in love with the city on site and became determined to know absolutely everything about it, including how the metric system worked. If Parisians used it, then Carla would, too. She recalled it being right around thirty milliliters in an ounce, so fifty would be a bit more than an ounce and a half. She looked again at the small pool of venom collected in the bottom of the test tube.

"Maybe fifteen?" she guessed.

"Not bad," Lisa said, admiration in her voice. "But you're a little high. It's usually between seven and ten."

"Wow, so you get around seven milliliters with each extraction?"

"Yes, right around there. And that also tells you

something about how potent the venom is, because a single bite from a king cobra can kill an elephant, and they don't always even expel all their venom in one bite."

Amazing. In spite of her fear, Carla began to see how someone could want to study these fascinating creatures. It also put a knot of nerves in her stomach when she thought about Jackson working with the cobras and doing the extractions.

Lisa had stopped walking and stood in front of what looked almost like a large square radio sitting on top of a table, with knobs in the front and a lid that opened on top, like where the CD tray might be. But it was definitely not a radio.

"This is the centrifuge," Lisa explained. "We'll put our test tube in this machine and let it run. It'll spin out all the impurities in the venom."

She opened the top of the device and set the test tube inside of it in a fitted container, then capped the tube.

"Impurities?"

"Mainly blood cells," Lisa said, closing the lid and pressing buttons on the front of the machine to start it. "But sometimes there can also be tiny bits of tooth fragments in there as well. Once the centrifuge has done its thing, the impurities will have spun to the bottom of the test tube and we can extract the purified venom and discard the rest."

The machine whirled to life and Lisa glanced at her watch. "How about we grab some coffee?"

"Perfect." Lisa had read Carla's mind. Now that the excitement of the extractions was over, a stifled yawn reminded her she hadn't gotten much sleep last night. Not that it wasn't worth it.

They walked out the door and headed for the caf. Outside, activity was brisk. Several researchers and other employees of the lab were moving quickly about, walking to and fro, as if their tasks were more numerous than time in the day allowed.

"What's going on?" Carla asked, glancing around.

"We've got a shipment coming in today."

"Shipment?"

"Of cobras. There's a small zoo in south central Florida that recently closed down and the owners were looking to relocate the animals. They actually had five king cobras, and Jackson's taking them all. They're being delivered today."

Despite the contents of the pending delivery, Carla was not immune to the buzz of excitement around them. She chuckled at her realization.

"I can't believe I'm excited, too," she said in response to Lisa's questioning look. "It feels like a new baby's arriving."

Lisa laughed. "You're right; it does. We actually don't get many cobras this way. Usually new additions to the enclosure are through hatchlings from the snakes we already have. It'll be fun to have some new kids around."

"*Kids*?"

"The snakes we're getting are all only a year or two old, so in king cobra terms yeah, they're still kids."

They turned the corner as they headed for the caf, Lisa laughing again at Carla's expression. "Listen, trust me on this one. You stick around here long enough and you find yourself really and truly caring for the snakes."

Carla adamantly shook her head. "Not me. Never."

"Never say never," Lisa warned as they headed into the cafeteria. "You'll get hooked, just wait and see."

Carla didn't answer. She'd sooner get hooked on a daily tooth extraction than hooked on king cobras, despite her momentary concern for Mariah the pregnant snake. That was just, well, maternal instincts. Like what many women have.

In a way, she envied Lisa's passion, her conviction that she'd found exactly what she wanted to do in life and pursued the dream. She'd never had the same passion, at least not yet. She thought maybe she'd find it at work but truthfully, although she threw herself into it as best as she could, she knew from listening to Lisa that her passion for her own work wasn't the same.

But she'd find what she wanted in Paris, she was sure of it, and she clung to that certainty like a lifeline. Truth was, if she didn't end up finding meaning and purpose in Paris…what then?

She stepped behind Lisa in the line, taking the largest cup available and filling it with thick, black French roast, a dollop of cream and several spoonfuls of sugar. Her stomach grumbled as she spotted nirvana among the available pastries. Apple crumb cake.

She unapologetically took the biggest possible piece. Nothing like carbs and caffeine to shake away sleep debt.

She followed Lisa to an empty table. It was the time of morning beyond the normal breakfast hour but still too early for lunch, so they practically had the place to themselves.

"Looks good," Lisa said, eyeing Carla's cake as she sipped her coffee.

"It is," Carla replied. "Have some. Please. You'll save me from eating the entire thing by myself."

Carla cut off a sizeable piece for Lisa and placed it on a napkin. They ate in silence for a moment and then Lisa said, "You know, you haven't been here very long, but I just want to say I really like having you around."

Carla's heart went mushy, but she couldn't help teasing her new friend. "Wow, cake really has an effect on you," she grinned, eyes sparkling.

Lisa laughed but insisted she was serious. "I mean it," she said. "We don't usually have people who are fun and interesting around here. The interns are often kind of duds. They're either super smart researchers who don't know what it means to kid around, or they're arrogant corporate know-it-alls who rub Jackson and the rest of us the wrong way the minute they open their mouths and begin talking about low hanging fruit. Whatever that means."

Carla smiled. Talking to someone outside her normal world was refreshing. But then she thought of that morning and of someone else who didn't appear to be as big a fan of hers as Lisa was.

"I don't think Kelly has the same positive feeling toward me."

"Oh, don't worry about her." Lisa swished her hand in the air as if shooing away an irritating fly. "She's all right once you get to know her. She just has kind of an edge."

"You think? She practically ignored me the whole time I was there."

"Well…" Reluctance shaded her friend's voice.

Carla looked up from her cake. "What? Is there something I should know?"

Lisa set down her cup and let out a small sigh, as if she'd come to a difficult decision. "Look, it's like I told you before. Whatever's going on between you and Jackson is between you and Jackson. I don't want to know and frankly, it's none of my business. But the thing is, with Kelly…" Lisa shrugged. "She likes Jackson, probably more than she should. Kelly doesn't come from money. She had to work her way up to get where she is, and she worked damn hard. It was tough for her to come up with the money for college, but she did it any way she could. Still, she couldn't afford to attend any of the top schools, so even though she has the degree she doesn't have the pedigree, if you know what I mean."

Carla nodded. The same thing was true in the business world. Simply getting your MBA wasn't enough; where you'd earned it also counted. Plenty.

"But if you know anything about Jackson," Lisa continued, "he doesn't put a lot of stock into superficial stuff. What counts for him is passion, heart, and love for what you're doing. And if you can show that through your work, it doesn't matter to him where you've done it. So he took Kelly on as a student intern and she's been here ever since. And because of what he did for her, I think there's kind of a hero worship thing going on with Kelly toward Jackson. She absolutely idolizes him."

Carla recalled the way Kelly lit up when Jackson walked into the extraction room, like a teenager seeing a movie star.

Lisa sipped her coffee, thinking. "As far as I know, Jackson's been straight with her that he's not interested in a relationship. But she's a girl who's overcome a lot, so one bit of initial resistance isn't going to matter to her."

Carla shook her head. "It seems like her efforts at a relationship would take away from the work. I'm surprised he keeps her around."

"Well, that's the thing. What I said about Jackson not caring about superficial stuff? To him this is a small inconvenience. What matters is Kelly excels at what she does. She's a born researcher. She can analyze something until the end of time and never get bored. She's tireless and she's smart, and she loves the cobras. That's what matters to him. As for her feelings toward him, he puts nothing by it." Lisa let out a small chuckle, though it was without humor. "Honestly, I think he views Kelly's attitude toward him as something akin to high school puppy love."

"But it sounds like her feelings are real." Oddly, Carla found herself coming to Kelly's defense. Feelings were feelings, after all.

"Like I said, it seems more like hero worship than anything else."

Carla nodded and went back to her cake. It was difficult to know how to feel about what Lisa had said, especially since she'd also once spoken about Jackson's heart not getting broken. Is that why he dismissed what Kelly felt? Because he was afraid if he got involved with her he'd end up feeling the same? But what, exactly, was so wrong with that? Why was he afraid of falling in love?

They finished up and returned to the lab. The centrifuge had completed its cycle, so Lisa removed the venom sample and showed Carla the rest of the procedure: extracting the pure venom, freeze drying it for storage, labeling the sample, and placing it in the cold storage unit along with the rest of the samples. There were vials and vials of snake venom samples in storage, all neatly labeled and dated, waiting for just the right scientist to come along and perform just the right test to unlock the venom's secrets.

Carla's throat tightened, awestruck by what it all meant. "Wow," she said softly as she stared as the vials.

Lisa glanced over at her. "Wow, what?"

"It's just that looking at all these samples makes me really understand I could be looking at the future cure for multiple sclerosis. It's a pretty amazing thought."

"And that's just the tip of it," Lisa said, shutting the storage door. "We're specifically focusing our effort on MS, but there's an entire world of medical mysteries out there. The possibilities of what we could find are endless. Unfortunately, the money's not."

"For research, you mean?"

"Exactly. But we do what we can, for as long as we can." She changed the topic then, instructing Carla on how to sterilize the lab equipment and prep the room for the afternoon extractions. One of the other researchers would be performing them, but Carla was welcome to watch if she wanted.

At that moment, Jackson and Kelly walked back into the lab, clearly in the middle of a heated conversation. The discussion halted when they entered the main room and realized they weren't alone.

"Hey," Lisa said to the two of them, "we were just finishing prep for this afternoon."

"Great," Kelly replied, her tone clipped. "When you're finished you can go." She looked at Carla directly. "Both of you."

Carla said nothing in response, but a slow burn of irritation began simmering her blood. She got it that Kelly'd had some knocks in her life, but the girl needed to ditch the attitude. She had half a mind to tell her when the sounds of the William Tell Overture drifted through the lab. She snatched at her phone.

"Yes?"

"Carla?" *Slurp, slurp.*

Shit.

"Hold on." She held the phone away from her ear and told Jackson and Lisa she would step outside. Kelly she ignored.

She walked down the steps and into a clear area where she stood off the main path so she wouldn't block the still-buzzing activity around her. "Okay, I'm back."

"What's going on? You haven't called."

She sighed; rolled her eyes. Prayed for strength. "I've been busy, Bryce. I'm not just sitting around twiddling my thumbs."

"Well, yeah, I know that." *Slurp.* "But this also isn't your real job, either. I mean, you're not exactly conducting experiments to end world hunger."

Oh joy. A dose of condescension to accompany the diet cola slurping.

"What do you want, Bryce?"

"I just figured I'd check up on you. Something wrong with that?"

"No, of course not." She let out a breath of air and did her best to strain the irritation from her voice. "What's going on with you?"

"Not much. I had dinner with your parents last

night."

Of course you did.

"And your mom told me you're working at a lab. So I did a little bit of my own research on it. It's weird, though. I couldn't find anything on the web."

"I know. I checked myself."

"Didn't stop me." *Slurp.* "I just searched university intranets."

Her eyes narrowed. "You don't have authorization to access university intranets."

"*I* don't," he agreed, "but Professor Dees does."

"My father's university colleague?"

"Sure."

Her hands gripped the phone as she fought back the urge to scream at him. "Bryce, what are you talking about? Did you lie to the professor?"

"Oh, Carla please. It wasn't lying. I told him I did research for your father and he'd entrusted me with the information. That was good enough for the old codger to give me his access."

"I can't believe this. You're such a weasel."

Slurp. "Cool it with the insults. I found some interesting stuff on this guy Jackson Rivard. Do you know him?"

Better than you ever will. "Yes, I know him. He's the director and owner of the research facility."

"He's also got a pretty impressive stack of honors heaped on him. For a lab guy."

"Oh?" She tried not to sound too eager, but in a rare moment since she'd known Bryce, she was actually interested in something he had to say.

"Yeah, lemme see…" In addition to the slurping, she could hear Bryce's mouse clicking. "Ahh, okay, here it is. He won the John Dystel Prize for MS Research, the Humboldt Research Award in Biology, the National Medal of Science. And last year he won something called the Max Plank Research award."

Wow.

Slurp. "Huh."

"What?"

"Well, it also says here, if this information is accurate, the National Medal of Science is given out by the President."

Carla's jaw dropped. "You mean the *president*, president. As in of the United States?"

"Yeah, guess so. At least that's what it says here." She heard a rustle that sounded as if he was settling in to his favorite chair. "So anyway, I was thinking..."

Carla's well-exercised sound filter strained out Bryce's annoying buzz. *The President of the United States had given Jackson an award?!* It was crazy. Of course, there was likely some kind of panel of scientists who chose the winners, but still.

Then a thought hit her like a ton of bricks. This must be why Bartlett Silver was so eager to get Jackson signed on as a client. It wasn't the money he would bring them—a research lab notoriously struggles for funds—but the prestige of his name. She knew one of Bartlett's strategic initiatives included expanding its portfolio in the scientific realm. Having Rivard Research as a client could potentially be worth millions since Jackson's notable name would open doors into the lucrative pharmaceutical market. *Greedy bastards.* Bartlett couldn't care less about Jackson. They only wanted to use his name.

"Carla? Still there?"

"What? I missed the last part." *And everything before it.*

"I said I was just trying to figure out my schedule for when I could come down and see you."

Ugh. She'd rather kiss a snake. "That's not a good idea, Bryce. I really need to focus on my assignment. I'm not even sure they'd allow it."

Slurp. "What do you mean, not allow it? I have a right to go where I want, Carla. Some snake jockey isn't going to keep me from seeing you."

Snake jockey? Where did he come up with this stuff? And since when was he so desperate to see her? What Bryce really wanted was being in her family so he could enjoy their money, and he seemed to be having no problem worming his way over for dinner and other visits while Carla was away. He had no need for her as far as she could tell.

"Listen, Bryce, we can talk about this later, but don't be making plans to come. I need to get back to work."

He let out an impatient huff of air. "Is there something going on there that you're not telling me about?"

"What? No." She swallowed. Since when did that self-aggrandizing jerk get so insightful?

"You can't put me off like this, Carla. We *will* talk about this later, so don't forget to call me. I don't need to be the one always chasing after you. Relationships are a two-way street, you know."

Or a highway to hell, depending on one's perspective. "Sure, Bryce. Whatever you say. Bye!"

She clicked off without waiting for his response.

Her eyes drifted closed and she let out long, slow

breaths of air, practicing her yoga class's relaxation techniques. She knew she ought to be getting back inside, but she needed to calm her thoughts before doing so. One phone call from Bryce had managed to stir an emotional pot of anger and amazement in the space of five minutes. Damn, he could be so exasperating, sticking to her like static cling and about as useful. She really needed to confront him when she got back to New York and make it perfectly clear they were not, in fact, the "couple" he seemed to think they were.

"Ow!" Something jabbed the bottom of her foot. Looking down, Carla spotted a sharp-edged stone she'd apparently just stepped on. *Evil little rock.* She picked it up and flung it, watching it bounce along the dirt path and out of her sight. If only she could get Bryce out of her life as easily.

She sighed. There was no ignoring this issue with him anymore, hoping it would go away on its own. First step, she had to talk to her mother. It wasn't going to be easy. Carla's mom thought Bryce would be good for her, had thought so for years. Bryce himself made sure of it. The fact that he was the son of Carla's mom's best friend didn't hurt his cause, either.

Still. This had to be done. As soon as she got back to New York she'd speak with her mom and let her know how she felt. It would be a tough conversation so she had to do it in person, face to face, without distractions like there always were on the phone. She couldn't risk any misunderstandings with her mother, especially since both she *and* Bryce's mother thought he was the perfect guy for her. Once that conversation was over, she'd talk to Bryce.

She let out another breath of air and opened her eyes, knowing she had to get back. But as she glanced toward the steps to the building, she felt a slow, delicious thrill skate its way across her heart. Jackson had come out of the lab, and was heading directly to her.

As he neared she had time to take in his shopworn jeans, untucked linen shirt, mussed brown hair with a stubborn lock draped sexily over his forehead. His ocean-blue eyes focused on her as if trying to burn her image in his memory. He approached with his seductive, loping gait, and she shivered with pleasure.

"Hey," she said as he approached. "I was—"

She could say nothing more before his lips crashed down on hers. He held her close, slipping his arm behind her back, deliberately pressing her against the bulge of his cock. Her response was automatic, like Pavlov's dog. Moisture began building in her pussy, dampening her panties.

His tongue searched her mouth, seeking more, deepening the connection. She kissed him back with everything she had to give, vaguely wondering what had brought on this sudden attack but enjoying every second of it. If Jackson Rivard had a sudden need to seduce her, she wasn't one to complain.

"Wow," she whispered when they paused for air. She closed her eyes for a moment as she breathed in the scent of him, her face pressed against his neck. "Where did that come from?"

He let out a shaky breath. "You opened Pandora's box when you let me fuck you," he said. "I can't get enough."

His honesty made her bold. She met his burning

gaze, smiling coyly. "Then let's take care of that right now."

He whistled low as his eyes raked over her, revealing his need. It was so exciting to know how much he hungered for her.

"Damn it, I want to. You don't know how much. But I can't, not 'til tonight. I've got tests to run, more extractions this afternoon, analysis to review. And there's a grant application due tomorrow that I—"

Time to silence him. Carla looked around and made sure there was no one in sight. Then without moving away from him, she slipped her hand down between their bodies and cupped his raging hard-on. Jackson hissed out a breath as her palm caressed him.

"Start thinking outside the box," she said, noticing beads of sweat dotting his forehead as he tried like hell to pretend there wasn't a woman caressing him outside his research lab. "It's what we corporate types do. Occasionally it has its usefulness."

She stroked up and down his jeans, against the granite bulge of his cock, thrilled by Jackson's quiet moans as she teased him mercilessly. "There must be offices not being used at the moment, or deserted basements in some of the buildings. Janitor's closet, maybe? Any one of those would do in a pinch."

She didn't need to say more. He took her hand to lead the way toward a building where Carla hadn't yet been. She nearly had to run to keep up with him, but she couldn't help but smile. If this wasn't a man in agony for her, she didn't know who was.

They reached one of the smaller buildings and Jackson pulled her inside. Carla looked around. There were shelves and shelves of books, just like in a library, stacks of them filling the main space of the room. Along each wall were rows of file cabinets. And in a smaller adjoining room were several desks with chairs, clearly a study area.

"This is a library?" Carla asked, behavior instilled since childhood compelling her to whisper.

"Yes," Jackson replied tensely. "It's for the researchers. It's also the place where I'm going to fuck you."

Her nipples tightened. She let out a breath. "Fantastic."

They walked between the stacks and quickly through the main room, continuing into the presently unoccupied study area. What Carla hadn't first noticed but did now were the number of doors leading off of the study room. Offices.

Jackson stuffed his free hand into his jeans pocket and pulled out his key ring. Flipping through the keys with impatience, he finally found the one he wanted, stuck it in the lock, and opened the door. Afternoon light streaming in from a single window revealed a small office. Jackson shut and locked the door behind them and led Carla over to a desk, shoving to one end the few items on it. Then he turned to her and kissed her again. Hard.

His drive was fierce, not cooled in the least by their walk to the building. As soon as he kissed her his hands roamed everywhere, sliding down her neck, across her breasts, between her legs. He caressed her through her jeans, sliding his palm back and forth over her mound in a deliciously wicked way. Carla sighed into his mouth as his fingers found her clit. Even through the material of her jeans and panties he was spot-on accurate, and she could feel the gush of wetness as she responded to his touch.

He broke the kiss and used both hands to unbutton her jeans and slide them down, along with her panties. He pulled off her shoes and then helped her out of the jeans and panties. With both hands he reached around her waist and lifted her to sit atop the desk.

"Spread your legs."

She complied, exposing her sex to his appreciative eyes, like a queen bestowing favors to a humble subject.

He smiled and licked his lips. "Wider."

Her thighs slid over the desk's warm wood, as far as she was able.

Jackson's scorching gaze roamed over her. He took a step forward and reached out, shoving up her blouse and bra, exposing her breasts. Her now bare nipples tightened.

He knelt down in front of her. "I like what I see."

As his hands rested atop each of her legs to hold them wide, he spread soft kisses along her inner thighs, his lips dancing across the sensitive skin. She leaned back and placed her palms on the desk behind her, supporting herself. Licking her lips appreciatively, she watched as his hot mouth traveled along her inner thighs to the center of her legs. His tongue found her pulsing clit.

"Ah!" She groaned and let her head fall back.

Jackson broke away and looked up. "Touch yourself while I make you come. Caress your breasts and show me what feels good. I want to watch while I lick you."

She looked down at him, saw the tar black of his

eyes and knew how turned on he was at the thought of her doing what he asked. For a moment a wave of shyness stilled her, but Jackson's obvious desire for her swept it away. She lifted her hands, smoothing them over the tops and sides of her breasts. The burn of passion in Jackson's gaze emboldened her. She smiled, using her fingers to pull and pinch her nipples, moaning softly as she did so.

"Yes, baby." He drew in a sharp breath. "Just like that."

He went back to work on her. With the tip of his tongue he swirled around her sensitive bud at first with soft as air strokes, growing stronger and more insistent as her arousal grew. He slipped two fingers through her wet folds, gathering moisture, before plunging deep in her hot core.

"Ohh!" She sucked in a breath, trying to stifle her cries, but Jackson made it impossible as he thrust faster and more deeply, curving his fingers toward her abdomen to brush her G-spot.

She cried out, parting her thighs wider still and pulling on her beet red nipples. "Jackson!"

"Give it to me, baby. Let yourself go."

His fingers drove into her wet core as she careened toward release. She rocked her hips against him and looked down. He worked his tongue on her clit, his fingers inside her slick walls, his breath hot on her mound. She met his gaze as he looked up and her breath caught in her throat at the lustful burn reflected back at her.

Suddenly she could no longer support herself and lay back down. She drew her feet up and rested them atop the desk on either side of Jackson's head. With both hands she continued to caress her breasts, pinching the sensitive nipples as she imagined Jackson's tongue swirling around them as he licked her clit.

Her eyelids fluttered closed and she groaned, heat flushing over her as arousal built. She spread her thighs wider and shifted both hands to grip the sides of the desk. Bracing for support, she ground her pussy against Jackson's face, increasing the pressure.

"More," she begged. "Faster." Blood roared in her ears as she rocked her hips, aching for release. Jackson's fingers thrust deep, spearing her with pleasure, as his tongue continued to work her clit. Seconds later, she screamed as the orgasm consumed her.

As soon as the pulses calmed, Jackson lifted her to the floor and turned her around to face away from him. He pressed one hand on her back and bent her over the desk, the warm wood smooth against her forearms. She smiled with anticipation, hearing the rip of his zipper as he pulled down his jeans.

"*Très belle*," he murmured as he slid his palms along her ass. He waited a beat to enter her, moving his body so it spooned behind her, his cock teasing, slipping between the crack of her ass. His arms came around and cupped her breasts, teasing the already pebbled nipples. She wished they were naked, desperate to feel the sleek skin of his body wrapped against her. But time for that later. Hopefully tonight.

She felt space between them. He'd moved back fractionally, enough to position himself. The condom paper ripped and the wet latex squeaked as he rolled it on. Then the tip of his cock pressed against her pussy, the thick mushroom head probing, gathering her juices, and thrusting home.

She cried out and bent forward even farther, shoving aside a pen to press her cheek against the desk, allowing Jackson as much access as he wanted. He buried himself in her, thrusting long and deep before pulling out and driving in again. His low, guttural groans, proof of his desire, heightened her own need. Arching her back, she met his thrusts full on, driving him deeper as he held her hips and pistoned away.

She loved the sexiness of it all—that they were in a library, that it was in the middle of the day, that there was a small element of danger in getting caught. But mostly she was turned on by how much Jackson wanted her. The man had practically dragged her into this room and tore her clothes off, and she loved every second of it.

His hand slipped around to her front, finding her clit. He began stroking her, timing his fingers with his thrusts, gently at first but then harder and faster. It excited her how well he already knew her body and responded to her signals. She tried to be quiet—who knew if anyone stood outside the door—but at some point she no longer cared. Jackson was too good a lover, and she was too turned on. If he chose to drive her wild, he'd damned well better be prepared for some noise.

Her heartbeat thundered against her chest like it was about to explode. Fiery heat burned through her body as her pussy clenched around his hard driving cock. She sucked in a breath as his slick finger continued to work her clit, expertly rubbing harder and faster as her arousal grew. Her lips parted and she groaned in ecstasy. A second orgasm hovered on the edge of a cliff. She was almost there.

Gripping either side of the desk, she steadied herself to meet Jackson's thrusts. As he pounded against her, his hand lightly slapped her ass and she gasped in surprise at the searing, erotic sting. Another spank and she cried out, pussy gushing in response as her release loomed. Jackson's heaving breaths signaled he was almost there, too.

"I can't get enough of you," he growled.

She opened her eyes and turned her head to look back at him. "Then give me more," she ordered. "Fuck me hard."

Just as she wanted, he pounded against her pussy, his balls slapping with every thrust, her ass pleasurably burning as he continued to spank. Her low groans filled the room as she pushed backward, reeling him deeper into her hot, wet core.

Suddenly she felt his thumb tracing the "o" of her parted lips before he dipped it in her mouth. She willingly sucked on it, her tongue swirling around and coating it with moisture. A second later he pulled away and his wet thumb slipped between her ass cheeks, probing her anus. She quivered in welcome response, pushing her bottom against the invasion. Never before had she felt so naughty, thrown across a desk as she happily fucked a gorgeous guy in a library.

She gasped as Jackson slipped the tip of his thumb in her ass, the tight stretch a fusion of pleasure and pain. He stilled, allowing her to adjust, and then slowly began plunging in and out. With his other hand he continued to work her clit, his quick expert strokes gliding over the swollen bud as she moaned low in her throat. She was exquisitely filled, the pure carnal sensation nearly overwhelming.

Her eyes squeezed shut, blood roaring in her ears. She thrust backward and seconds later screamed, shuddering with release. As if in the distance, Jackson groaned, his shaft swelling inside of her, pulsing as he came. Then he collapsed against her.

He covered her body like a shield, his chest hard and heaving against her back, his cheek resting against her neck. She felt the warm panting of his breath against her skin and wished they were in bed. He could hold her, and they could rest, and then they could do it all over again.

When he found the strength to stand up straight, he pulled wads of tissue from a nearby box on the desk and buried the condom inside a handful before chucking it in the trash. Then he pulled on his jeans and stepped back, giving Carla room to do the same. They faced each other, reassembled.

"*Mon Dieu*," he said, running hands through his hair. "That was outrageous." He stepped forward, circling his arms behind her neck. "More than outrageous," he amended, leaning in to dot her face with soft kisses. "More like *incroyable*."

The very tip of his tongue touched her lips as he spoke. Just like that, she wanted him again.

"I'll settle for *incroyable*," she purred in response. "Until tonight, that is, when I'll be sure to be *fantastique*."

He chuckled. "*Fantastique*? Are you trying to kill me?"

She glanced down at his cock. "And cut off my access to *that*? Do you think I'm crazy?"

His eyes warmed as he looked at her, and he

nodded. "Yes, I do. But I like it."

They left the office with Jackson leading the way, letting Carla know they still had the building to themselves. "I would have known if someone came in because I'd have seen the lights beneath the door," he said.

Once they were outside, he released her hand. "I'll leave you here for now," he said. "You're due back at the lab, and I've got work in my office. I'll see you tonight."

"Hope so." She knew he had a tendency to work late, and didn't want to make assumptions about where she factored into his day.

"You will. How about dinner in the cafeteria? Eight?"

"Sounds good."

"Okay. I'll see you later." He gave her a quick kiss and was off, just as if they were a couple leaving for the day's work. Carla sighed, as relaxed as if she'd just had a massage. Sex with Jackson melted away all the stress she'd felt after Bryce's call.

Except remembering Bryce's call also reminded her she hadn't asked Jackson anything about what Bryce had told her, about the prizes, and the medal. No doubt he had them shoved somewhere in a drawer. Flaunting that stuff wasn't his style. But she wanted to at least know what it felt like to get those prestigious awards and what kind of meaning, if any, they held for him.

She was just about to call out and ask him to come back when something inside of her halted it, and she fell silent. An inner voice reminded her that the good feelings between her and Jackson would turn to ice if she asked him about those awards and forced him to talk about himself.

It was more than time to get back, but her body still hummed from Jackson's touch and her flushed skin would give her away. A walk over to the shore of the bayou for a few minutes would be just what she needed to get back under control.

She headed through a grove of live oaks, their dense branches cooling the air around her and muffling the outside noises as if entering a cave. The worn path stretched long before the canopy of oaks thinned and gave way to the bayou. The air filled with sounds of birds and insects.

Ahead of her, stately cypress trees stood proud in the water, their branches heavy with Spanish moss. Abundant plant life filled the stream, so lush and dense that the water looked pea green. An ibis picked its way through swirling water hyacinths and thick rushes, fishing for lunch. On a downed tree, whose large trunk was still partly above water, turtles basked in the sun. Carla took a step forward to get a better look.

"I wouldn't go any closer. There are gators in these waters," a voice warned quietly.

Carla turned, startled. Jackson's sister, Amy, wearing a light summer dress with her hair up in a loose bun, stood a short distance away. Carla held a hand to her heart, laughing. "You surprised me," she confessed. "I didn't see you standing there."

Amy headed toward Carla, her steps slow and careful. "I'm not shocked," she said. "You looked pretty caught up in your own thoughts."

"Oh well, I…" Carla's voice trailed away, embarrassment creeping in. Jackson's sister obviously couldn't read her mind, but there was a certain perceptiveness about Amy that made her wonder.

She waited while Amy approached, and then realized Jackson's sister walked unaided, wheelchair nowhere in sight. Carla wondered if maybe the last time she'd seen her, Amy had been healing from a leg injury. She stepped toward her to see if she needed help.

"I'm Carla," she reminded her. "We met once before, at your house."

"Sure, of course I remember." Amy accepted Carla's outstretched arm. "Thank you. I think I may have overestimated my energy level today. Let's head over to that fallen tree. It'll make a good resting spot for a minute."

They reached the tree Amy mentioned and took a seat next to each other. Once Amy had settled, Carla's curiosity got the better of her.

"I'm sorry," she said, "but I have to ask. The time before when I saw you, you were in a wheelchair. But now you're walking."

Amy chuckled softly at Carla's confusion. "I'm not always wheelchair-bound," she explained. "Just occasionally when I'm having a particularly bad flare up."

"A flare up?"

Amy glanced over at her. "Jackson didn't tell you?"

"Your brother hasn't told me much of anything where he or his family is concerned. He didn't even tell me right away you two are related."

Amy let out a soft sigh. "That sounds like my brother." She shifted on the log so she could face Carla more directly. "What he also failed to tell you about me, in addition to many other things I'm sure, is I have MS."

Carla sucked in a breath as pieces of the Jackson puzzle clicked into place. His frenetic drive, the relentless focus on finding a cure for MS now all made perfect sense. His source of inspiration sat right next to her.

"Oh, I'm sorry."

"Thank you, but there's no need. I cope just fine. Oh, there are days where I'm fatigued, or my legs are numb. But then I'll have stretches where I'm not feeling any of the symptoms at all." She shrugged. "It's an unpredictable disease."

"So I guess when I first saw you, it wasn't a good day?"

"No. I'd had a flare up and felt dizzy. I don't take chances when that happens, so I use the chair."

"How long have you had it?"

"I was diagnosed when I was fifteen, and I'm twenty-four now, so MS and I have known each other awhile." She spoke matter-of-factly, without a trace of self-pity or remorse. Carla couldn't help but admire Amy's courage.

"There's a lot you don't know about my brother," Amy continued. "Which is understandable. You haven't been here long, and he's a tough nut to crack. But since you and he have a relationship, there are things I should probably let you know about."

Carla unexpectedly felt her face grow warm. How did Amy know?

As if reading her thoughts, Amy continued. "Jackson's said nothing to me, of course. Relationships are one thing he and I don't generally discuss. But I can tell."

"Is it that obvious?"

"Not from you." Amy gave her a reassuring smile. "As you pointed out yourself, we've only just met. But Jackson and I are close, and I know when there's something going on with him, especially when that something is a relationship. He doesn't have many of them but when he does, he's different. He tends to tense up, be more on edge."

Carla frowned. "That doesn't make it sound like they bring out the best in him."

"Well…" She looked out at the water, her fingers working loose bits of bark on the log. "I should probably talk to you about that."

Carla's heartbeat kicked into high gear and a knot of tension settled like a stone in the pit of her stomach. Whatever Amy was about to say wasn't good.

"Has Jackson told you anything about our parents? Anything at all?"

"He told me they were killed in a car accident two years ago."

"Wow." Amy's eyebrows lifted in surprise. "I'm astounded he even told you that much. He must really have it bad for you."

What? "No, I'm sure that's not it. Jackson and I…we're just…" Just what, exactly? "We've been spending some time together."

Amy chuckled. "That's a polite way to put it. And I'm glad, I really am. Jackson needs to have someone in his life."

"So why doesn't he?"

"Well…" Amy took a breath and stretched her legs in front of her, easing out the kinks. "The thing is, he's shouldered the burden of our parents' deaths for two years and can't shake it loose, despite everyone's efforts."

"But why?" Carla frowned. "I didn't think he was in the car, was he?"

"He wasn't even in the country. Our parents were on holiday in England. They'd always wanted to go, and two years ago Jackson made it happen. He paid for the entire trip."

Understanding began to dawn in Carla's mind. "So because he sent them there he takes responsibility for their car accident?"

"Yes," Amy confirmed. "But it's more complicated than that. At the time, Jackson was having a relationship with a woman named Katherine Carlisle, a fellow researcher. The affair was intense, particularly for Jackson. He was very much in love with her."

A cold, hard fist, as bitter and toxic as venom, grabbed hold of Carla's heart and squeezed. The air whooshed from her lungs. "I see," she managed to croak out.

"Katherine was brilliant and beginning to earn praise on some of her papers. But it wasn't fast enough for her. Above everything else, Katherine was outrageously ambitious. She wanted honor and distinction, she wanted recognition. She wanted the scientific community to know her name, and she wanted everything right now. Today. She wasn't content to earn her stripes in time; her ambition didn't have the patience. So what better way to advance her career than by teaming up with one of the leading MS researchers in the country, if not the world?"

"Jackson."

"Of course. In the world of MS research, Jackson's a rock star. He's made breakthroughs with cobra venom the scientific community thought they wouldn't see for years. He's relentless in his pursuit of a cure for MS and his venom studies are world-renowned."

"It's incredible," Carla said, impressed. "Everything Jackson's done would take some scientists a lifetime, yet he's still only in his thirties. You must be proud."

"I am." Amy nodded. "My brother's an amazing man. But getting where he has takes work, and because he worked so intensely, he didn't have enough time for Katherine. At least not according to her."

Carla frowned. This Katherine girl was sounding pretty self-centered. She wondered, with more than a little jealousy, what the attraction was. "Wasn't she here with him?"

"Not on site, no. She lived in Baton Rouge and would spend weekends here, or he'd go there. But it wasn't enough for her. Problem was, Jackson and my father were research partners. They did all their work together and Jackson didn't want to take time off if my father wasn't. They felt like they were so close to a breakthrough. But Katherine insisted. She nagged and nagged until finally Jackson caved. He convinced my father and mother to take their dream vacation in England, even paid for the whole trip. With them gone, Jackson felt like he could take time off and be with Katherine."

"And on that trip they died."

Carla's chest tightened; she couldn't breathe. In that single moment she understood it all; Jackson's relentless guilt over his parents' death; his dark, brooding nature; the drive in his work. His reluctance to have a relationship, even a temporary one. She understood why he'd tried so hard to resist it, and felt like a fool for pushing him.

"The accident wasn't his fault," she whispered hoarsely.

"Of course it wasn't. But you'll never convince him otherwise. Jackson feels he forced them into the vacation, and forced them to their deaths. He denied my father the opportunity to find a cure for MS for me, his daughter. And all because of his desire to be with Katherine.

"At the funeral, Jackson made a promise to my parents that he'd look after me and he'd find a cure for MS. He devotes practically every waking second to fulfilling the pledge."

"Which leaves no time for anything else in his life."

"Anything or anyone." Amy sighed, a deep mournful sound coming from a place of true sorrow. "Jackson's never explicitly said it, but I strongly believe he feels any time spent on a relationship is time away from the pledge he made to our parents."

"But that's crazy. I can't believe your parents would ever think that."

"Of course not," Amy agreed. "But remember, the relationship began the chain of events that led to their accident. In Jackson's mind, the only way to make up for that is by not having another relationship and instead spending all his time finding the cure.

"The sick irony on top of everything," she concluded, "is Katherine left Jackson shortly after the accident. Turns out her ambition was intense, but not her loyalty. With Jackson grieving and driven to find the MS cure, he no longer had time for her, so she latched on to someone else who did."

Carla was shocked. "She didn't stand by him?"

"No. She wasn't Jackson's top priority anymore so she moved on. Remember, it was always all about Katherine. If Jackson wasn't going to help advance her career, she'd find someone who would."

The selfishness was almost too much to comprehend. A sick swell of anger consumed her, causing her hands to shake. Yet she was grateful Amy had told her the story, because it helped explain a lot about Jackson.

Amy continued. "I think Jackson feels if he finds a cure for MS it will help to make up for what he perceives as his crime."

"Crime? But he didn't commit one."

"I know that, and you know that. Someone has to convince Jackson." She shrugged. "Still, he's a man, and he's no monk. A man has needs."

Her frank talk was surprising, but refreshing. Amy wasn't a blushing schoolgirl and she wanted to see her brother heal.

Carla looked at her, eyes narrowed. "Why are you telling me this? I'm only here for a month, and then you and Jackson will probably never see me again."

Amy pressed her hands against the log and lifted herself from her seat. Carla stood as well and held out an arm to help her.

"I'll be all right, Carla, but thank you."

"Of course."

Amy turned to face her. "I'll say one more thing before I leave. You asked a minute ago why I told you

Jackson's story since your time here is short. But the truth is, I don't really believe that's true. Do you?"

"Well, of course I…" But the assurance wouldn't come. Carla hesitated. Of *course* she believed it was true. Success in this assignment would earn her the big promotion to vice president. And she wasn't even thirty yet! She'd even have a leg up over her powerhouse siblings—none of them had ever worked internationally—not to mention her über-competitive parents.

Her mom talked about Carla's career climb endlessly, her voice swelling with pride whenever the topic came up. This promotion ensured her corporate success, and the cherry on top was Paris. Just the thought of it conjured up sweet songs of French accordion music and walks along the Seine. She'd had this dream for years and no way was she giving up on it now. It was *Paris*, after all. What she really wanted.

"Yes," Carla said firmly, able at last to speak the words. "I do believe it's true. I'm really only here for a month. I'm going to Paris after this."

"Paris? Hmm." Amy mused. "Do you speak French?"

"Well, no, but—"

"Jackson does." She said no more but turned away, back toward the compound, leaving Carla alone with that thought.

Jackson does. Well, yes, she knew that. But so what? It's not as if she was going to Paris with him. And anyway, she'd be going nowhere at all if she didn't get Rivard Research signed on as a client. That had to be priority one. Once that happened, Paris was a lock.

She watched Amy carefully make her way along

the path, her last statement about Jackson speaking French knocking around her mind like pinballs in a machine. She had to admit, strolls along the Seine would be a whole lot better with him by her side. Her heartbeat stuttered as she envisioned him slipping his hand into hers and then drawing her toward him for a kiss, lights of the French city glittering in the background.

She turned toward the lab, deciding she needed to ditch that last bit ASAP. She'd focus on her fear assignment, getting Jackson to sign on as a client, and banish all craziness like thoughts of him accompanying her to Paris. In order to get there in the first place she needed to do her assignment and do it well. And in order for her to do *that*, all thoughts of Jackson being in Paris with her had to go away. Because, well, crazy ideas like that could put dreams in a girl's head that were no good. No good at all.

Chapter Seven

The cobra bit down hard. Thick, deadly venom slid down the side of the glass collection vessel and pooled at the bottom. Half a minute later, the snake had released all she was going to from the bite, and Jackson gently steered her away from the vessel with a firm grip at the base of her head. Maintaining his hold on the cobra, he instructed Kelly to lift the snake's body with her handling hook and together they quickly set her down inside the holding container. Carla could finally breathe again.

It was the last procedure of the day so she walked into the extraction room to collect the instruments for sterilization. Jackson was still there, giving instructions to Kelly.

"We'll start tomorrow morning on the cobras we got from the zoo. I'll see you here at eight."

"Of course." Kelly shot a glance over at Carla as she entered the room, then swung her gaze back to Jackson. "See you soon, Jackson," she purred, slapping on a giant beauty pageant smile right at him. As she walked out of the room, she glanced over her shoulder at Carla, her pouty lips curling in a sneer.

Carla watched her go, ignoring her teenage mean-girl manners. Part of her pitied Kelly, part of her wanted to smack her. She did her best to ignore the latter impulse, which was easy enough to do once she approached Jackson

"Bonjour, *ma chère.*" His gaze flicked down and then lingered on Carla's bare legs. "You'd better not wear that skirt again if you're going to watch me extract."

"Oh?" A flush of warmth eased through her blood like a lazy river. "And why not?"

"Too dangerous." He cast a quick glance around to ensure they were alone. "You distract me from my work. I need to have a hundred percent focus when I collect venom." He pulled her into his arms and bent forward, nibbling on her ear lobe then down along her neck. "I could get bit otherwise," he said, his voice low and smooth as whisky. "You wouldn't want that, would you?"

His hot breath and kisses sent tingles dancing along her spine. She leaned into him as her eyes drifted shut.

"Of course not," she whispered. "Why should the snakes have all the fun?"

"Naughty girl." He chuckled against her skin. "That doesn't sound like something a strategic corporate executive should be saying."

"Well..." His lips brushing her skin made her want to purr like a cat. "Maybe you're right."

"Definitely am. In fact, I should be rewarded for putting up with your unprofessional behavior." He slid the tip of his tongue inside her ear.

"And what...*ooh.*" She struggled to think. "What did you have in mind?"

"I'm thinking along the lines of an integrated solution." His hand slid down her front and slipped beneath the waistband of her skirt. "Like fucking you silly."

"In that case," she reached between their bodies until she felt the rising mound in his pants, "let me help you leverage your assets."

"Oh, fuck, Carla." Jackson groaned as she caressed his cock through his jeans. She started thinking they were going to need that library again when the click of the door froze them in place.

Someone had entered the building. Although the extraction room couldn't be seen from the front entrance, they jumped apart like guilty teenagers. A few seconds later, Lisa stood in the doorway.

"Hey." She nodded to them both. "I hope I'm not interrupting anything?"

"Of course not." Jackson propped a hip against the table, carefully folding his hands in front of his lap. Carla choked back laughter, staring at the floor until the urge passed.

Jackson cleared his throat. "What's up?"

"I've been reading over the paperwork we're submitting for the Atlantis grant and had a few questions I wanted to run by you." Lisa glanced over at Carla who was busy trying to look busy. "Unless this is a bad time?"

"This is fine." Jackson gave a professional nod to Carla, transforming himself in a nanosecond from her lover to her boss. "You know what to do with the equipment. Is there anything you need?"

"Nope. I'm good here."

"Okay. I'll…ah." He lowered his voice so Lisa wouldn't hear. "I'll see you tonight in the caf, around seven?" She nodded and Jackson turned to go, but before leaving, he let out a slow, deep breath, as if getting himself under control. She looked back down at the equipment, hiding the smile that tugged at her lips.

Once she finished everything she needed to do, she remembered he'd asked her earlier to bring out additional handling equipment from the storage room for the next day's extractions. She went to the room and turned the knob, only to find the door locked. Jackson was supposed to have left her the keys but, as he had admitted, she'd distracted him.

Crazy man. She'd give him a hard time about that later, although right now she needed to figure out how to get the room open. What about the large key ring in his office, the one she usually saw on top of his desk? Would he mind if she took it to see if one of those keys opened the storage room?

It'd be easy enough to give him a call and ask, she decided, pulling out her phone. Her finger tapped on his name, quickly found since it was already stored in her favorites. She shrugged off her internal cringe of embarrassment about having done that as she waited for Jackson to answer. No such luck. Once connected, the call went straight to voicemail.

Carla thought for a minute. She didn't want to invade Jackson's privacy by going to his office without asking first; on the other hand, he'd asked her to do something and she meant to do it. Besides, it's not as if she were going to snoop.

Minutes later she arrived back at the house and stood in the hallway in front of the office door.

"Jackson?" she called his name upon entering, but the room stood empty. Switching on the lights, she walked toward the desk, her gaze searching the smooth, polished wood. No keys. Damn.

Now what? She looked around. Maybe one of the

desk drawers? She pulled the top one open, ignoring the illicit little thrill shooting through her as she searched his personal things.

Pens, pencils, paperclips, phone charger, USB drive, notepads, envelopes, glasses cleaning cloth, and no keys. In other words, a whole lotta nothin'.

Sighing, she shut the drawer and pulled out the one below. It was a file drawer and, to no surprise, filled with files. No keys there, either. She carelessly flipped through the files, not even sure why since clearly she wouldn't find what she was after. But as she went to shut the drawer, she heard the clink of metal. Could that be the keys?

Frowning, she opened the drawer wider and resumed her search. She sorted through the files, jiggling each one to find the source of the sound. At last she came across a thick brown folder, stuffed full. Something in there clinked. She pulled it from the drawer.

Easing the file on top of the desk, she opened it and her eyes flicked over the words on a somewhat crumpled letter stuffed inside. *Dear Mr. Jackson, It is our esteemed honor to present you with the Jenson-Hobart Award for outstanding scientific research in monoclonal antibody for the treatment of relapsing-remitting multiple sclerosis...*

Behind the letter was an elaborate gold-leafed certificate printed on heavy card stock. It seemed as if the certificate should have been in a frame and hung on the wall, not here, haphazardly stuffed in a folder. As she scanned the rest of the contents, her mind flashed back to the conversation with Bryce. Awards, certificates, letters of merit, just like he'd said. But why did Jackson seem to have such little regard for all this distinction? Everything was shoved in the file as though they held no higher meaning than the monthly electric bill.

Finally her fingers alighted on the last item in the folder, a small wooden container, much like a jewelry box. Unable to resist temptation, she opened the box and found, lying atop soft velvet lining, a gold round disc hanging from a ribbon, like an Olympic medal. This was the source of the clinking. The medal had come loose within the box and must've knocked against it when she pulled open the drawer.

Also in the box was a photograph of no less than the President of the United States placing the award around Jackson's neck. She sucked in a breath. This had to be the National Medal of Science. Her fingers skimmed the raised letters and engraved drawing of a kneeling man on the front.

Unable to resist, she lifted the medal out of the box. It had a solid, prestigious weight to it. She held it by the ribbon and then, because she just couldn't help herself, placed the medal around her neck. What would it be like to receive such an award?

"My esteemed colleagues," she muttered to herself, "I'd like to thank all of you for this distinguished honor. It's such a tremendous—"

"Looks good on you."

Her head snapped up and she gasped, mortified. Jackson stood in the doorway, eyes glinting as he studied her.

"I...I didn't mean..." She didn't mean what? Not to snoop? To invade his privacy? But she had, and he'd caught her, and now she sat feeling like a naughty child with her hand in the cookie jar.

He stepped toward her, arms crossed. She was reminded of the day she'd first met him, Mr. Grunter, intimidating yet sexy as hell. Just like now. Except, if she wasn't mistaken, a ghost of a smile broke through his stern expression, like peeks of sunshine chipping away at black clouds.

He took a seat opposite her.

"You wanna tell me what you're doing here?"

"Of course. I'm sorry. I was looking for keys. To the storage room."

He raised an eyebrow. "In my office?"

"You were supposed to have left them for me in the extraction lab. But you forgot them."

The right-hand corner of his mouth rose in a smooth grin. "That's right, I was. But I recall getting distracted. Something about a short skirt comes to mind." He eyed her legs once more, his gaze slow and deliberate as it traveled the length of them.

She relaxed in her chair, grateful he wasn't angry. Still, she owed him an apology. "I remembered seeing the large key ring usually on top of your desk and thought maybe the storage key would be there. But it wasn't, so I started—"

"Snooping?"

"*Looking*. For the keys." She let out a light breath. "But you're right. It ultimately turned into snooping and I'm sorry. I didn't mean it."

His quiet chuckle was like music. "If you didn't snoop, I'd assume you have no curiosity."

"There's curiosity and then there's manners. Something I showed very little of just now."

He brushed his hand in the air, as if waving aside a

fly. "*T'en fais pas*, Carla. Don't worry about it."

"Well… Okay. Thank you."

They sat for a moment in companionable silence, and Carla wondered if she'd be pushing her luck if she asked him about the awards. He seemed to have so little interest in them. Then again, could there be some painful association, something he preferred not to talk about? A shadow passed through her mind as she considered whether Katherine had anything to do with Jackson hiding the awards. She nibbled at her bottom lip, wrestling with whether or not to ask the question.

Jackson nodded toward her. "That medal looks better on you then it ever did on me. Why don't you keep it?"

"Keep it?" she sputtered. "But this is a major award, such an honor. It would be like giving away your Oscar, or Nobel prize, or—"

"Not to me." His voice was quiet yet firm. In the back of his jaw a muscle jumped, outward indication of his steely determination.

Suddenly she knew why the awards didn't matter. "Your eye is still on the prize you haven't achieved."

He sat still as granite, gaze boring into her, before at last giving her a tight nod.

"That's right."

She understood how he felt. The cure was his prize; nothing less would do. She equated that with Paris. The promotion, the new title, successful completion of her fear assignment…those were all fine. But Paris is what she'd always really been after. Nothing less would do. Or so she thought, anyway.

She looked back at Jackson. "Everyone always says to enjoy the ride."

"What?"

She reached up to finger the medal still hanging around her neck. "You know, the ride. The journey you take on your way toward the prize. We're supposed to be enjoying that."

He nodded. "And are you?"

Funny how easily he turned the conversation around to her when it was supposed to be about him. Still, talking to him felt easy, comfortable. Like being with an old friend. Things were so different now compared to the day they'd met. Mr. Grunter's icy exterior had melted.

"I'm not sure." The words surprised her the minute they left her mouth, but she realized they were true. She didn't honestly know if she were enjoying her journey or not. "I sometimes feel as if I'm…"

He waited, relaxed, not pressing her to finish the sentence before she was ready. She liked that about him. He had a way of putting her at ease, his calm composure a tonic for her nervous anxiety. He also gave her the courage to admit things out loud she'd never even admitted to herself.

Her voice was soft as she finally said, "As if I might be on someone else's journey."

His eyes filled with understanding.

"Do you ever feel that way?"

He shook his head. "That I'm on someone else's journey, no. But I can't say I'm enjoying my own ride."

Her brows lifted with surprise. "Why not?"

He shifted in his chair and she wondered if she'd gone too far, made him uncomfortable. But he didn't look as if he wanted to bolt. On the contrary, he looked as if he were settling in. "Like I said, I know I'm on the right path. I'm on *my* path. I know what I'm supposed to be doing. But I'm not a patient man, Carla, and I always feel like I'm racing against the clock, charging ahead of time." He let out a slow, deep breath. "It can be...unsettling."

"At least you know you're headed in the right direction."

"Am I? Sometimes I wonder."

"Of course you are." She nodded vigorously, emphasizing her point. "These awards, these prizes." She held up the medal. "All of this is your proof, Jackson. Proof you're going the right way. The discoveries you've made confirm you're getting closer toward the ultimate prize. These are all victories, and they shouldn't be stuffed in a drawer. You need to bring them out and celebrate your achievements." Her voice rose with the passion of her conviction. She felt her cheeks heating and ordered herself to calm down before Jackson started thinking she'd gone off the deep end.

"Maybe you're right," he said, nodding. "Perhaps I've been thinking about them in the wrong way. I'd always thought they diverted my focus away from what I really want. Maybe they're actually proof that my focus is on track."

He stayed silent and stared off in the distance for another minute, as if contemplating his own words, before seeming to remember Carla was still in the room. A slow grin eased its way across his lips. He rose from the chair and in a couple of short steps closed the distance between them.

"In any case, I still think you should keep that," he said, touching the medal where it hung down just below her breasts.

"No way. It's a huge achievement and it's yours."

He reached down and put his arms beneath hers, lifting her from the chair. Her body molded against his, curves fitting perfectly along his muscled planes. She squirmed as his hands slid along her back to cup her ass. He bent down and kissed her, hot and hungry, like he'd been denied her lips for far too long. She groaned as his tongue slipped into her mouth, sliding next to hers in a sensual mating.

He broke the kiss only to nibble his way down along her neck. "Then at least wear it while you're here," he murmured against her skin.

"What?" His kisses fogged her brain; she struggled for coherent thought.

"To celebrate my achievement. Just as you said." He traced the fine line of her collarbone with the tip of his tongue. She groaned.

"Wear the medal when I make love to you. Just the medal and nothing else." He pulled away for just a moment, tossing her a wicked grin. "Then I'll feel like I really got a prize."

****

"Right here," Jackson tilted the small pitcher in his hand so its contents drizzled directly onto Carla's erect nipples, "is really the best place to pour the honey."

Over the past week they'd settled into a pattern of having dinner in the caf, dessert in Jackson's bedroom. He'd insisted dessert tasted a whole lot better in bed, and Carla wasn't about to disagree. Besides, he was absolutely right. Having mind-blowing sex with Jackson every night beat chocolate soufflé by a mile and was fat free to boot.

He bent forward and began with slow and careful

precision to lick away every drop on her skin. The thick, amber liquid dripped down her nipples to the sides of her breasts. Before it trickled to the bed sheets Jackson was there, licking away the honey with sensual swipes of his tongue.

"Don't want to miss any," he said with a wicked smile.

Carla let out a long hiss and settled back on the pillows, content to give him as much time as he wanted for this little tongue bath.

His lips captured her nipple and he swirled his tongue around the distended nub, making it hard as a cherry pit. Slow and steady pulses throbbed in her pussy, matching her heartbeat. Although she loved the way he sucked her nipples, even using his teeth to lightly bite and scrape her sensitive skin, she began losing patience with his game. She needed the delicious stretch of his thick cock in her pussy. Now.

Her thighs opened, invitation for Jackson to satisfy her hunger and fuck her.

"Need you in me," she begged, arching her pelvis toward him.

"Not so fast." He waved a scolding finger at her. "I'm not finished here."

His attention returned to her breasts as he continued to clean off the sticky honey. But, as if granting a small concession to her demands, he dropped his right hand between her legs and made a leisurely exploration of her slick folds. His finger trailed through her juices, skimming her clit only enough to make her think she might lose her mind in frustration. He stroked, rubbing the swollen kernel just the way she liked it, then backed off as soon as her hips began to rock.

"Jackson, please." She could hear the desperation in her ragged voice.

"You need something, *chère?*" he asked with feigned innocence.

"You know what I—ah!" He plunged two fingers deep inside her.

Oh, sweet heavenly bliss. She cried out, raising her hips to meet his sublime thrusts. She wove her hands through his hair and then dropped one of her hands down to trace the curve of his back and the sexy rise and fall of his ass. And what an ass. Tight and sculpted, like Michelangelo's David.

With his thumb he made slow circles around her sensitive clit, his touch quick yet light. Carla closed her eyes and slipped further down the pillows, surrendering herself to his touch. She let her thighs drop open even further, allowing him as much access as he wanted. Her breaths grew quicker and more shallow and she couldn't help but undulate her hips as he increased the pressure against her G-spot.

She tingled everywhere, from her hair to her toes, reaching, reaching to grab hold of the orgasm that was building but yet not quite there. So close, going full steam ahead to the edge of the cliff.

"Oh yes, oh please!" She rocked against his thrusting fingers, hips flailing, her fingers twisting the bed sheets into knots as she held tight. "Don't stop don't stop don't stop. Give me more. More, Jackson, please!"

He gave her what she wanted and then some, his fingers driving into her pussy until she reached the summit, nerve-sizzling pulses of pleasure rushing through her body like a storm, blissful spasms she hoped would never end.

When she finally floated back to reality, Jackson propped above her against his arm, trailing his fingers along the smooth skin of her breasts.

"That was beautiful," he murmured, fingering her still swollen nipples.

"Yes," she purred like a contented cat, "it was." She looked at his body and his jutting cock, hard as a marble pole. "But I want that. Now."

"Greedy."

"For you."

She adjusted herself, assuming he would climb atop her. But instead he rolled her to her stomach. *Nice*, she thought. *Doggy style.* She loved that position for the ease with which she could meet his thrusts. She heard the quick tear of the condom pack, but was surprised when Jackson settled his body atop hers, his weight pressing her into the cool sheets.

"You don't want me up?" she asked.

"Not yet." He swept aside her hair so he could lick and kiss her neck. "Need to hold you first."

She sizzled with pleasure, loving the intimate feeling of his body draped over hers as she lay on her stomach. Jackson slipped his hands beneath her pelvis just for a moment, raising her hips and positioning himself before he slid deep inside.

She gasped as he entered, balling her hands into fists against the pillow as his thick cock stretched her. His rock hard abs were coated with a light sheen of sweat and slick as they glided over her back. It was difficult for her to meet his thrusts in that position but Jackson didn't seem to care. He set a slow, almost leisurely pace, plunging into her but then pulling out nearly all the way and pausing before he thrust once more.

His hands braced on either side of her face, his fingertips skimming her cheeks, and she turned her head so she could take one of his fingers in her mouth, sucking it like a treat. He picked up the pace, plunging harder, and she curved her back so she could bring him more deeply inside of her. His arm slid beneath her belly and he brought her up to her hands and knees.

"Time to get serious," he murmured, reaching forward to caress her breasts as he buried himself deep. His balls slapped her pussy as he pounded against her, his labored groans filling the air. He straightened and rested one hand on her hip while slipping the other around her waist to play with her clit.

Sensation overwhelmed her. She cried out, sure she wasn't ready yet. It was too soon, she'd come just minutes ago. But even as the thought flitted through her mind, a seed of desire unfurled and she burned for him once more.

His skilled touch knew just the amount of pressure she needed. His fingers swirled around her swollen clit, circling faster; harder. A pleasing sharp sting of his hand landed across her buttocks. She groaned, savoring the addictive pain.

Jackson leaned forward again and turned his attention back to her neck, kissing the nape, his labored breathing gusting across her skin. Her eyes squeezed shut as the orgasm danced before her, just out of reach. Her pussy swelled, growing heavy, readying for release.

She reached between her legs to caress Jackson's balls and was rewarded with his low, throaty groan. A couple more thrusts and he cried out, swelling and pulsing inside of her. She rocked her hips forward, pressing her clit hard against his hand, and seconds later joined in the release.

Jackson pulled out and made a quick trip to the bathroom to get rid of the condom. Then he settled back down on the bed, bringing Carla with him. He lay on his back and she rested her head against his arm. His warm skin emitted his scent, faint but distinct. She breathed deeply, basking in the familiar smell.

Jackson noticed and raised a questioning brow. "I take it a shower is in order?"

She looked up at him. "Only if I can join you."

"I wouldn't object."

He made to roll away but Carla placed a hand on his chest to stop him. "Not yet."

"I thought by the way you were sniffing around I'm getting a bit ripe."

"Not at all. I'm actually enjoying the scent of you. It's wonderful."

He chuckled. "You're definitely unique."

"Unique?" She lifted herself up and rested her head on her arm. "That's generally euphemistic for 'different' or 'weird.' It's not usually much of a compliment."

"But in this case it is."

"Yeah?"

Jackson propped himself up on the pillows and absently swirled the tips of his fingers across her cheek. "I think you know me enough by now to realize I'm a bit off the beaten path."

A perfect opening; she couldn't resist. She propped herself up on the pillows as well, putting some distance between herself and him. She pulled the sheet up as well, not feeling comfortable being naked at this very moment.

"Actually," she began cautiously, "I don't know if that's true. About how well I know you, that is."

It wasn't her imagination; she was certain of it. He visibly tensed. "What do you mean?"

"I…" She hesitated. Did she really need to have a "serious" discussion with him? Two weeks of her assignment were already gone. Why not just enjoy the remaining time they had together and call it a day? But in her heart she knew it felt wrong. Like it or not, sensible or not, Jackson had begun to mean something to her. She tried like crazy to deny it, but after a while the truth just wouldn't go away. She knew herself well enough to recognize feelings, and she was starting to get them, big time, for Jackson.

Before she could begin again, Jackson said, "You talked to Amy."

She winced against the accusation in his voice. "It's not like I was spying on you, Jackson. She came to me, not the other way around. Ask her yourself."

"I don't have to. I know Amy well enough." He sighed, a long, tired sigh, as if just learning he had a monumental amount of work to do and limited time in which to do it.

"How much did she tell you?"

"I already knew about your parents, because you had told me. But she talked about how you blame yourself for the accident." She turned to face him more directly. "Which, by the way, you shouldn't because—"

"Save it for someone else." His voice had taken on a hard edge. "I know what I did."

She heard the toughness in his words, but as she

studied his face she could see the trauma in his eyes. He had put on a mask, the same one he donned for everyone else when the subject of his parents' accident came up. Jackson shielded himself from anyone trying to help him while bearing the pain of their deaths squarely on his shoulders alone. He acted tough in a feeble effort to fool people. Maybe sometimes it even worked. But not with Carla.

"So do I," she said. "You made them happy."

"I got them *killed.*" He ran his hands through his hair and turned the other way, toward the night table. He grabbed his glasses from the stand and put them on.

Silence stole into the room like an intruder, robbing them of the intimacy they'd known mere minutes ago. She scooted off the bed and grabbed for her clothes, pulling them on and then walking around the room to stand in front of Jackson, who remained sitting on the edge of the bed.

"I know you didn't want me to learn this about you," she began, "but I did so I think we should talk about it."

Even before she finished her sentence he shook his head. "No." His voice was soft, barely above a whisper, but his conviction was undeniable.

She frowned. "Why not?"

"Because there isn't anything to talk about."

He rose from the bed and began reassembling his own clothes, pulling on jeans and a T-shirt and then looking for his socks.

Carla trailed after him, sputtering. "Nothing to talk about? How about the fact that you blame yourself for your parents' death? How about the overwhelming guilt eating at you every single day, driving you to the ground? Shouldn't that be talked about?"

He whirled around as if she'd physically grabbed hold of him and forced him to face her. He stared, eyes blazing fire, then he clenched his jaw and shook his head.

"Not with you."

His tone was purposely cold. He wanted her off his back. But giving up easily wasn't her style. "Jackson, this is a huge part of your life. We should discuss it."

His face contorted with anger. "Why?" he asked, the word brittle with frost. "Why should I discuss something like this with you?"

She blinked, taken aback by the bite in his tone. But she held firm. "Because it's a part of your life, and so am I."

She took a risk making that declaration, and she knew it. She'd opened herself up to a deeply painful attack, where he could launch into her like a machete and slice her wide open, exposing her feelings and vulnerabilities. But she *was* part of his life, even if only temporarily, and she hated the way he hid from her.

Jackson's breath left his chest in a whoosh, as if someone had slammed a fist into his gut. She sensed the truth had hit home. He sank down on the bed, slowly, like a deflating balloon. "You're right," he quietly admitted, swallowing hard. "You are a part of my life, even if it's only for the next two weeks."

His reminder of their waning time, even though he hadn't said it to hurt her, nonetheless stung.

"But I asked you for a level of trust before, and I'm asking for it still. I just…" He took several deep breaths, as if to steady his nerves. "I just don't want to talk about it."

"Then why do you think Amy told me?"

"Carla, please. I—"

"I've told you I respect your wishes, Jackson. I do. And I'm not asking you tell me anything you don't want to. But the one person in the world who you're closest to told me everything. I'm just wondering why."

He shrugged, but Carla knew he was hiding from her. Again. And she was getting pretty tired of it.

"What?" she said, her voice sharp. "What is it?"

"She thinks..." He shook his head, changed his mind. "*Zut alors*. It doesn't matter."

She knew he was clamming up, stopping the conversation. She refused to accept it. "It *does* matter. Tell me."

"Fine." He let out breath. "Amy thinks I need someone in my life, and I think she's hoping it's going to be you."

"So she wants me to know who you are, warts and all?"

The smallest of grins started to touch one corner of his mouth. "Something like that, I guess."

"And you?" She sifted out any notes of hope or expectation from her voice, though her heartbeat slammed against her ribcage like a conga player on steroids.

"Don't worry, I don't have any intention of ruining your planned-out corporate life. Your trip to Paris and your big promotion are right on track. I'll give your firm a great recommendation and you'll be on your way."

He looked at her as if expecting her to be grateful and really, why wouldn't she? Everything she'd planned for herself—and her parents had planned for her—moved along like a well-oiled machine. As far as Jackson knew, that's what she wanted. She'd told him as much, so why would he think she'd changed her mind?

Wait a minute, *had* she changed her mind? Why did she think like this? She wanted Paris and the promotion…right? Suddenly she felt as if the room had constricted, sucking out the oxygen and leaving her gasping like a fish out of water.

She turned to slip on her shoes and toss Jackson a grateful smile, hoping it masked the tortured anguish eating away her insides. An image of that old game show flashed through her mind, the one where the contestant had to pick what's behind door number one or number two. The audience yelled out their choices, demanding to be heard, all the while the confused contestant stood on stage, biting her lips, searching for help among the masses.

Paris or Jackson? Door number one or door number two? Which one would give her what she really wants? Carla bit back an urge to scream. She had to get out of there and go someplace where she could think. Alone.

"Thanks for the evening." She made to leave, but Jackson sprang from the bed, capturing her by the door.

"I didn't scare you away, did I?" A curious vulnerability was etched on his face, eyes wide and hopeful.

Carla was struck with a clear insight of how much her answer meant to him. Tension slid from her bones, realizing her feelings of insecurity didn't lack for company. She shook her head, wanting to reassure him. "Scare me? No. Why?"

"Well, you know." He shrugged. "With Amy's crazy idea about us being together. She knows I don't want a relationship and neither do you. We've both got plans. But for the next two weeks, my plans include you."

I don't want a relationship. I don't want a relationship. Jackson's words echoed in her head, mocking her like a spiteful child.

She closed her eyes and released a long breath. *Remember, you don't want a relationship either. Right?*

Yes, that's right. Her future was her career and Paris, and she had to remember that.

Just focus on the time left, Carla.

He turned her around and gave her a soft kiss, his lips lingering for a moment before he pulled away. "After that, I promise to set you free."

Her heart twisted. Could he free someone who doesn't want to be let go? Confusion spun like tumbleweeds in the wind. She didn't know what to do or what she wanted. Except that right now, with Jackson's eyes fixed on her, blazing with intensity, she knew one thing—she wanted him.

The atmosphere transformed, becoming as hot and sultry as the bayou. Carla heard Jackson's breath hitch and knew his hunger for her began building once more.

"*Mon Dieu,*" he groaned. He bent forward, lips and tongue sliding along her throat. "Sex with you is so fucking good."

Her lips fell open to say something in response, but the words wouldn't come. Confusion mingled with the hot thread of desire that always seemed to flow between them. Already a warm gush of wetness dampened her panties. She wanted to think, but need for him won out.

"I should go," she protested, even as he began unbuttoning her blouse. Once it fell open, he unhooked her bra and feasted on her breasts.

"Come back to bed," he murmured, pulling her in that direction.

"Jackson, please, I—"

"Now."

Argument failed. His demanding tone turned her on as quickly as if he flicked a switch, because she knew it meant he wanted her. Badly. He had her on the bed, lying on her back. He stood next to the bed, lording over her as though she was his captive. With deliberate, agonizing slowness he undid his jeans, his eyes never leaving hers. He shoved them down, then just as quickly got rid of his shirt. Her appreciative gaze roamed over his sculpted torso, his thick shoulders, the ladder of muscles forming his abs. He stood naked before her, a bead of moisture clinging to his rock hard erection.

"Do you see what you do to me?" he asked, taking his cock in hand. He stroked himself, gripping the head before sliding down the swollen shaft. He cupped his balls for a moment, panting as arousal deepened, then continued to stroke. A trickle of sweat rolled down his chest as it rose and fell with desire. Carla's heartbeat crashed like thunder. Her pussy clenched as she watched Jackson masturbate.

"Do you see why you can't leave yet?" He climbed onto the bed and kneeled before her, continuing to stroke. "Take off your clothes. Slowly."

Carla's lips curved in a smile as she sat up in front of him. She shrugged out of her already open blouse and bra, then lay back down. She undid the buttons on her jeans and lifted her hips, sliding them down.

"These, too?" she asked coyly, thumbs hooked in the top of her panties.

Jackson nodded, his gaze glued to her.

She scooted to the edge of the bed and slipped off. He shifted himself on his knees so he could look at her as he continued fisting his cock.

She slowly turned around, hips swaying like a vixen until she stood with her back to him. With tortuous languor she slid down her panties, bending forward so Jackson could fill his gaze with her exposed ass and pussy. Once she stepped out of her panties, she stood before him. Placing her spread hands against her hips, she traced upward to the curve of her waist, and then over her belly and up to her breasts. She played with them, pinching her nipples as Jackson kept stroking himself. His mouth dropped open. She smiled as let out a long, low groan, loving the powerful feeling he gave her.

Fully undressed, she walked back to the bed and sat, knees folded beneath her. "Now," she said, "let me relieve you of your agony." She leaned forward and took his cock between her lips, relaxing her throat so she could draw him in deeply, tasting his saltiness on her tongue as she sucked. Then she pulled back until he was nearly out of her mouth, teasing just the head of his cock with long, slow licks.

"Fuck, Carla," he hissed. He wove his fingers through her hair, guiding her. She swirled her tongue along his length as he swelled in her mouth, and she savored the salty drop of pre-cum that beaded at his slit. With one hand she cupped his balls, and his groan filled the room. His free hand played with her breast, light teasing pinches that had her crying out even as she took him deep once more. Suddenly he pulled his cock from her lips.

"Not yet," he said, in response to her questioning gaze. He lay down on the bed then curled his index finger back and forth, gesturing for her. "Let me make you come first, Carla. Move over here."

She crawled toward him, thinking he wanted her on top, but as she began positioning herself Jackson shook his head.

"Not there." He pointed to his mouth. "Here."

A spear of lust shot straight to her pussy. She moved forward until she straddled his face, her hands braced against the headboard. Jackson placed his hands on either side of her hips and lowered her. The hot wet swipe of his tongue circled right on her clit.

"Ah!" Her eyes squeezed shut, hips swaying against his mouth.

The tip of his tongue circled her clit with agonizing torture before he swiped her slick folds and dove deep into her entrance. The pleasure was intense, her legs trembling as Jackson licked and teased.

She grabbed the headboard for support, the first flutters of orgasm building. Her thighs gripped his face as her hips swayed against his probing tongue. She cupped her breasts as her fingers pinched the swollen nipples. Jackson gave her just what she needed, his magical tongue flicking hard and fast across her clit. Seconds later she found release, keening long and loud as the climax consumed her.

Once the spasms slowed, she positioned herself over Jackson's jutting cock.

"Your turn," she whispered with a smile. She

grabbed a condom from the dresser drawer and rolled it on him. Then, resting her hands atop his chest, she slowly impaled herself, her pussy sizzling from the tantalizing stretch of his thick cock.

She writhed atop him, her hips mimicking the sensual sway of a belly dancer. She wanted to torture him, to draw out his climax so he could savor the ride, but Jackson was having none of it. He grasped her hips with his large hands and set the brutal pace.

"Need you fast and hard," he panted.

She smiled at his agony. "Say no more."

Gripping her thighs against him for support, she rode him hard, plunging up and down in a frenzied pace. She felt behind her for his balls, fingering them as he raised his hips to meet her thrusts. Beads of sweat dotted his forehead and his breaths were quick and shallow. He reached up so he could tease her nipples and she arched her back in response, filling his hands with her breasts. She loved his generosity as a lover, never forgetting about her needs even as he teetered on the edge of release.

Knowing he was close, she contracted her pelvis muscles and milked his cock as he thrust, wanting to increase his pleasure. They kissed, tongues mingling as she drove down, again and again. Seconds later Jackson exploded, his body going still as the climax pulsed deep inside her pussy.

She collapsed atop his chest, the thumping of his heartbeat echoing in her ears. They stayed that way, swirling back to Earth, until Jackson shifted out from under her and made a quick trip to the bathroom to get rid of the condom. He came back to bed and lay on his back, cradling her beside him.

They were good together, no doubt about it. Sexually, at least. But again, Carla found herself just where she'd been only minutes ago, filled with doubt and wonder. Two more weeks of really great sex and that was it. Wham bam, thank you, ma'am, and both went on their way. She should be happy about the lack of complication. No strings, no messy feelings to deal with. He was setting her free, he said so himself. That hollow feeling, the one pressing against her chest and growing bigger every day, would just have to be ignored.

She shifted to prop her elbow on the bed and her head against her palm. She peered over at Jackson. His eyes held a mixture of satiety and confusion. Perhaps her doubts reflected in her gaze?

"Is everything all right?" he asked.

His earlier words echoed in her mind. *She knows I don't want a relationship and neither do you.* It was true. It had to be. So why did those words feel so wrong?

She swallowed back the golf ball-sized lump in her throat and gave him a shaky smile. "Of course."

She needed to leave—*now*—before the maddening threat of tears began welling in her eyes.

"I'm just going to get some fresh air," she said, rolling off the bed and pulling on her clothes. "You work me up into such a sweat, I need to cool off."

She tried to grin, even felt the corner of her mouth tugging upward. But from the tightness of his furrowed brows, she knew her acting skills needed work. Still, he held up a hand to wave as she left.

"Okay, but don't be long," he said. "The bed will get cold."

Somehow she managed to get out of Jackson's room and make her way downstairs and outside before she had to brush away the tears. Once she stepped into the sultry bayou night, grateful for the cover of darkness and lack of passersby, she gulped in air and tried her best to settle her pounding heart. *Damn, damn, damn.* She'd vowed not to fall for Jackson and look how that had turned out. Like an idiot, she'd not only fallen but fallen hard.

Good going, Carla, she scolded herself. *You couldn't have screwed up your Paris dreams any better if you'd planned everything out ahead of time. Falling for a herpetologist who lives a thousand miles away. How convenient!*

Of course, in the end, it really all meant nothing. Jackson had no intention of asking her to stay. He'd made that abundantly clear. They'd have a good time for a month and that was that. He'd continue his research and she'd go to Paris. Except a tiny part of her questioned if she even wanted to go anymore. Another much larger part of her wanted to know how exactly she was going to do it with the piercing pain of a broken heart.

She brushed aside more tears and decided to walk around the perimeter of the research facility when she heard Jackson calling her name from the house.

She turned back and saw him standing on the porch, holding her cell.

"You left your phone on my nightstand," he explained as she approached his outstretched hand, "and someone named Bryce called."

Carla cringed as she took the phone. "You talked to him?"

"No. But I saw the display on your phone when it rang. It said Bryce Betts." He cocked his thumb toward the front door where he was headed. "I'll give you some privacy to call him back."

She took a deep breath, readying herself for the upcoming conversation with Bryce, when her phone rang again and she saw it was him. What was going on? A shiver of dread skittered down her spine. Had something happened at home?

Her hands shook as she held the phone to her ear. "Bryce? What's wrong?"

"Wrong? Nothing, I—no, I don't think this is the road." His voice became muffled as he held the phone away and spoke to someone. Then, "Carla?"

"What's going on? Bryce, who are you talking to?"

"The driver. I think he's lost."

She didn't bother softening her tone as she shifted gears into annoyance mode. "What driver? What are you talking about?"

"Listen Carla, I'm in the middle of the backwater bayou here and there's not a damn thing in sight. No streetlights, no houses. Oh, and this hick of a driver says his GPS doesn't work out here." He expelled a huff of frustration. "There's absolutely nothing to guide our way."

Her heart sank as she realized what must be happening. *Please, dear Lord, let it not be true.* But even as she uttered the prayer, she knew it was too late for help from above.

"Are you in Louisiana?"

"Of course I am. I told you I was coming for a visit."

A storm cloud of rage formed above her head.

"And I told *you* it wasn't a good idea. Why did you ignore me?"

"Because I knew you didn't mean it. You don't actually expect us to not see each other for a solid month, do you?"

"Actually, I do. I'm busy here, Bryce, and I don't have time to entertain you. This is a business assignment. You need to respect that."

For a few seconds he was quiet, probably shocked into silence at her outburst. But Bryce recovered quickly. "If I didn't know better, Carla, I'd think you weren't interested in seeing me."

Good try, she thought. *But not good enough.* She wasn't about to be baited into reassuring him of something that wasn't true.

"You really shouldn't have done this, Bryce. Now I'm going to have to scramble around and inconvenience people to try to find someplace here for you to stay."

"There?" He cackled into the phone as if she'd just told a dirty joke. "Carla, we're not staying at the snake farm. What kind of boyfriend do you think I am to let you suffer there over the weekend? I'm whisking you away to New Orleans."

"New Orleans?!"

"Of course. As long as you have to be down here, you may as well take advantage of the one thing these hicks have to offer."

She bristled at his conceit. "I'm not going to New Orleans, Bryce, or anywhere else with you. My assignment here is for a month and it's not a nine to five, Monday through Friday job. It's all day, every day. Your assumption that I can just leave for the

215

weekend is misguided."

"No, it's farther down the road. There's supposedly a turn-off sign. Just keep going, you idiot." Bryce returned his attention to Carla. "Sorry, I missed what you just said. Anyway, let me focus on getting there and I'll see you soon. Bye!"

He clicked off before she had time to respond, making her so mad she felt like throwing the phone.

Fuming with rage, she turned and stomped back toward the house. She had little choice but to let Jackson know what was going on. This was his property, after all. His land, his company. His home. She put her foot on the first step, dreading the conversation with Jackson when the man himself came through the front door.

"Everything okay?"

She looked up, took a breath. "Yeah, definitely."

Jackson stepped onto the stairs, sauntering toward her in his lupine gait. When he reached the bottom he stood directly in front of her, studying her face. "Why are you lying to me?"

Carla felt her cheeks color, embarrassed to be called out so easily.

"I, ah…" she shrugged as her voice trailed away. "That was Bryce."

"I know. Who's Bryce?"

"He's a…well, I guess you could say he's a family friend."

"And?"

There was an edge to Jackson's voice he didn't bother to hide. Was he jealous? In some ways she was flattered; but in others it filled her with dread. He wasn't going to like what she had to tell him. She sighed and ran her fingers through her hair. May as well just get this over with. "He's on his way here."

Jackson stilled, and she saw a muscle jump at the back of his jaw. Aside from that, his face was like stone. "You've invited your friend here? Without telling me?"

His voice was soft, but a current of lethal anger vibrated through his words. Carla knew she needed to set things straight right away, although a small part of her felt irritation as well. Jackson jumped to conclusions awfully quick.

"I didn't invite him," she clarified. "In fact when he brought up the topic of visiting me I told him not to. But I guess he didn't listen."

"Or you weren't very persuasive."

Now she was definitely angry. "You're out of line."

"Am I?" He raised an eyebrow as he looked down at her. "You've just told me someone I've never met before is invading my work and my home, uninvited and unwelcome, and my reaction is out of line?" He took a step back, apparently not as comfortable being so close to her as he was a moment ago. He jammed his hands in his pockets. "Who is this guy to you?"

"I told you, he's just a friend. His family and mine have known each other for years. Our mothers were childhood friends."

"So he's just casually stopping by at ten o'clock at night to say hello? After flying down here from New York, I assume?"

Obviously Jackson believed she held out on him, and if she looked at it from his perspective she could understand why.

"Could we go inside and sit down?" She looked toward the door.

He stared at her though narrowed eyes, jaw tightly clenched. Tension seemed to vibrate from his every pore. Without a word he snapped around and headed back up the stairs. He held the door open for her and they went inside to his office.

"Everything I've told you is true," she began, taking her seat in front of his desk. "Bryce is someone my family has known for years. He and I more or less grew up together. His family and mine used to visit each other all the time and even took a vacation together one year. We go back a long way."

Jackson's only response was a curt nod, but at least he listened.

"Lately, I mean over the past year or so, my relationship with Bryce has changed."

"Changed how?"

"Bryce has begun assuming he and I are more than just friends."

Jackson stiffened in his chair, crossing his arms across his chest. A muscle jumped in the back of his jaw but he said nothing in response.

She took a breath and plunged ahead. "My family would like that, I think. I mean, if he and I were, you know, involved."

His eyes were cold. The silence dragged out and when it looked like he wasn't going to speak she cleared her throat to continue. But then he said, quietly, "And would you like it as well?"

"*No*. Absolutely not. I don't want Bryce in my life, Jackson. And it has nothing to do with anything between us. I've never wanted Bryce for more than a friend. In fact, he's not even a friend. He's not someone I'd ever confide it, or miss when I'm away, or want to hang out with. Anything defining what a friend is, is unrelated to how I feel toward Bryce."

"But you haven't told your family."

"No." She shook her head, her admissions resurfacing guilt she'd had for a long time. She owed her parents the truth, but had never been able to bring it up. It felt like they'd be so disappointed in her.

"Why not?"

"I don't want to talk about it." She threw his own words back at him, his plea that he not speak about certain pieces of his life. She hoped he would give her the same respect she'd given him.

He shrugged. "Fair enough. So what happens now?"

"He's on his way here. That's why he called, because he wanted to let me know."

Her hands, which she'd folded primly on her lap when she first sat down, now fell helplessly to her sides. "I'm sorry, Jackson. Please believe me that I never invited him."

"I do."

She gave him a grateful smile. "Thank you."

"I can assume he's not going to be sharing your room?"

"You are correct."

A satisfied grin spread across his face. He rose from his chair. "Then we'll need to find a place for him."

"It's just for tonight," she said, rising as well. "I'll insist he leave tomorrow." The scraping of tree branches against the windowpane distracted her for a moment. "Wow, it's getting windy."

"A storm's coming." He stepped toward the door, then turned back toward Carla holding out an arm. "After you."

She walked over to him, stopping directly in front of his tall, muscled frame. She looked up at him and gently removed his glasses. "Do we have to go so soon?"

She set his glasses atop his desk and then placed her hands on his chest, feeling the thumping of his heartbeat. Suddenly need for him overtook her. Her hands began trembling as her breathing quickened. Shivers of anticipation raced down her spine.

Jackson looked down at her, eyes stained black. She saw the tent in his jeans and stroked her hand over it. He let out a groan. "Carla, what you do to me…"

He kicked the door shut and flipped the lock. He bent down to kiss her while gently moving her backward until she pressed up against something hard.

He broke for a moment and looked behind her. Her eyes followed his gaze.

"You like desks?" he asked.

"Yeah," she replied, continuing to stroke him. "I like them a lot."

Chapter Eight

The soft patter of summer rain tapped against the window like handfuls of tiny pebbles. In the distance, a rumble of thunder. Normally those were soothing sounds to Jackson, easing him to sleep like a lullaby to a child. But not tonight. His mind was too busy for rest, distraction endlessly churning like clothes in a wash machine. And the distraction's name was Carla Saunders.

He lay in bed, on his back, arms folded beneath his head as he stared into the darkness. Hard to believe he wasn't sound asleep after the way she'd exhausted him. Just the thought of her grinding on top of him, hips swaying, pinching her nipples as she pounded his cock... *Holy fuck.* A rush of blood beat a path straight to his groin.

Sex sure wasn't his problem. Not with her. After two long years of abstinence he was back in the saddle big time. He had half a mind right now to walk over to her room and join her in bed. His lips curved up in a half smile. They still slept in their separate rooms when they finally actually wanted to sleep. It was at Carla's insistence, for "appearance's sake," even though he didn't give two hot damns what anyone thought. And if he were to stroll on over there now she'd welcome him, he was sure of it. Even after their marathon session tonight she'd be up for another go-round. She was so sexy, so uninhibited, the most trusting, generous lover he'd ever had. Probably would ever have again.

Merde. He swore softly and swung his legs over the side of the bed. No way would he be sleeping any time soon. He got out of bed and walked over to the window. The rain continued to fall and the breeze had kicked up. Droplets of water filtered through the window screen, sprinkling his torso and legs. He didn't mind. With where his thoughts had just been, a cold shower wasn't a bad thing.

But it wasn't the sex thoughts keeping him awake. It was the silence after Carla went back to her room for the night that made sleep so elusive. He knew that Amy— Well. His sister had thoughts better left unsaid, except it had never been her way to stay silent. Not around him. People made the mistake of thinking she was a quiet, introverted woman who kept to herself and made no waves. But they didn't know his sister like he did. With her, still waters ran deep.

Amy thought Carla would be good for him. Long term. As in the future. Despite his restlessness, Jackson chuckled. If anyone had told him a month ago that he'd be losing sleep over a city-slicker corporate girl who could talk endlessly about strategic business plans and low hanging fruit he probably would have decked the person. But that was before he met Carla.

Amy had immediately seen the real person beneath the corporate façade. She'd been insistent since day one that Carla's soul didn't rest with the kind of work she was doing, and Jackson was inclined to agree. Didn't matter, though. After Carla's time here she'd get a huge promotion and then would finally go to Paris, something she said she'd dreamed about since childhood. Good for her. So why did he care if she left?

He blew out a frustrated breath and ran a hand through his hair. The answer was easy. Admitting it? Not so much. But here alone, in the dark, with nothing but raindrops for company, he acknowledged the truth. For the first time in two years, he finally felt *alive*. And it was all because of Carla.

For a long time even just the thought of another relationship froze his blood cold. After what he went through with Katherine and then the death of his parents… It was a hell he'd barely survived. The only way he'd done so was by plunging head-first into work, pushing a relentless, all-consuming pace so anything and everything around him would be forgotten. He would drive himself to the grave if that's what it took. It didn't matter. Or so he thought.

Carla made him see his world differently. She infused him with…*admit it, dickwad. You're by yourself.* Fine. She infused him with joy. He felt happy around her. She made him laugh and enjoy life, which in turn made him a better scientist. After only a few short weeks, he saw his life differently and understood things he hadn't before—like the pointlessness of blaming himself for his parents' death. It was all Carla's doing. She was good for him, no doubt. But could he be good for her?

He sank into a nearby chair. His hair ruffled in the breeze streaming through the window, and the cool air prickled his naked skin with goosebumps. Jackson barely noticed. His mind drifted to the evening's unexpected arrival, that drip of a guy, Bryce. What a jerk, just showing up where he hadn't been invited. At least he didn't mean anything to Carla. Oddly enough, though, the jealousy Jackson felt toward Bryce wasn't a bad thing. It told him a lot about himself, and about his feelings for her.

The rain had stopped, at least for the moment. A shaft of moonlight broke through the thinning clouds and seeped into his room. Carla would be gone soon, away to Paris for a year. He let out a slow breath. He had a decision to make.

****

Carla rolled over and pulled her pillow over her ears as the loudly soughing wind tried its best to wake her. She should be up and dressed by now, but it was tough going when she'd only been asleep for three hours. When she remembered the reason why, she groaned and buried her head beneath the covers.

A sharp rap against the door ten minutes later startled her out of sleep. What the hell? More knocking, louder this time. Then she heard it. A soft but distinct slurping. She bounced out of bed and grabbed her robe, cinching it tightly before opening the door.

Just as she'd known, Bryce stood out in the hallway, diet soda in hand. He was dressed in the usual country club look he favored, although his herringbone twill trousers were decidedly rumpled, testament to yesterday's lengthy journey.

"Morning." He took in her robe and slippers and raised a surprised brow. "You're not dressed yet?"

"Shh!" She put two fingers to her lips and looked down the hallway. Luckily, Bryce appeared not to have woken anyone. Not yet, anyway. But she didn't want to risk it.

"Come in for a minute," she said, stepping aside to let him through. Bryce accepted the invitation and she shut the door behind him.

Once inside, he took a look around the room and gave a sniff of disapproval. "Awfully small in here." He pressed the soda can to his lips and took a long swill. "Although a little bigger than the closet you stuffed me into last night."

"This isn't a beach resort, Bryce. It's a scientific research facility."

"Doesn't mean you actually have to live here. You could stay in a hotel for the month."

"There's nothing close by. Besides, I like it here."

"Whatever." He shrugged. "I just hope you're not going all native on us."

"What exactly does *that* mean?"

He didn't answer at first, instead strolling about the room like an investor assessing the space before purchase. He glanced out the window, thumbed through the books atop Carla's desk, and poked his head inside the bathroom. She was just about to tell him to get out of there when he turned to face her once more.

"It's a reminder your life isn't here, Carla, it's back home in New York with us. You've been distant since you got here and frankly, we're all a little concerned. That's one of the reasons why I decided to come down. That, and the fact that of course I missed you."

She was unable to prevent her eyes from rolling at that last statement. Bryce was so full of it. He missed her like a tax dodger misses the IRS.

Although she hadn't invited him, he went ahead and plopped himself down in the chair at her desk. With a sigh, she sat down as well on the edge of her bed.

"If my parents were concerned they would have called."

"They didn't want to disturb you on your fear assignment. You *have* to succeed in this, after all. But your behavior has been somewhat out of character, and we've all noticed."

She kept silent, because there was every possibility it was true. She hadn't called as much, even though her mother had specifically requested it. Somehow, out here in the remote and beautiful Louisiana bayou country, with its swamps and snakes, its miles of empty space, its stunning natural beauty, she'd found herself feeling like she didn't need to call home. Here she'd found fascinating people doing fascinating things, and the opportunity to actually do good in the world. She'd also found Jackson.

"Look, I appreciate you troubling yourself to come all the way down here and check on me, but it really wasn't necessary. Or, frankly, wanted."

She felt a surge of satisfaction when his jaw dropped open.

"I'm going to need you to leave," she continued. "Today."

The crash of a heavy object just outside interrupted further conversation. Both she and Bryce rushed to the window where they saw Jackson and the facilities chef, Jean Auber, struggling to right an overturned dinner cart. All around them were stainless steel bowls of what appeared to be rotting vegetables. From all appearances, it looked as if Jean had been taking peels and trimmings to the compost bin when a gust of stiff wind flipped the cart over.

"Gross." Bryce wrinkled his nose and took another sip of soda.

Carla ignored his comment. "I need to change

clothes, Bryce, so could you step outside, please? Maybe go and see if you could lend Jackson a hand? After all, he gave you a room for the night after you showed up out of the blue."

"Which wouldn't have been necessary if you'd just come with me to New Orleans like I planned instead of holing me up in this viper pit." His face scrunched into a nasty sneer. "I'll wait for you in the hallway."

His arrogance was too much. Her temper exploded.

"You conceited, self-indulgent jerk! You've got some nerve coming here without an invitation, imposing on people you've never met, and on top of it all acting like a spoiled brat."

His mouth fell open like a trap door. He narrowed his eyes and his voice grew low. "What did you say?"

"You heard me. I'm not happy you're here and I'm not going to pretend otherwise." She stood up from the bed and pointed toward her door. "I want you to leave. Get out of my room and get away from this facility." When he didn't budge, she added, "Now."

The two bright red spots of color on his cheeks were evidence she was getting to him. Bryce became angry. Very angry. The flush spread over to his ears and down his neck. His fingers crunched the soda can as he took a step toward her, eyes flashing. "You're out of line, Carla. No one talks to me that way, especially not you."

"Get out!"

"You're going to regret this."

"Now!" she snarled. "I'm not telling you again. Go make arrangements for getting back to New York."

"You bitch!" he spat. "This isn't the end of this." He grit his teeth and stormed toward the door, slamming it behind him as he stalked out.

She sank down on the bed, giving her legs a minute to stop shaking. She'd never had a conversation like that before with Bryce or actually, with anyone she could recall. Sure, she lost her temper now and again, but she'd always put a lid of control over it. A satisfied grin slipped across her lips. Letting loose felt pretty damn good. Still…

She glanced at the door as a cloud of unease cast a shadow over her triumph. She'd better go see where Bryce went. Like it or not, as long as he was here he was her responsibility, and she was nervous he would do something to screw up her results on the fear assignment.

After a five minute power shower and another five to sweep on light make-up and get dressed, she was out the door. Bryce was nowhere in sight.

When she reached the back of the house where the cart had overturned, the only evidence it had even happened was a meager scattering of compost vegetables here and there. Otherwise, no Jean, no cart, no Jackson. And no Bryce. Had he actually left, or was he stalking around the property?

Her hair whipped across her face from the wind. As she eyed the sky she could see black thunderclouds gathering in the distance. Looked like the storm Jackson had predicted was about to come down hard.

She wondered where she should go to look for him when she heard someone calling her name. It was Lisa, running toward her from the direction of the cafeteria.

"I'm glad I found you," she said when she was close enough for Carla to hear. "There's someone looking for you in the caf."

Shit. Not gone yet. "Thanks for letting me know," Carla replied, nearly shouting to be heard above the blowing wind. She looked up at the sky. "That storm looks close."

Lisa glanced in the same direction. "Sometimes we get these scary looking black clouds and it blows for a while and then nothing else happens. But I'd bet money we're going to get dumped on this time. Come on." She nodded in the direction of the caf. "Better go get your friend."

Carla reluctantly followed behind, still fuming at Bryce. The sooner he left the better she'd feel, but she supposed it wasn't smart to send him out in this storm. *Damn.* She may have to wait until it blew over.

They reached the caf just as breakfast was winding down, although Bryce had a full plate of food in front of him and tucked into a mountain of scrambled eggs. He looked up through black, slitted eyes as Carla approached. The anger in the room was palpable.

Although Lisa said nothing, Carla could sense her discomfort. She decided to do what she could to patch things over. She and Bryce could settle their differences in private.

She turned to her friend. "Lisa Martin, meet Bryce Betts. Bryce is visiting from New York, although he's leaving today."

His jaw tensed when she said that, but to Bryce's credit he held his tongue in front of Lisa.

"Nice to meet you," he mumbled.

"Likewise." Lisa turned to Carla. "I've got to get to the lab," she said. "Nice to meet you, Bryce." Before he could even respond, she was off.

"Friendly," Bryce said, the sarcasm unmistakable.

"She actually is," Carla defended, "but you made her uncomfortable with your rudeness."

"*Me?*" He looked up from his plate and scowled. "You're the rude one, Carla, with the way you've treated me."

Carla sighed; she'd lost her appetite for fighting with a spoiled brat. Time to set him straight, once and for all. She'd wanted to talk to her mother first, but what did they say about the best laid plans? Another saying took precedence now—seize the moment. She took a seat across the table from him.

"Listen to me, Bryce. I never invited you here in the first place and I don't want you here now. You're jeopardizing my performance on the fear assignment. As much as it may surprise you, I actually like it here."

His hoot of laughter was so sudden he spewed a chunk of eggs onto his plate. Carla sat back, disgusted.

"You're kidding me? You like a snake farm? You, who are more afraid of snakes than a mouse is of a cat? You're actually trying to convince me you like it here?" An edge of disbelief coated his laughter. "Don't lie to me. Your parents would be so disappointed."

How like Bryce to pretend he was a stand-in for her parents, sent here as some sort of ambassador to check up on her. Her voice grew steely. "I don't need you to tell me how to deal with my parents so leave them out of this. Just finish your breakfast and be on the next flight to New York. We're not going to New Orleans or anywhere else together. Not now; not ever."

The crestfallen expression on his face was so potent that if she didn't know better she'd think it was real. But his manufactured disappointment was nothing but a joke. Bryce was a manipulative, using, petulant narcissist, motivated solely by greed, and she needed him gone.

She caught a flash of lightning in the corner of her eye from a nearby window, and seconds later the rumble of thunder. Leaves and other bits of debris swirled in the air as the trees bent from the wind's growing force. The storm approached.

"I'm not your girlfriend, and I never was," she continued. "I think it's time you accepted it."

His lips tightened into a thin stubborn slash across his face. "That's not what I was led to believe."

"If you think otherwise then the fault is yours. I've never done anything to lead you on."

"You've never done anything to steer me away."

She sighed. He wasn't going down without a fight.

"Fine. Point taken. Then let me be perfectly clear. We're never going to be a couple. It's not meant to be."

"You don't know that for sure," he argued. "You can't see the future, Carla."

"I—" He was right on that point. She couldn't see the future, but she could *feel* it. In her heart. "It's true I don't know what the future will bring. But I do have an idea of what I want. And it doesn't include you. I'm sorry, Bryce."

Her softened tone seemed to have no effect on his mood. His face remained as dark as the approaching thunderclouds and she knew his anger had not abated. "It's that guy with all the awards, isn't it? The one I met last night. Jackson?"

Her eyes flashed to the floor as she remembered Jackson making love to her while she wore one of those very same awards, the heavy gold medal bouncing between her breasts as he ground against her, thrusting over and over. Heat rushed to her cheeks.

"I knew I sensed something when I saw you two together," Bryce snarled, voice laced with contempt. He set down his fork and rose from the chair. "We'll talk about this in New York. But this isn't the end, Carla. You don't know what's best for you, but I do. And I need to be a part of your life."

Needed to be a part of her parents' life. That was what he meant. As much as Bryce tried to pretend he was brokenhearted over not having her as a girlfriend, Carla knew what galled him the most was losing out on the exciting lifestyle her parents provided. Their interesting friends, fascinating trips. The house, the cars. The money. That's what this was really all about. The malevolent power behind Bryce's ambition was impossible to overstate. He would let nothing and no one stand in the way of him getting what he wanted. Including her.

"You'll see clearly again once you get out of here," he continued. "I don't think this place is having a positive effect on you. You're..." He looked at her, shaking his head as he speared her with his stare, as if trying to discern where the old Carla had gone. "You've become different."

"Different how?"

"More...assertive, I guess. More stubborn."

She straightened, lifted her chin. "More confident?"

He shrugged and set his napkin atop his plate of unfinished food. "Call it what you want. All I know is in the time you've been here you've changed, and not for the better. You need to get out of here."

"When I'm finished, and not before. But you've

got to leave today, Bryce. As soon as this storm is over."

"Yeah, whatever." He walked away without another word. Carla breathed a sigh of relief. It had been a difficult conversation, one she should have had months ago. She knew she hadn't led him on but maybe he had a point. Not wanting to disappoint her family, and especially her mother, she hadn't done enough to discourage him, either.

A half hour later, the storm's fury broke wide open. Lightning crackled and lit up the sky, followed by explosive roars of thunder threatening to rip the world apart. The rain came down in sheets, falling so hard and fast the ground had no time to soak it up. In minutes the dirt tracks around the facility turned into raging rivers. Carla experienced it all while sitting with Lisa and Quinn in the data lab, saying little, waiting out the storm. The relentless roar of the wind made it difficult to concentrate on anything else.

When it was finally over they went outside to survey the damage. To everyone's dismay, it was extensive. There'd been hail with the storm, the size of golf balls, and they'd done their work. Dented rooftops on cars, broken windows in several buildings, downed trees, branches and leaves everywhere. In many places where large tree branches had fallen they were blocking the road, making entering or leaving the compound impossible.

No one, however, paid any attention to the material damage until they could confirm the cobras were okay. Jackson had had the facility built with Louisiana weather in mind. A native of the area made him all too aware of the destructive force of the storms the state was prone to. No one's nerves would be calmed until they'd checked on the cobras. Once they could finally leave the data lab, Carla, Lisa, and Quinn raced over to building eight.

They were not alone. Half the staff had already arrived and the rest were on their way. As soon as Carla entered she spotted Jackson already at the monitors, frowning at a sea of black screens. She rushed over to where he stood.

"What happened? Did we lose power?"

"Yeah." Jackson kept punching various buttons on the console. "There's a back-up generator installed for that very reason. If we lose juice from our main power source, the generator kicks in." He frowned, stabbed at a couple more buttons. "At least that's what's supposed to happen. But I'm not getting a thing."

He stood and asked one of the researchers to help him as he raced over to the main circuit room. As Carla's eyes followed him, she noticed Bryce standing in the back of the room, a smug sneer plastered across his face.

"Looks like you won't be able to get rid of me as fast as you wanted, Carla," he said when she'd walked back to him.

Her eyes narrowed with suspicion. "What do you mean? The storm's over."

"Have you seen the roads? There's no coming or going out of this place for probably several days. There are downed trees everywhere blocking the way." He flashed her a self-satisfied smile. "Guess you'll just have to put up with me a little bit longer."

She clamped down on her teeth, waiting for the rush of anger to pass and praying for strength not to strangle him.

"Then you'll have to do some work around here," she said tightly. "Jean can always use help in the kitchen. Maybe you could cut up some vegetables or even wash dishes. Something to make yourself useful. This isn't a free hotel you know."

"Have you gone insane? It'll be a cold day in hell before I start washing dishes."

Her blood pressure rocketed as she balled her hands into fists, a hair's breath away from socking him. "You arrogant, son-of-a—"

"What's going on?"

Both Bryce and Carla turned at the sound of the female voice. Of all the people she least wanted to see, aside from Bryce, here was the other one. Kelly. Carla gritted her teeth.

"Bryce," she said, "this is Kelly Grassle. She's one of the researchers here." Bryce nodded toward her, and as he did so Carla noticed his eyes lingering on her lavishly displayed cleavage. On her left breast was a tattoo of a snarling dragon, drops of blood falling from its fangs. Lovely.

"Kelly, this is Bryce Betts. He's a friend of mine who had planned on visiting just for the day."

"Nice to meet you, Bryce." Kelly murmured as the two shook hands. "I take it your plans changed after the storm?"

"I can't get out," Bryce explained. "So it looks like I'm stuck here for a bit."

A coy smile crossed her lips. "Well, we can always find something for you to do around here."

An undercurrent of sexual tension passed between the two of them as Bryce gave Kelly a smile back, and

Carla was relieved. If Bryce's attention focused on someone else, all the better for her.

"Bryce, I need to see what I can do to help around here," she said. "Can you find your way around?"

"Don't worry about it," Kelly answered for Bryce. "I'll help out your friend."

"Ah, yeah. Okay." Carla turned to leave. "Thanks, Kelly."

"Don't mention it."

The researcher had all of her attention focused on Bryce, so Carla made a quick getaway. She left the building and walked around to the back, by the circuit room, wanting to find Jackson and ask if she could help. An empty room greeted her when she entered. She walked around the property, picking her way through the debris, but she couldn't find him in any of the other buildings, either. She began getting worried when she spotted Cheng Li. He removed twigs and branches from around one of the outer buildings, trying to clear the path.

"Cheng," she called out to get his attention as she approached.

He looked up and gave her a polite nod. "Hello, Ms. Carla," he said, continuing to collect branches.

"Cheng, have you seen Jackson?"

"Mr. Jackson came here a few minutes ago," Cheng confirmed.

Carla's face lit up. "Did he say where he was going?"

"He's going to go into the cobra holding facility. I will join him shortly, as soon as I can get into this building and gather supplies. We are very concerned about the gravid female. She is weakened due to long periods of time sitting on the nest, and she needed to exert much energy protecting her nest from the storm. The camera closest to her was broken by the storm so we are unable to monitor her. We must enter the enclosure to check the female and fix the camera."

Carla's heart sank and she trembled with fear. The back enclosure held over one hundred king cobras, and Jackson was about to walk directly into it. On top of that, he wanted to retrieve a nurturing female whose mate, close by and standing guard, would not be receptive to her being disturbed.

"It's so dangerous. Do you really have to?"

"Yes. We must ensure the female and her unborn hatchlings survived the storm."

He finally had the path cleared enough so he could enter the building, and with a polite parting nod he was gone. Carla turned and raced back to building eight.

The first thing she noticed upon entering was the generator problem had been fixed. All the screens were running as Lisa tapped at the keyboard, bringing up various angles of the enclosure. The second thing she noticed was Jackson, in with the snakes.

The camera picked him up as he made his way through the strewn branches and high natural grasses in the enclosure. He protected himself with thick boots and leg chaps that wrapped around his calf and knee, and he walked slowly but with confidence, ever mindful any given step could put him directly into the path of a king cobra.

Carla dashed over to the nearest monitor where Lisa operated the console.

"He's all right so far," she said in relief as Lisa pressed a button and brought up a different angle.

Walking into the picture of one of the cameras was Cheng, who'd accessed the enclosure from one of the outside entrances. He, too, walked carefully through the debris, mindful of the snakes but moving as quickly as possible to catch up with Jackson.

"Yeah, Jackson's fine," Lisa confirmed, but her expression remained serious. "What we're concerned about are the cobras, especially Mariah."

"But it's stormed here before, right? And everything has been okay?"

"Of course. But this was a bad one. I heard on the radio the wind gusts were tropical storm strength. They said something about the low pressure intensifying unexpectedly and causing a lot of damage." Lisa clicked on to another camera angle. "All I know is, I want those cobras to be okay."

"Me, too," Carla replied, meaning it. This place and everything about it—the mission, the people, even the snakes—had become important to her. But right now all she could think about was Jackson.

For the rest of the time Jackson and Cheng were in the enclosure, she stayed glued to the monitors. She could tell by his body language the damage was bad; luckily the nest and eggs seemed to be all right. It didn't take long for them to fix the downed camera. Over the two-way Cheng said Jackson replaced a blown out bulb, and as soon as he'd completed the work the men jumped into view from that camera onto the monitors back at base. But then, just as Carla heaved a sigh of relief, her heart leapt into her chest.

The camera picked up Drew, Mariah's partner, dangerously threatened by the presence of the two men. The cobra raised himself high, well over two feet, and the ribs around his neck flattened into a hood. The men were aware of it and were backing away, but not fast enough to satisfy the threatened male. With a flash quicker than lightening he struck, head streaking toward his prey, and his fangs sunk deeply into Jackson's thigh.

Fear shot through Carla like venom from the cobra. Her hands flew to her mouth but did nothing to stifle her terrified scream when she saw Jackson cry out and clutch his thigh. She seized Lisa's hand in a death grip while her eyes clung to the monitor as the horrifying scene unfolded.

Cheng Li grabbed from his side pants pocket a slim black case. It looked like an oversized wallet folded in half, but as Cheng opened it she could see on the camera it was a first aid kit containing, among other things, several syringes. With calm but quick efficiency he began using the syringes on Jackson, plunging one needle after another into the veins of his left wrist.

In the meantime, Jackson took a small scissors from the kit and cut away his pants leg. Two red puncture marks, almost mockingly small compared to the damage they inflicted, were surrounded by angry, swollen blisters.

Trickles of cold sweat rolled down Carla's face and in the valley between her breasts. Her stomach churned with fear, but she knew she had to stay strong. If there was anything, *anything* she could do for Jackson once he and Cheng emerged from the enclosure, she'd do it. She'd be there for him.

Cheng did little talking on the two-way except for a check-in to ensure everyone knew what happened. "Cheng to base."

Lisa picked up the radio. "Base here, Cheng."

"You saw what happened?"

"Confirmed."

"Unfortunately it wasn't a dry bite."

"Help's on the way."

After that exchange, the monitor area grew silent as a tomb, all eyes riveted to the cameras as they watched Jackson and Cheng. Two senior researchers had raced into the enclosure with a stretcher to carry Jackson out. The rest of the staff knew they could do nothing more and a pervasive sense of helplessness, like a thief, stole into the room.

Carla swallowed back her fear as she watched Cheng giving Jackson the antivenin injections.

"What did Cheng mean by a dry bite?" she asked Lisa.

The researcher's eyes never left the screen as she replied. "It's when a snake bites without discharging venom. It happens sometimes. Unfortunately not this time."

Once Cheng finished, he retrieved bandage wrap from his kit and began winding it around Jackson's leg, above and below the bite but not onto the injury itself. They had propped Jackson up against a tree with his legs sticking straight out in front of him.

"Why doesn't Jackson lie down?"

"He needs to keep his heart above the bite," Lisa replied.

"And the bandage?"

"Helps slow the blood flow to his heart. You don't want to restrict it, just slow it."

Just as Cheng completed his administrations, the camera picked up the two researchers who'd arrived with the stretcher. The men lifted Jackson onto it, all the time moving slowly, wanting him to exert as little effort as possible. Movement increased blood flow, and blood surging through Jackson's veins would carry the poison with it.

When the men were finally ready, they left the area and headed back to the building, careful not to startle any of the snakes and risk another bite. Once out of the enclosure, they were met by Quinn who waited with a golf cart that could navigate around the strewn branches and he drove Jackson to his room. By then his skin was warm and he had difficulty breathing. As they hurried along the hallway toward his room, they passed the door to Amy's room. Quinn pounded on it.

"We need your help, Amy," he called out as he banged. The door swung open immediately. Amy's face reflected a picture of calm, even when she spotted the gurney upon which Jackson lay.

"Get him on his bed," she instructed. "I'll be right there."

She turned away, shutting the door behind her. Carla marveled at how she could be so composed in the face of crisis, but then she remembered Amy was a trained nurse.

They entered Jackson's room with Amy right behind, carrying an oxygen tank and tubes. Methodical yet quick, she set up the equipment and intubated his nose. In seconds oxygen flowed and Jackson's breathing began to settle. Amy placed the listening device from the stethoscope she wore around her neck against Jackson's chest. The room fell silent while she listened to his heartbeat.

"Hand me that," she said to Carla, pointing to a

blood pressure cuff. Carla gave it to her and Amy strapped it around Jackson's bicep and stuck the earpieces in her ear. She inflated the cuff and then slowly turned the valve to let out the air, keeping an eye on the gauge.

"Sixty over forty," she announced, and the nervous tension already in the room shot up like a rocket. Even with the antivenin that Cheng had administered, Jackson's blood pressure had plummeted dangerously low.

Jackson himself was unaware of what was going on around him. He had fallen unconscious.

Amy opened a black packet of syringes, similar to the one Chang had had in the field, and withdrew a small bottle of clear liquid. She filled the syringe and injected it into Jackson's arm.

"What's that?" Carla whispered to Quinn, but Amy answered.

"Isotonic saline. It should help get his pressure back up."

In fact, the first bit of good news since the wretched ordeal began came minutes later when Amy rechecked her brother's blood pressure. It had rebounded to eighty-six over fifty-nine. Not great, but better.

"There's nothing else we can do but let him rest," she said to the nervous gathered group, "so I'd like everyone to go. I'll monitor him and call for help if I need it. At this point we've done all we can."

With reluctance, the group began shuffling out of Jackson's bedroom, most of them giving Amy's hand or shoulder a squeeze of thanks for everything she did. She acknowledged their gratitude, but her face remained a mask of concern. Jackson was her patient, but he was also her brother.

Carla waited until she was finally alone with only Amy and Jackson in the room, and then she pleaded with Amy to allow her to stay. "I'll help you in any way I can. Whatever you need me to do. But please, I can't…" Her throat grew tight, forcing her to pause before going on. "I can't bear to leave him," she finished in a whisper. "I just can't."

She knew she asked a lot. She'd only been there for a few weeks and was requesting privileges well beyond her status. At the same time, she knew she'd ingrained herself in Jackson's life, and he in hers. Amy knew it, too.

"You might be able to help," Amy said, nodding her consent. "Talk to him; try to keep him calm." She glanced down at her brother, her lips a thin tight slash across her face. "I know he looks relaxed, but emotionally he's under stress. He's worried about the sanctuary, his staff, the research, getting funding. Hearing your voice, reassuring him he'll be okay, might be just what he needs."

"He can hear me?"

"Yes. Research has shown snakebite victims appear to fall into a state of unconsciousness but are still aware of ambient noise around them, including the sound of people's voices. So if he hears you telling him everything will be all right, it'll help in his healing."

"All right." Carla pulled a chair up to the side of his bed. At first she wasn't sure what to say, but at Amy's encouragement the words began to flow.

"Okay, so I'm sure the first thing you'll want to know," she began telling Jackson," is the status of

Mariah. You went to check on her, that's what you and Cheng were doing before you got bit, in case you don't remember. Anyway, she's fine. We all watched you on the monitors and all indications checked out. She and the nest are in good shape."

She leaned back in her chair, warming up to her own monologue and actually beginning to enjoy herself. "And you know, the more I think about it, the less surprising it is she survived so well. I mean there is *no way* a strong female like that is going to let anything get in between her and the ones she loves. We girls protect our own, whether it's people or cobras. We protect who we love, and we don't let adversity get in the way of the bonds between family. That's just the way it is. That's why Amy's going to do everything she can for you, and so am I. Because Amy loves you, and I—"

She stopped before she went too far. Casting a hurried look toward Amy to see if she'd been paying attention, she knew from her soft smile that Jackson's sister had heard every word.

"I was right," Amy said, her eyes moist. "The minute we met, I knew you were the one for him."

Carla quickly shook her head, her objection palpable. "No," she insisted. "I was just talking, trying to make him feel better, like you said." Preposterous though it was, she could actually feel her cheeks go warm. "It's nothing."

"So you don't love my brother?"

"I—" She couldn't quite take that leap, but she couldn't exactly deny it, either. At the moment Carla felt as if she were in the middle of a suspension bridge hanging precariously between two steep cliffs. She couldn't go back to where she'd been, but moving ahead had risks as well.

"I don't know," she finally admitted, a welter of emotions roiling in her mind. She cast a glance back at Jackson and then bent forward to tenderly brush aside a lock of hair from his forehead. "I know I care for him."

"I know you do, too," Amy said, her voice hitching in her throat. "Just don't hurt him. He's been through enough."

At that Carla only nodded, acknowledging what Amy said but unwilling to go further. She didn't want to make a promise she wasn't certain she could keep.

She kept vigil with Amy in Jackson's room for the remainder of the day and through the entire night, fear for Jackson prohibiting her own sleep. At one point, Chef Jean brought over a tray filled with sandwiches and a container of jambalaya. Although both girls were touched by his concern, the delicious food went largely uneaten.

Carla talked to Jackson throughout the night, sticking mostly to banal topics like the weather or movies she'd seen. Amy chimed in now and again, but as evening wore on her contributions waned. When it had been over half an hour since Amy last uttered a word, Carla glanced over to the chair where she was sitting, only to see Jackson's sister with her legs tucked under her, fast asleep.

"Well," she chuckled, returning her focus to Jackson, "apparently Amy is about as thrilled with my analysis of the best late night TV as you are." She took a cool washcloth from the night table and pressed it lightly to his forehead. "Maybe it's time for a topic change."

Returning the washcloth to the bucket of ice where it kept cold, she settled back in her chair.

"You know, the last time I was in this chair we were doing something a little more interesting than me watching you sleep." Her pulse jumped at the searing memory of Jackson thrusting into her as she sat atop him. She lowered her voice, even knowing Amy was sound asleep. "So let's just make sure that you get yourself feeling better so we can have a repeat session of that one, okay?

"Of course, we'll have to make up for lost time since my assignment's nearing the end. Hopefully I'll have convinced you to sign on with Bartlett Silver. We can do a great job for you, you know. You shouldn't downplay the value of corporate consulting, Jackson, even though I know you do. But really, our firm—"

Hearing herself being pitch girl for Bartlett Silver suddenly made her stomach churn, and the truth slammed into her like a semi. She was trying to convince herself of a lie.

"Oh, fuck it," she sighed. "I can't do this anymore. I just, it's all wrong. Everything. Maybe Bartlett Silver could actually help Rivard Research. I don't know. But you know what? The truth is, I really don't care."

She glanced over at Amy, whose calm, steady breathing reassured Carla that she still slept. Nevertheless, her voice dropped even lower and she pushed up in her chair to lean toward Jackson.

"I don't even know whether I'm cut out for the corporate life. I know my family thinks I am. My mom's always talking about me climbing the ladder. My promotion to V.P. is important to her. It's like another notch in her belt, you know? A notice to the world that her kids are successful. Whatever success means, I suppose. But people have different definitions of that word. Maybe mine just don't match everyone else's."

A knot lodged in her throat and the hot sting of tears misted her eyes. Blinking against them, she continued. "All I really want is to be happy. Be close to my family. I even wish I was better at sports because I'd love to share that connection with them. But they love me in spite of my klutziness. And in the end, that's kind of what this life is about, isn't it? Family, friends, love. I think if we have that, we don't need much more."

Jackson's sheet had slipped down, baring his chest. She looked longingly at him, wishing she could slide her fingers across his smooth skin, along the ripples of his rib cage and his hard muscled abs. Her nipples grew tight as she imagined him playing with them as she had her fun.

Soon, she hoped. He'll be better soon. For the time being, her mind needed steering away from that thinking. Paris came to mind, but she found herself unable to muster up the enthusiasm. She told herself the stressful situation had something to do with it. A trip to Paris seemed like a frivolous luxury. But in her heart of hearts she knew that wasn't the reason.

Jackson's condition changed little, but according to Amy it was a relief. She periodically checked his bandages, making sure they were snug but not too tight as his thigh swelled from the bite. Shortly after midnight, Amy said the swelling had stabilized, and by dawn it had even subsided. There was also no tissue necrosis, something Amy admitted to Carla she had greatly feared.

"It happens more commonly when digits are bitten," Amy said the next morning as she changed Jackson's dressing. "The tissue around the finger or toe develops gangrene and the affected digit has to be amputated."

Icy terror rose prickled Carla's scalp. "So Jackson could have lost his leg?"

"Jackson could have lost his *life*." Amy's shoulder slumped forward as she leaned over the bed, once more checking her brother's blood pressure, and Carla realized how exhausted she really was. After all, Amy had her own physical challenges.

Carla stood up from where she sat and hurried around the bed to Amy's side. "Come here," she said, placing her hands on either side of Amy's arms and steering the girl toward a chair. "You making yourself sick isn't going to help your brother," Carla said firmly, taking a seat beside her. "You've got to get some rest."

Amy slowly blinked, her lashes sweeping over the dark circles beneath her eyes. "I've got to make sure—"

"I'm fine."

The deep, gravelly voice from the bed had both women jumping to their feet. They rushed across the room to his bedside, where he was in the middle of pulling out the nasal tubes.

"My lungs are clear," he said to Amy's questioning look, "and I don't need these anymore. Really."

"Well, all right," Amy acquiesced, although Carla sensed she would have left them in a little longer if the decision had been hers alone.

Amy cleared away the oxygen tank and breathing tubes, and then Jackson told her to get out of his room and get some rest.

"Listen to Carla," he told his sister. "I can tell you're exhausted. If you don't get some rest you're liable to have a flare up, and that's the last thing I need."

Amy raised an eyebrow toward her brother. "The last thing *you* need?"

"Of course. How are you going to wait on me hand and foot if you're too weak?" His teasing brought enormous relief to both girls because it assured them Jackson was truly recovering from the bite. He was still very weak, but he would most definitely live.

Amy took her things and left after Carla promised to stay with Jackson until he fell back to sleep. Once she'd gone, a strangely awkward silence filled the room. Carla pretended to busy herself, checking Jackson's bandages, fluffing his pillow, pressing a cool damp towel to his forehead, but she knew her busy work was nothing more than a diversion.

There were things she wanted to say to him, but should she? Would she be crossing into dangerous territory? There was an assumption between them that when her assignment ended she'd be on her way, off to Paris as she'd always dreamed, and he'd be here continuing with his work. There was no "after" once she was gone. So why stir up trouble by telling him how worried sick she'd been? That she thanked God he was all right? That she wasn't sure what she'd have done if something had happened to him? No, she decided. Keeping quiet was best for everyone.

"Did your friend leave?" he asked.

She turned away from the window where she'd been adjusting the A/C gauge, knowing Jackson referred to Bryce.

"Actually, no. Not yet. The roads aren't passable after the storm. That's why you're here and not in the hospital. We couldn't even get a helicopter to land."

He nodded, absorbing the information. He withdrew his hand from beneath the sheet and held it out toward her. "Come over here."

She went to him and grasped his hand. His skin was cool and his grip weak, but he was alive and he was with her. Happiness flooded her, giving wings to her soul.

She smiled. "You better not do that again," she said in a lightly scolding voice. "You gave us all a scare."

"I've been bit before. No big deal."

"No big deal?! Jackson, you could have died."

"But I didn't."

He acted unconcerned, but Carla knew differently. Jackson had too much respect for his cobras to know that what happened was very definitely a big deal.

"Listen," he said, and Carla had to lean forward to catch what he said. He was weak and needed sleep.

"I might be out of it for a few days, and you only have a week left on your assignment. If you want, I can..." His voice trailed away as he gathered his strength, breathing in deeply and then slowly releasing the air. "I can sign the papers you need for completion of the assignment. Then you can go."

If he'd told her he wanted her to sleep every night in the cobra enclosure her heart wouldn't have sunk as much as it did at that moment. She felt as if she'd just been socked in the gut. Her breath hitched; she couldn't draw air. Just like that, he was sending her away. The night before they'd made unbelievable love in his office, the very place where they'd first met. Tonight he wanted her gone. A wave of sorrow washed over her, so all-consuming and potent she feared she might get sick. She held a hand to her lips, choking back a sob as the taste of bitter bile coated her throat.

"I—"

"You don't have to say anything." He smiled, faintly, clearly an effort for him to do so. "You've been amazing and I'll give you the highest marks possible. Then…" He grew weaker by the second. He had to sleep. "You can go to Paris." His voice faded to a whisper as his eyes drifted closed. His hand went limp and he could no longer grasp hers.

With tears rolling down her cheeks, Carla gently placed his arm against his side and pulled up the sheet to tuck beneath his chin. She crept out of the room and shut the door behind her.

Her heart felt like a block of lead in her chest, except lead doesn't ache. Or shatter. Dispirited, and with apparently no other choice, she walked down the hall to her room and began to pack.

Chapter Nine

"What do you *mean* you let her go?"

Jackson winced at the fury in Amy's voice. Twin spots of red dotted her cheeks. Her brow was furrowed and her jaw clenched tight. She sat ramrod straight on the edge of Jackson's bed, hands balled into small fists. He shifted uneasily and pulled up the sheet to cover his chest, a thin barrier of protection between himself and his outraged sister.

"She wants to go to Paris. You know that."

"She *thinks* she wants to go to Paris, but it's just an escape from that hellish corporate life she's stuck in. *You* know that."

Jackson sighed, turned his head to look out the window. Steel grey clouds covered the sky and blotted out the sun, the dull atmosphere symbolic of his mood. "I don't think that's it entirely," he finally said, turning back toward Amy. "She said it's a dream she's had since childhood, *before* she ever set foot in an office. Anyway, what's the point? Even if she weren't going to Paris she'd return to New York."

"Well, of course she would. Where else? Because she hasn't been invited to stay!" Amy pushed herself up from the bed and stepped over to study the heart-rate monitor, probably more as a distraction than anything else, Jackson thought. His sister was an excellent nurse and insisted on studying his vitals even though it was clear by now, two days after the bite, he'd pull through. Still, she needed to reach that conclusion on her own.

A surge of guilt darkened his thoughts, realizing how much pain he'd put her through over the past two years. Their parents' accident had been brutal for both of them, and on top of that he'd plunged into his own private hell for months afterward. Amy must have been just sick about it, but he'd been too caught up in himself to notice. What a selfish ass.

He drew his arm from underneath the sheets and held out his hand to his sister. "Amy, come back over here." She turned to face him but didn't budge. "Please."

Her jaw was still obstinately set, but she relented and walked back over to his bedside.

"Could you sit down?" He patted the spot on his bed where she'd been minutes before. "Help a poor snakebite victim out?"

He grinned, doing his best to turn on a little charm, wanting to melt the ice that had formed between them.

She didn't answer the grin, not yet, but at least she sat back down. When she'd settled, Jackson took her small hand in his.

"I know you want the best for me," he began. "You always have."

"Of course. You're my big brother." Her voice trembled slightly.

He saw a sheen of tears in her eyes. Amy's love for him had always been so strong, as his was for her. He felt his own throat grow tight.

"She's good for you, you know. That's why she should be here."

"I—"

"Don't deny it, Jackson. You know I'm right."

"Who said you're not?" He held up his free hand to surrender. "Geez, you're so bossy."

Her lips finally revealed a faint smile. "And you're so stubborn."

He sighed. She was right about that, too. Stubborn as an ornery mule, some would say. And did. He'd also been called driven and forceful and relentless, all of which were true but none of which factored in to why he wasn't trying to keep Carla for as long as he could.

Amy squeezed his hand and he looked up. Worry lines etched the corners of her mouth. Her gaze searched his face and she frowned, as if unsatisfied with what she saw.

"You need to convince her to stay."

He shook his head. "I don't need to and I won't." Storm clouds formed in Amy's eyes, but he ignored them, just as he ignored the spear of pain jammed deep in his heart. He'd made up his mind.

"But why? This makes no sense. Jackson!" Her voice grew sharp when he turned away. "Don't try pulling your ignoring trick on me. It won't work."

He blew frustrated air from his lips. "I'm not ignoring you, but there's nothing more to say." It sucked like hell that he was hurting Amy. He knew she liked having Carla here. They'd formed the beginnings of what could be a strong friendship if it'd been given a chance to grow. If only...

For an instant he allowed himself to indulge in fantasy, imagining having Carla around. Being with her, talking to her, hearing her laughter during the day and moans of desire at night. A rush of blood flew straight to his cock. Sexy, sensual Carla. Snakebite or not, he ached from wanting her. It was way beyond physical, though. In the short time she'd been here she started meaning something to him. *Damn it.* He swallowed hard against the lump tightening his throat.

Breaking into his thoughts, Amy said quietly, "She's not Katherine, you know."

"Who said anything about Katherine?" It came out harsher than he intended, but he didn't pull back. "That was a long time ago. Carla's nothing like her."

"That's exactly my point! You've met someone who cares about you, *really* cares about you, and you're letting her walk out the door." Amy huffed with annoyance and actually gave him a light shove, as if to knock sense into him.

"I can tell how much this hurts you, too," she continued. "It's as plain as the nose on your face."

"Doesn't matter."

"Don't go all heroic on me, Jackson. It *does* matter, so stop trying to deny it. That's why I don't get—" But then she stopped, and what looked like understanding washed across her face.

"I just realized."

He said nothing, didn't have to. Amy and her insightfulness. He knew his sister had figured it out.

"If you ask her to stay, she just might do it. She'd give up on her dream of Paris and you'd feel like you ruined it for her."

He nodded, briefly closing his eyes. A fierce ache burrowed deep in his chest at the thought of Carla not having what she'd wanted after working so hard for it. "I couldn't do that."

"Which is why you're letting her go."

His gaze flicked back over to his sister, meeting

her crystal blue eyes. "You know the saying." His voice grew thick. "About letting someone go."

"If you love them." Amy breathed in deeply, nodding. She understood.

"She'll come back to you, Jackson." Her eyes sparkled with the conviction of her belief. He smiled at his sister, the faint spark of a dream briefly lit.

"Hope so."

****

Carla spent the next two days saying goodbye. The researchers were surprised by her early departure, but when she told them Jackson had authorized it because he wasn't able to supervise any more of the assignment, they understood. Still, there were a fair amount of protests against her leaving, which brought fresh pain to her heart every time it happened. She'd forged some unexpected but lasting friendships.

She stopped by Jackson's room several times to check on him and to help Amy, but each time she was there, Jackson slept. Maybe it was for the best. A sign, perhaps, that her time with him was well and truly over.

She called her mother the day before she was scheduled to leave to let her know she'd be returning early.

"I don't understand why you're finished early, Carla. What went wrong?"

"Nothing went wrong. In fact, I'm getting the highest possible recommendation from Jack—er, Mr. Rivard, the director of the facility."

"Try SAS, Betheny. I'm sure you can get me a direct to Copenhagen. Listen, honey, I'm still not convinced it's a good idea for you to return early, despite what the director says. What's the firm going to say? They'll wonder what you're doing back at work."

As if she hadn't thought of that herself. "It's been taken care of, Mom. The paperwork explains everything."

"A little snakebite seems like a pretty flimsy excuse for a career-making assignment to be cut short. Someone needs to be talked to. Should I get involved? Betheny, what was that morning flight time?"

What the fuck! Carla stabbed the mute button on her phone, too angry to immediately respond. Something she'd regret later might come spewing out. Instead, she took a deep breath while she grabbed for the bag of chips on the desk. While trying to be helpful, her mother was actually way out of line on so many levels. Carla chomped down on a handful of chips, not caring that she stalled in responding to her mother's question. She needed a moment.

"Carla? Have him picked up in a limo, Betheny. He's never going to sign with the Celtics if he thinks they're stingy with cash. Carla, are you there?"

She swallowed her mouthful of salty fortification and unmuted the phone. "I'm here."

"You know, another idea is for Bryce to speak with someone there."

"Bryce?"

Indifferent to Carla's outrage, her mother calmly replied, "Why not? He's stuck there until the roads clear and he already told me he's been speaking to one of the key research directors about conducting six sigma quality improvement. Apparently she's very impressed. I'm sure he'd have some influence over the decision to terminate your assignment prematurely."

Carla shook her head. No more. She'd wanted to

have this conversation in person, but too late now. She'd already broken her news to Bryce; now she needed to deal with her mother. She just couldn't go on allowing her life to be led by her parents. To allow *their* hopes, and *their* aspirations to serve as hers. She was her own person, flaws and all, and she would live her life as she wanted. She would be Carla Saunders instead of Linda and Robert Saunders's daughter.

Her face lit with a hope-filled smile. "Actually, Mom, everything Bryce has told you is complete bullshit."

"Carla!"

She wanted to shock her mother, and it felt as good as she'd imagined. "That's right, Mom. Bullshit. As in a pack of lies. Bryce hasn't spoken to any key research director, I can assure you."

"Well…what…" Linda Saunders was actually speechless.

"Let me ask you this." Carla rose from her bed and began pacing the room, consumed with so much energy she could no longer sit still. "Did Bryce happen to mention the name of this 'key director'?"

"Yes, he did."

"And was it Kelly Grassle, by any chance?"

"As a matter of fact, yes. I've been meaning to do a search on her but haven't found the time."

"Don't bother."

"Why not? Doesn't she work there?"

For once Carla had her mother's undivided attention. She didn't talk to Betheny at the same time, firming up her schedule or making airline reservations. Linda Saunders focused entirely on her daughter.

"She works here all right—as an entry level

researcher. She's about as far from a director here as I am."

Silence on the line as her mother digested the information.

"He lied to you because he wanted to impress you," Carla continued. "Like always. That's what Bryce does. He'll say or do absolutely anything to get in yours and Dad's good graces. And it seems like it's worked."

Her mother's voice was laced with skepticism. "I have a hard time believing I've been so easily duped."

"Bryce is smart. He's devious and driven, he's a master of deception, and he'll do what it takes to get what he wants. And what he wants is to be part of our family. He doesn't care about me, but he does care about being associated with our family. He views it as glamorous. From where he comes from, maybe it is. But I can tell you this: I'm not going to marry him. I don't even want to see him again. Ever. I'll make my own choice about who I marry, Mom, and it's not going to be Bryce."

It felt fantastic to say it, as if an ox yoke had been lifted from her shoulders and she was finally free of the horrendous weight and restriction that had been with her for so long.

"I'd never want you to marry someone you don't want, Carla. I just, it seemed like Bryce was so perfect for you."

"Maybe that's because..." She sucked in a breath. *C'mon, say it.* "Because you never actually took time to get to know him. He's your best friend's son, so you assumed that's good enough."

Crickets. Her mother didn't say a word, but Carla knew she was there. She heard the gentle puffs of her breathing, certainly, but more than that, she felt her presence. For once in her life, Linda Saunders wasn't dividing her attention between multiple conversations. Instead of talking, she was finally listening. For Carla, winning a gold medal couldn't be a sweeter victory.

"Good enough is never good enough for any of my kids," Linda finally said, a waver in her voice. "Including you. *Especially* you. It's possible that I—" She let out a heavy sigh, then her voice took on an edge. "That I'm harder on you because you're a woman. I've pushed you because I know how damn hard it is for us to make it in this world if you don't have a set of balls strapped between your legs."

Carla simultaneously choked and laughed, gasping as a crumb of potato chips shot from her mouth. "Wow. I never knew you felt that way."

"If you didn't, that's my fault. I love you, Carla. You're my only daughter. I want what's best for you, not what's good enough."

The room wavered through her suddenly misty eyes. "I love you, too, Mom."

She spoke to her mother for several more minutes, their relationship taking a crucial step forward as Carla slowly but surely convinced her of the truth about Bryce. Carla had stood up for herself and she'd sensed her mother was proud.

She had dinner in the caf, purposely eating late in order to avoid the painful goodbyes so much a part of her routine for the past couple days. She knew she had no choice, but leaving this place, and the people, felt so wrong. In just a short time, Rivard Research had become like home. She let out a sigh and realized she needed to get some air. She'd let the soul of the bayou ease her broken heart.

The storm took with it the oppressive humidity, leaving in its wake dry, clear air, perfumed with the heady scent of magnolia blossoms. Twilight edged closer, and all around her she could hear the symphony of birds settling in for the night. Above her head tiny dots of starlight, like pin pricks, began to fill the sky. She chose a path and began walking, destination unknown. She only knew she needed time to think.

She rounded the bend and began walking north, toward the snake enclosure. Funny how she felt a need to check on the snakes. She wasn't a scientist, or a researcher. She didn't even know what she should be checking. But it felt important to reassure herself the cobras were okay after the storm. It felt right.

She stopped walking, stuck in her tracks as if she'd stepped into glue. Checking on the cobras felt *right* ? Had she lost her mind?

She frowned and resumed walking, kicking pebbles along the way. Up to now she'd defined herself by what she was doing. Climbing the career ladder, competing knowingly or not against her successful siblings and parents, trying to find her place in life. But all that ignored the person she was inside. The curious, kindhearted, passionate Carla. The one who cared about friends and family, about people and nature, and about her work.

Ah, yes, but there was the rub. What kind of work? What did she want to do? She finally had to accept that corporate life wasn't what she wanted. It didn't feed her soul like the research facility did. It was absolutely, astoundingly crazy, but she couldn't deny the truth. She liked it here. She liked the bayou. And, of course, she really liked Jackson.

She didn't know what it meant, or what the future held, but when she thought of him her heart did a dance, telling her everything she needed to know. She wanted to stay here. She wanted to give up the corporate life and turn her focus on helping Jackson in his mission to find the cure for MS. She wasn't a scientist but whether he liked to admit it or not, Jackson's research facility was a business, and a business needed to be run. She could help him with that, in so many ways. Everything about the idea felt right to her. She hoped it did to him, too.

She approached the clearing before the enclosure, so eager to get back and speak with Jackson she nearly started to run. The trees were thick here, the live oaks above and around her like a tent, blocking out the sky and dimming the light. She could hear the croak of frogs as night descended, and the distinct cries of barrel owls. Then she heard another sound that stopped her cold: a moan of passion.

She stood frozen, unmoving, not wanting to make a single sound until she knew from where the sound came. She looked around her. She didn't see anything, so she wondered where—

In the distance, a couple was having sex, wrapped in each other's arms and too caught up in what they were doing to have seen or heard Carla. The woman's top was pulled down around her waist and she wore no bra, allowing her lover to feast away on her exposed nipples. She moaned as he did so, thrusting her fingers in his hair.

Carla gingerly stepped behind a tree, taking care not to make a sound. She thought to walk the other way and approach the enclosure from a different direction, allowing them privacy. But then her eye caught something on the ground beside them, some kind of white, cylinder-shaped object.

She stuck her head out, leaning forward as much as possible while still affording herself the protection of the tree. She focused hard on the object, allowing her eyes to adjust to the dim light. When she finally realized what it was, it took monumental restraint not to burst into laughter. The identification of the white fountain soda cup also gave her the identity of its owner. Bryce. Silent as a ghost, she slipped her hand into her pocket and pulled out her phone.

The couple changed positions and Bryce stood with his back braced against a tree. His companion, whose dyed blonde hair looked remarkably similar to Kelly Grassle's, kneeled before him with his cock in her mouth. She pleasured him with admirable enthusiasm, using her lips and tongue all along his length while her fingers caressed his balls.

"That's it," Bryce moaned. "Suck me, baby."

He fisted his hands into her hair, guiding her head, and Kelly eagerly took him in. She moaned around his cock as she worked his balls, and Bryce's head dropped back against the tree.

"Deeper," he growled, thrusting his hips forward. Kelly responded, her lips sliding all along his length. With one hand she continued to stroke his balls while she slipped the other hand behind him. Carla couldn't see exactly what she did, but when Bryce jerked forward and cried out as Kelly appeared to caress his ass, she had a pretty good guess as to what was going on. She made her decision to step out from behind the tree.

Strolling toward them, she took no precautions to muffle the sound of her footsteps. She stepped on a tree twig, and the couple before her froze.

"Hey, Bryce. What's going on?"

"Carla?!" With lightning-fast speed—who knew Bryce could move that quickly—he shoved Kelly off of him and jerked up his pants.

"What are you doing here?"

"I was on my way to check on the cobras," Carla answered, her voice as mild and unaffected as if they were discussing the weather. "How about you?"

"I…ah…"

"Actually, I could see what you were doing. No need to elaborate." She turned her attention to Bryce's companion. "Hi, Kelly."

To her credit, Kelly had the decency to look mortified. Not only was she caught in *flagrante delicto*, but she did it with another woman's boyfriend. Or so she thought.

"Listen, Bryce," Carla continued, ignoring Kelly, "when you go home tonight—and by the way, I don't care if you have to walk every step but you *will* be leaving tonight—feel free to mention to my parents that you've decided you need some space, and then feel free to never call me or them again. Ever."

"Carla, listen to me—"

"Actually, I've done all the listening to you I'm ever going to do. Now it's time for you to listen to me." She held up her phone, waving it before him.

"What I just told you is a non-negotiable requirement for me not to post and e-mail to everyone you know—including my parents—the video I just made of you and Kelly. If you say anything to them other than what I told you, or if you try to visit them on the sly and I find out about it, this feature presentation goes viral. Period."

For once in his life, Bryce had nothing to say. He didn't even try to challenge her and demand she show him the video. Carla imagined her tone and determination were probably proof enough.

Carla turned her attention to Kelly, who'd taken the time to adjust her blouse so she was at least a little more covered up.

"I don't see the need to mention this to Jackson, Kelly. What you do when you're not working is your business, but take a piece of advice. Have a little more self-respect. Spruce up your wardrobe, and conduct yourself like the professional you've worked so hard to be. Giving someone a blow job in the middle of the woods on company property isn't exactly the hallmark of an esteemed scientist."

Kelly looked away, cheeks burning.

"Goodbye, Bryce. Safe travels. And don't forget what I said."

Without waiting for a response, Carla turned and walked away, leaving Bryce and Kelly to reassemble themselves. What a day! Standing up to her mother, now Bryce. Confidence had its rewards.

She emerged from the woods by the monitor building and ducked inside. Lisa sat at the controls. When Lisa heard the door open, she turned and spotted Carla.

"Hey." Lisa's attention returned to the monitors. "Come over here. Quick. You're about to see something amazing."

Carla hurried over to the monitor where Lisa's eyes were glued. She had the camera focused on the nest of eggs, but the expectant mother was nowhere in the frame. A trickle of alarm skittered along her spine.

"Where's Mariah?"

"Right next to the nest but just out of the camera angle."

"Why isn't she tending to the eggs?"

"Because they're hatching." Lisa beamed as if she herself were giving birth. "Look at the egg on the right. You'll see a small hole just near the top of it on the far end."

Carla studied where Lisa had pointed and sure enough, the little hatchling broke through. Carla gasped.

"I see it!"

"And there." Lisa pointed to another egg on the monitor. "That little one is coming out as well."

For the next two hours, Carla stayed transfixed to the monitor. The birthing process was slow, little hatchlings struggling to break through the shell bit by bit. When the first one finally had enough room to wriggle out of its shell and into the world, Carla was astounded by how much the experience touched her. Never in a million years would she have thought watching a snake with anything other than revulsion and fear was possible for her, and yet here she was growing emotional over little baby cobras. Crazy.

After seeing five hatchlings emerge from their shell, Carla excused herself and headed back to Jackson. She wanted to see how he was doing and tell him about the newborns. And she had something else to say to him as well.

The house was quiet, although she could hear the sound of typing coming from one of the rooms where a researcher from Turkey currently lived. From another room, the muffled sound of a TV. Who knew a place dubbed *The Snake Pit* could be so cozy? Jackson's home had the community feel of a dorm but without the obnoxious parties and noise.

She reached his room and gave a quiet knock. To her surprise, Jackson himself opened the door.

He stood before her wearing nothing but a loose pair of sweats. His feet and chest were bare, as if taunting her to come run her fingers along his hard, muscular pecs. Not that she was complaining.

"Hey," he said, opening the door wider to let her in. "I wondered where you were."

"Taking care of a few things," she replied, but then turned the focus toward him as he shut the door behind her. "Should you be out of bed?"

"I'm fine. Just tired."

"Then let's sit." They walked over to the reading chairs in the corner of the room and sat down. A brief memory flashed through Carla's mind of when she and Jackson had made love in the very chair where he sat now. He'd been trying to talk to her, and she'd taken his hard cock in her mouth...

She pushed the memory aside. Time to focus on creating new ones.

Carla said, "You look a lot better than you did the last time I saw you."

Jackson looked away for a moment, his gaze unfocused, as if trying to remember something. He took his glasses off and rubbed his eyes, but finally he shook his head. "*Merde*. I don't have a clear grasp of time yet.

When were you here?"

"Two days ago."

"Two days?" He frowned as he put his glasses back on. "What kept you away?"

"I've been in to check on you. You were always asleep. The last time we actually spoke was a couple of days ago."

He strained to remember, but she could tell it wasn't coming. Carla heard his quiet sigh of frustration.

"Don't worry if you don't remember the conversation." She tried to comfort him. "You were practically asleep then, too."

To her surprise, he cracked a smile. "What fascinating company I've been."

"Doesn't matter. I'm just so glad you're okay."

"Yeah," Jackson nodded. "Have to admit I am, too."

They fell silent for a moment. There were so many things she wanted to say, but she couldn't think where to begin. She decided for the moment on the safe route. "Hey, I've got some good news. Mariah's babies are hatching. Right now, as we speak. I've just been sitting with Lisa at the monitors for the past couple of hours."

"*Fantastique*," Jackson said, a spark of light in his eyes. "Any still births?"

"None that I saw."

He grunted at the news, reminding Carla of the Jackson Rivard she'd met on her first day here. It seemed like ages ago. So much had happened between then and now, and so much she wanted to say. She cleared her throat, ready to start talking, but faltered before she could begin. Her earlier euphoria faded as she realized one crucial detail had been left out of the equation when she'd made up her mind to stay. Would Jackson want her to?

"You still with me?"

His voice startled her back to Earth. "Sorry. What did you say?"

"Lost you for a minute. Were you thinking about Paris?"

"Paris? What makes you say that?"

"Easy guess," Jackson replied. "Your face usually gets that faraway, wistful look whenever the topic has come up, so I figured that was going on now." He paused, then his voice grew softer as he added, "I know how much you want to go."

Once upon a time, she *did* want to go to Paris. The idea of moving there had made her burn with passion, body and soul. She wanted to live there, to become fluent with the language, to immerse herself in a culture and a country different from everything she'd ever known.

But looking at it now, in a new light, Carla realized it wasn't so much that she wanted to go to Paris, but that she wanted to escape from New York. Not so much the city, because she truly loved it there. What she didn't love was the life she led. But here in Louisiana, with Jackson, she'd found her Paris.

"I do want to go," she confirmed.

His response was a stiff nod.

She couldn't know what it meant, but no time like the present to find out. She plunged forward. "Do you want me to go?"

He looked up, brows knit in confusion. "Of course."

Well, what were you hoping for, silly girl? Her

inner voice chided as she turned to look at the window. *That he'd pledge his undying love and beg you to give up the dream you yourself have said you'd always wanted? He wouldn't do that to you. Besides, he's got his own dreams to fulfill right here.*

"That is, if you want to."

She looked back at Jackson, who leaned forward in his chair, his intense gaze so sharp it could cut. She took a deep breath.

"What if…" Her heart pounded with nervousness, the roar of her blood like thunder in her ears. "What if I told you I'd changed my mind?"

"About Paris?"

"About everything."

He shook his head. "I don't know what you mean."

She couldn't sit for another second. Springing up from her chair, she paced the room like a political candidate awaiting polling results. She put several steps of distance between herself and Jackson and then turned to face him once more. "I've been doing some thinking."

"About?"

"About everything. Work. My family. My life and what I want to do with it."

"That doesn't sound so bad." He watched her move across the floor. "So why the pacing?"

"Well, for starters, I realized I'm not cut out for the corporate world."

"That part I knew."

She spun around, doing a double take. "You what? You knew that?"

He shrugged. "Of course."

"Well, what…why…" She paused, gathering her

thoughts. "Why didn't you say anything? You could have saved me a lot of time."

"No, not at all."

"What—"

"There wasn't anything anyone could have said to you. It's something you had to figure out for yourself."

She knew he was right. If he'd said something to her, she simply wouldn't have believed him. What a mule she could be.

"It was pretty obvious in the first couple of days after I met you that you've been living the life of someone you're not," he continued. "But you had to look in the mirror and see for yourself."

"I guess I finally did." She gave him a shrug. "Wish it hadn't taken so long."

"Everyone's path is different."

"You, ah…you also factored into my thinking. In a crazy kind of way."

"Oh?"

"The thing is…" She took a deep breath; let it out. "The thing is, I'm pretty sure I'm in love with you."

"I see." He said nothing more, receiving her information as calmly as if she were a researcher discussing her latest findings.

Hi, Dr. Rivard. My research over the past month has shown I go mushy over snake babies, my dreams of Paris aren't really what I want after all, and I hate the corporate life. Oh, and I'm in love with you.

She shook her head, crossing her arms in front of her as if warding off a chill. "Told you it's crazy."

When at first he said nothing, she repeated, softer, "It *is* crazy. Right?"

She stood there, biting softly against her bottom

lip, looking over at Jackson as he stared off into the distance. It was impossible for her to know what was in his mind. His expression was smooth, unblemished, like a statue carved from marble.

At last he returned his gaze to her. "No," he replied, his voice quiet. "I don't think it's crazy. Least not the way I see it."

Carla could do nothing but nod and swallow around the giant goose egg that had formed and now stuck fast in her throat, blocking the words from coming out. She suddenly had a wild urge to clap her hands to her mouth like a game show contestant who's just been told she's won a new car. Her heart hammered wildly, at once thrilled and terrified. If Jackson was saying what she thought he was saying, she'd won something a thousand times better than a car.

With pulse racing, she waited for him to elaborate, but Jackson had never been a man of many words. Apparently he felt he'd said all that was needed. But it wasn't enough for Carla.

Walking over to where he remained seated, she knelt down before him and looked into his hooded, serious eyes, searching for her answer. "So?" she prompted.

"So yes." He released a soft breath. "I love you, Carla. Have for some time now."

"Oh. I—"

He pulled her up and into his kiss, his mouth soft but demanding, claiming possession of her. His tongue pried open her lips and he swept in, exploring her warm and willing mouth. It was curiously, wonderfully like being home, back to the tingly, seductive embrace of Jackson Rivard that she was getting to know oh so well.

She groaned, melting into his kiss, the palms of her hands gently caressing his warm, muscled chest.

At first she was reluctant to rest her full weight on him because of his weakened condition from the bite, but Jackson was having none of it. He settled her more firmly on his lap by curving his hand around her back and onto her ass, pulling her against him so she could feel the bulge of his arousal pressed beneath her thigh. She moaned into his mouth.

He slipped his hands beneath her blouse and in one smooth movement released the snap on her bra so her breasts spilled free. Then his hands were everywhere, sliding his palms across her breasts, gently pinching the nipples between forefinger and thumb. Carla squirmed against him, feeling the insistent pulses between her legs as her body readied itself for him.

But she didn't want to go on, not like this. Not until they finished their conversation. With a willpower of iron, she pulled away.

"Not yet," she panted softly against his ear.

"Why not?"

She extracted herself from his lap and sat in the chair next to him, straightening her top and refastening her bra. She couldn't think straight sitting across from him halfway undressed.

"There are things I need to say. Important things."

He let out a breath, bringing his desire under control. For the moment.

"As I was saying, I love you, too, Jackson. At least I think I do."

He frowned. "You're not sure?"

"I've never been in love before." She shook her head, gave him a shrug. "This is all new to me, and it's

273

confusing as hell. I thought my life was all set. I had a job, I knew where I was going to live. I even, according to my parents, had someone who would marry me. In a few short weeks, my life turned upside down."

She leaned forward, a pleading look on her face as she strove to make certain Jackson understood.

He nodded. "Even though it doesn't look that way from where you sit, Carla, I'm sorting through the same feelings."

"You are?"

"Yes. I have my research facility, my mission, my goals. Everything I want and need has been perfectly put in place and moving forward just as I envisioned. At least that's what I thought. But then you came along, and suddenly things started looking different. What I thought was so well planned out didn't appear that way anymore."

"What do you mean?"

Jackson took a deep breath and slowly released it. "I know you know about Katherine. Amy told me."

She nodded reluctantly. "I'm sorry."

"There's no need. That relationship taught me well."

"About having your heart shattered?"

Jackson's mouth set. "I decided afterward I didn't need to spend my time looking for a woman to love. I love my sister—not in the same way, of course—but my love for Amy fuels me toward my goal of finding a cure for MS, and I figured that's all I needed. Wasting energy on loving someone else was just distracting and unnecessary, and it screwed up my plans. But then you came along."

"How did I interfere?" Carla's brow wrinkled in

confusion. "Even if you did fall in love with me, your life, your goals—everything—is here."

"I'm ready to go to Paris with you, Carla."

Her heart stopped. "What?"

"I know how much you want to go, and that you're moving there after this assignment. I want to be with you, so I decided that if you felt the same way, I'd put my part of the research on hold. I'd denote Quinn as head researcher. He takes my place until your Paris assignment is over."

Her eyes filled and the image of Jackson before her became unfocused and watery, like looking through a windshield during a storm. She blinked back the tears, trying to stop them from tumbling down her face, but even so she could feel her throat tightening and knew she'd be losing the battle.

"You'd do that for me?"

He closed his eyes briefly and nodded. "Of course."

"But your research. Your goals."

"They go on. Just in a different way than I first thought." He reached out and took her hands in his, lacing their fingers together. His focus was locked to the floor for a moment, as if collecting his thoughts. Then he looked back up, piercing her with his stare. "Turns out getting bit was the best thing that's happened to me in a long time. Apart from meeting you."

"What?" She frowned, shaking her head. "What do you mean?"

"For two years I've spent every waking minute searching for the MS cure. I think of nothing else; I do nothing else. My entire life has been put on hold trying to make up for the accident. And my parents' deaths."

"But you didn't—"

"I know what you're going to say. I didn't cause the accident. But it's something I have to come to terms with on my own."

She gave him a cautious smile. "And have you?"

"Don't think I'm quite there yet, but almost. What I do know is I have other reasons to live." He lifted one of her hands to his lips and pressed a kiss against the back of it, his warm breath caressing her skin. Then he said, "Those reasons include you. It's time for me to put the past behind and move on."

He released her hands and gave her a wry grin. "Besides, you can't go to Paris with that horrendous French of yours. You need a translator."

The tears she'd been battling against finally won, and she felt their warm wetness against her cheeks. But even through the tears she could see Jackson's smile, lighting the room—and her heart—like a thousand watt bulb. She swiped at her tears, chasing them away.

"I'd planned on learning French while I was there."

His eyes sparkled with a wicked gleam. "But *mon ange,* that's such a boring way to learn."

"Is it?"

"Let me show you a better one."

Jackson rose from the chair and held out his hand toward her. She took it and stood. He brought her toward him, into his embrace, surrounding her with his warmth. She sank into him, resting her cheek against his shoulder and closing her eyes as she took in the surprising softness of his skin and the heady male scent of him. He began caressing her back, long smooth strokes that had her purring like a contended cat.

"*Viens au lit*," he said, still stroking her back while planting whisper soft kisses against the nape of her neck.

"What does that mean?"

He stepped back, enough so he could bring his hand around to place a finger beneath her chin, tipping it up to look into her eyes. "Come to bed."

He took her hand and they walked across the room, stopping when they reached the side of the bed.

Jackson looked down at her, one side of his mouth curving upward in a devilish grin. "*Déshabille-toi*."

"I—"

He thrust his arms beneath her blouse and lifted it up and over her head. "Take off your clothes."

"That's not fair," she protested, nonetheless unbuttoning and then stepping out of her jeans. "Just because I don't speak the language doesn't mean you get to decide everything."

"*Au contraire*. I'm your teacher, and this is my lesson plan."

She loved this playful side of him, something she hadn't seen nearly enough of. But before they continued, she had to finish what she'd come here to say. "Jackson, wait."

Her pleas were ignored as he leaned forward to begin sliding down her bra straps. Suddenly she remembered one of the few French words she did know. "*Arrête!*"

It worked. He paused and nodded his approval. "*Très bien*."

"*Merci*." She stepped back to give herself some space. "I just need to know if you're sure."

"I told you—"

"I know. But I didn't get to say everything I wanted so I just…you have to hear the rest." She stopped, getting her thoughts together. "When I said before that I was wrong about everything, I meant about the path I was on. I tried to make the corporate life work, but there was always something inside of me that didn't feel right."

"Stuffing a square peg in a round hole."

"Exactly. The thing is, though, the skills I have are solid. They just need to be used in the right place."

"Like Paris."

"No." She let out a breath. "Here."

Confusion furrowed his brow. "Here? What do you mean?"

"I mean I want to work for you. Here at the lab. I don't want to go to Paris, Jackson. At least not to live. Not now. What I want is to stay and work here. Not as a researcher of course, but maybe as your operations person."

"Operations?"

"In charge of communications, public relations, fund raising, marketing. You don't even have a web presence, did you know that? I couldn't find out a thing about this company before I came. You don't have anyone doing any of that, except yourself, and frankly you're about as good at that as I am at French."

He feigned insult. "*Pardon*?"

"Your brilliance is in your research. That's where you need to be spending your time."

His serious expression returned and he nodded his agreement. "It's true. I try to put focus on it, but…"

"What I'm trying to say is, I want you to hire me."

He closed the space between them, taking her in

his arms. With gentle pressure he pushed her down on the bed and sat beside her. He returned his attention to the bra straps he'd been in the middle of pushing away when she'd interrupted him.

"I'd love to hire you," he said between soft kisses along her shoulder. "But I couldn't afford you."

"You'll pay me through the grant money I raise. I promise it'll be more than you've ever had before. Besides, I'd work for cheap," she responded, a small gasp escaping her as Jackson removed the bra and her breasts tumbled free, instantly stroked by his insatiable fingers. "And you could throw in some sex on the side," she added. "As extra compensation."

"Mmm." He leaned forward to flick his tongue across her nipple. "That could work."

"You'll also continue with my French lessons." She hissed as he took the hardened nub into his mouth. "For free."

He pressed her back against the bed and settled himself alongside of her. With the tips of his fingers he skated them across her breasts, her stomach, and then lower still, pushing down her panties.

"*Bon.* You're hired. I'll continue your French lessons, and we *will* go to Paris. Don't give up on your dream, Carla. We'll make it happen together."

"Okay. But still, I…ohh." She groaned as he slid his hands between her legs, softly caressing the smooth skin on her inner thighs.

"*Tu es si belle.*"

"I know what that means! It's—"

He silenced her with a kiss, whispering something else to her when they finally broke for air.

"I know that one, too," she said, her eyes dark and

hazy with desire.

"Then say it back to me."

"*Je t'aime.*"

"Nice," Jackson praised her. "*Très bien.*"

"*Merci.* I like these French lessons."

"Then let's continue with the most important one." He swirled the tip of his tongue around her ear. "It takes constant practice and repetition to master the skill. But the French are famous for it."

"Oh? What's that?"

"Making love."

She sighed as he continued caressing her and slipped her hands down the curve of his back, stroking the lean, corded muscles. She turned her face toward his so she could whisper in his ear. "Then get ready, teacher. I'm going to ace this class."

About the Author

Being born and raised in Wisconsin means Elizabeth Shore will always be a Cheesehead at heart, but for many years she's lived with her husband in New York. They also travel frequently to Finland, her husband's home country. All that time in cold climates means she's shivering a lot, but finds no better way to shake off the chill then by writing erotic romance—the hotter the better.

Elizabeth likes brooding, complicated heroes and is also a fan of horror. One of her geekiest moments was traveling to Bangor, Maine, so she could have her picture taken in front of Stephen King's house. She writes both historical and contemporary romance, is a passionate lover of Renaissance art, and a devoted animal advocate. She's grateful to her husband for his ardent, unyielding support, and to their passel of cats who allow them lodging in their apartment so she has a place to write.

Visit Elizabeth Shore at
www.lizshore.com

To chat with Elizabeth Shore and other Wild Rose Press authors of erotic romance, join us at www.groups.yahoo.com/group/thewilderroses.

Also Available

Big Bad Easy

by

Ursula Whistler

http://amzn.com/1628301430

A grueling unsolved murder case is the tipping point for detective Jameson Kelly. He's ready to hang up his holster for early retirement when Zara Robinson walks in to his precinct, the victim of a car break-in. She's everything Jameson likes in a woman—tall, blonde, beautiful and athletic. More than enough woman to take him down and make him beg for more. One more case can't hurt to help pass the time, especially one he knows he can solve.

Zara is a woman who knows what she needs, and top of her list is closure on this spree of car break-ins. And there's Jameson—he's big with an air of bad despite being a cop and all man. Man enough to easily make her feel soft and womanly. But when clues to the theft lead to something bigger, she's glad to have his brains as well as his skills on her side.

Turn the page to read an excerpt.

Chapter One

Jameson Kelly had an eyeful this morning. A few times a week, usually on a Sunday morning, there would be legs sticking out of short skirts and boobs barely contained by tube tops or halter tops. But this was a Monday, when the hookers weren't lounging around the station waiting for transfer to central lockup. There shouldn't have been a well-dressed, tall woman with long, muscular legs making a splash with the male officers who were beginning their morning with a review of cases and a cup of coffee. Yet, there she stood, with an equally muscular ass cupped by a mid-thigh length business skirt.

Without a case to review, he felt free to watch her as she shifted from one high-heeled foot to another. He guessed she waited on the captain, which meant he would have a nice long time to day dream about what the rest of her body would look like in a black lace bra and matching thong. He wouldn't mind working with her.

Getting a view of those legs each day might inspire him to keep his job as a detective for the New Orleans Police Department. The firm, toned biceps on the woman drew his eye as well. The cap sleeve of her simple white blouse covered her deltoids, but he bet that he'd be able to see the definition there as well. All of the muscles were well complemented by her long dark blonde hair and tanned skin.

He'd never been able to resist a well-built, athletic woman. It was their attitude for life that attracted him as much as their bodies. A healthy physique meant a healthy mind, ready for challenges, changes, and the seemingly insurmountable problems that came with living in New Orleans. That's why he'd kept exercising well past the age that most men called it quits.

At forty-two, he looked better than some of the younger beat officers. He prided himself in that. What he didn't have was their enthusiasm for keeping the Crescent City a safe place with less theft, less violence, and definitely less murder. He'd seen too much, too many ups followed by dispiriting downs. Jameson wanted to hang up his gun and holster, permanently.

The woman tapped her foot loudly and leaned over the desk at the entrance in an attempt to get the desk officer's attention. Jameson snorted. Good luck there, lady, but keep leaning over. His cock stretched his pants with this new view of her solid and curvy ass. The woman had to be an expert at developing her legs from the toned calves to the tight hamstrings. He flexed his hands, wishing he could caress those muscles as he made a slow journey to her strong, round globes.

He shook his head. The captain needed to give him a case. Otherwise, he'd start ogling the hookers on the weekends, and that never led to good things.

Another sergeant, younger, with a developing pot belly, passed behind his chair and gave it a kick. Jameson jolted upright and growled at the cop who'd kicked his seat. "Stop being an ass, Decker."

Decker grinned. "Stop looking at hers, or go over and make her feel more comfortable. An old guy like you will calm her, you know, with your grandfatherly ways."

"Shut the fuck up." Jameson pushed his chair away from his desk. He'd show Decker just how he could affect a woman. Her hand wouldn't be on her hip long. It would be on his chest, then his abdomen, and she'd gasp with delight at the size of his dick. Decker wouldn't ever know any of it since Jameson wouldn't ever be that public with his caresses. And, this woman was worth exploring. Those thoughts he'd keep to himself. Maybe he could spend some time with her to keep her calm before the captain showed his face. She had a folder, he noticed. So, he had an opening to talk to her. It couldn't hurt.

As he got five feet away from her, the captain's door opened. The lady's body snapped to attention, and her shoulder-length golden hair whipped about her tanned face. She gave a small smile, but it vanished as she walked to the captain.

Jameson knew that his superior officer carried more woes than anyone else in the district. This one was supposed to be the quieter police district, but lately, small crimes and a few larger ones were making headlines. Despite the work of the detectives, two of the biggest cases were still unsolved. A rapist and a murderer still walked the streets of Uptown.

Based on the tightened mouth of the woman a few feet away from him, he figured she was a victim of some crime. He highly doubted she'd been raped. Nothing about her showed that look—that empty, glassy-eyed appearance of a woman who'd been assaulted. Plus, he bet she could kick any man from here to Sunday if one tried to take advantage of her.

Then, he had a wild thought. Was she here for a job? Transfer from another city? Former military? His heart raced with the possibility of working next to her. Strong, confident, determined. He swallowed hard and tried to think of something besides her hard body next to his as their partnership became more than business related. If he didn't get his lust under control soon, Decker would have some quip ready about the growing tent at his crotch.

"Captain, don't even try to reschedule." Her voice and the accompanying scowl wiped away all imaginings of sex with her. Shrill, angry, and laced with bitterness. Not what anyone wanted to hear first thing in the morning. She took a few steps toward Captain Usner and shook her file folder at him. "You've put me off for weeks, and I'm not leaving until I get an officer assigned to this case."

"Certainly, Ms. Robinson." Usner didn't even try to hide his exasperation.

Jameson figured she must have called four times a day or more. The captain had complained about a shrew constantly bothering him. With a glance, he sized up the lady again. Banging hot body, pleasing face, bad attitude. He'd retreat now. Maybe the captain wouldn't notice him. He most certainly didn't want to work with her.

"So," her foot tapped again, "who?"

The captain pointed right at Jameson's face. "Sergeant Kelly just cleared his case load on Friday. Three solved in one day. He's all yours."

Jameson cringed. Too late. He'd barely turned to hide at his desk when the captain called his name. Not willing to catch the ire of his boss, he stuck out his hand to the lady. "Ma'am. I hope I can be the one to help you."

"Me, too." She tossed her hair in what Jameson took as a sign of triumph. "Zara Robinson, and I've been waiting weeks to hear something from you guys. Shall we begin?" Her grip of his hand matched his expectations, firmer than many men's.

Out of the corner of his eye, he watched the captain back into his office with a grin and a wave. "Sure. Let me get your case file."

"No need." She shook the well-worn folder at him. "It's all here. Where's your desk?"

From the sound of Decker's snickering, Jameson knew he didn't want to hear what she had to say within ear shot of anyone at the station. "How about I buy you a cup of coffee at the cafe across the street? Better than what we have here, and it gets you out of a place you don't like so much."

"Fine." She adjusted her shoulders downward, relaxing some tension. "That's a good idea. I don't like this place. At all."

One mark in his favor. Of course, he was fighting her image of New Orleans' cops, which surely involved laziness, excessive force, and general sloppiness in their work. "Let me get my jacket, cover all this hardware." He patted his firearm that hung around his shoulders on a harness.

"I'll wait outside." She narrowed her eyes. "Don't think you can ditch me, though."

"Ma'am, I wouldn't even think of it." He'd solve her case and leave the force with a good taste in his mouth. This would be a parting gift to his captain, keeping Zara Robinson off his voicemail.

As he passed Decker's desk, he kicked the man's chair, mostly to stop the man from laughing so loudly.

"Kelly, if you get some from her, make sure you use a gag. That way you won't hear her complain."

"Shut the fuck up, Decker." He had to get a better come back for the man. Of course, the best retort would be to get a taste of Zara Robinson's body. It would be for his satisfaction only. He sure wouldn't share that with a prick who couldn't keep in shape.

Thank you for purchasing
this Wild Rose Press, Inc. publication.

If you like this title, you might also like:

Man Of Few Words by Ursula Whistler
http://amzn.com/B00ASZT4EK

Heartbreaker by Monica Robinson
http://amzn.com/B00BJ5ZUY6

For other wonderful stories of erotic romance,
please visit our on-line bookstore at
www.thewilderroses.com.

For questions or more information
contact us at
info@thewildrosepress.com.

The Wild Rose Press, Inc.
www.thewilderroses.com